Life At All Costs

Life At All Costs

AN ANTHOLOGY OF VOICES
from
21st Century Black Prolife Leaders

Dr. Alveda King
and
Dr. La Verne Tolbert

To order additional copies of this book, contact:
Xlibris Corporation
1-888-795-4274
www.Xlibris.com
Orders@Xlibris.com
113113

CONTENTS

We Are Pro Family

Lift ev'ry voice and sing,
Till earth and heaven ring.
Ring with the harmonies of Liberty;
Let our rejoicing rise,
High as the list'ning skies,
Let it resound loud as the rolling sea.
Sing a song full of the faith that the dark past has taught us,
Sing a song full of the hope that the present has brought us;
Facing the rising sun of our new day begun,
Let us march on till victory is won.

Stony the road we trod,
Bitter the chast'ning rod,
Felt in the days when hope unborn had died;
Yet with a steady beat,
Have not our weary feet,
Come to the place for which our fathers sighed?
We have come over a way that with tears has been watered,
We have come, treading our path through the blood of the slaughtered,
Out from the gloomy past,
Till now we stand at last
Where the white gleam of our bright star is cast.

God of our weary years,
God of our silent tears,
Thou who has brought us thus far on the way;
Thou who has by Thy might,
Led us into the light,
Keep us forever in the path, we pray.
Lest our feet stray from the places, our God, where we met Thee,
Lest our hearts, drunk with the wine of the world, we forget Thee,
Shadowed beneath thy hand,
May we forever stand,
True to our God,
True to our native land.

—The Black National Anthem by James Weldon Johnson

Open your mouth for the speechless,
In the cause of all who are appointed to die.
Open your mouth, judge righteously,
And plead the cause of the poor and needy.
(Proverbs 31:8)

ACKNOWLEDGMENTS

 On our cover is a photo of prolife political activist and legendary leader, Mildred Fay Jefferson (April 4, 1927-October 15, 2010). Dr. Jefferson helped launch the National Right to Life Committee (NRLC) and served as its Vice President (1973), Chairman of the Board (1974), and President (1975-1978). In addition to being a founding member of the NRLC, Dr. Jefferson launched Black Americans for Life and served on the Board of Directors of more than 30 prolife organizations.

Dr. Jefferson's passion for saving the lives of the unborn may have been inspired by her education and subsequent career as a physician. After receiving a B.A degree summa cum laude from Texas College in Tyler, Texas and a M.S. degree from Tufts University in Medford, Massachusetts, she entered Harvard University in 1947 and became the first African American woman to graduate from Harvard's Medical School in 1951. She continued with a string of firsts . . . she was the first woman to be a surgical intern at Boston City Hospital and the first woman admitted to membership in the Boston Surgical Society.

Her interest in medical ethics and jurisprudence and their impact on law and public policy led her to the White House. President Reagan credited Dr. Jefferson with changing how he viewed abortion and wrote, "You have made it irrefutably clear that an abortion is the taking of a human life. I am grateful to you."

And we are grateful, too.

Along with Dr. Jefferson, considered to be the mother of the black prolife movement, we acknowledge the countless leaders—men, women, grandmothers, grandfathers, pastors, and politicians—who lobbied for life in their families, churches, and communities. This legacy inspires *Life at All Costs: An Anthology of Voices From 21ˢᵗ Century Black Prolife Leaders.* Our prayer is that we will ignite passions in generations to come.

Rescue the unborn. Restore the family.

Dr. Mildred Jefferson's Bio was retrieved on March 7, 2012 from *http://en.wikipedia.org/wiki/Mildred_Fay_Jefferson#cite_note-youtube.com-4* and *http://www.thehistorymakers.com/biography/biography.asp?bioindex=1251*

INTRODUCTION

This collection of articles, essays, sermons, and research papers from the multi-faceted voices of the National Black Prolife Coalition sounds the alarm. From pastors and ministers to post-abortive women, activists, authors, physicians, professors, and political activists, the black prolife movement exposes the truth about life issues that for too long have been silenced by the media.

But *we* have not been silent. Whether in the classroom, sanctuary, crisis pregnancy center, bus tour, or billboard, we have sounded a warning that abortion is murder and challenged America that it has to end. Our collective experiences are powerful witnesses to the horrors and falsehood surrounding this issue. No white lie is big enough to cover up what God has revealed. In this anthology, we share His truth.

Preserving the Author's Passion

Co-editor Dr. Alveda King summoned the troops to submit their work. My task was to organize and to compile these submissions. In so doing, I resisted the temptation to line edit in order to preserve each author's passion, style, and voice, but I did add subtitles to make reading easier along with very minor changes that unify this anthology so that we speak with one voice.

Throughout this book, you will be astounded by the numbers of children who have been aborted. Figures may vary from chapter to chapter due to the source of the information and/or the date of the original writing. Pick a number, any number—15 million, 15.5 million, or 20 million—you decide. No matter your choice, you must agree that abortion's death toll in the African American community is nothing less than staggering.

And so is the death toll in other communities, as well. Our concern is not just for black babies, although African American preborn children die at astounding rates. Our concern is for *all* children, no matter their ethnicity. Yes, abortion primarily targets blacks, but the blood of the mutilated also flows in the streets of Hispanic/Latino communities, Caucasian communities and in the neighborhoods of the wealthy and affluent as well as in the poor.

We affirm the founding principle of this great nation—the guiding force of our forefathers—which is the Word of God, the Bible. Each author in this anthology adheres to this Christian heritage and writes from a biblical presupposition.

Scripture passages in this anthology are from the New King James (NKJ) or the New International Version (NIV). Designations are not specifically noted unless the quotation is from the Amplified Bible.

Easy Reading, Profound Impact

Because most chapters are brief, reading this volume is easy. Nevertheless, you will be profoundly impacted by what you discover between these pages. It is our prayer that this anthology speaks for the speechless and pleads the cause of the poor and the needy. It is our hope that convictions are challenged, minds are changed, hearts are healed, and prolife passions are refueled.

In publishing this volume, we humbly acknowledge that these are not *all* of the voices in the black prolife movement. There are many who share this legacy. Would that we could include everyone who has lobbied for life and against abortion!

From state to state and city to city, in neighborhoods, churches, and on street corners, there are millions more voices that join with ours to champion the cause of life. May our cries echo with theirs to raise high the banner! And as Dr. Martin Luther King, Jr. often quoted, "Let justice run down like water, and righteousness like a mighty stream," (Amos 5:24).

—La Verne Tolbert, Ph.D.

WE ARE PROLIFE

An Africa proverb says,
"No one knows whose womb holds the chief."

An African customs asks every expectant mother,
"Are you the one?"

CHAPTER 1

History of the National Black Prolife Movement And the National Black Prolife Coalition

Dr. Alveda King

And now abide faith, hope and love. The greatest of these is love.
I Corinthians 13:8

In the early beginnings of the 21st century, a group of valiant yet war torn prolife African American individuals began to coalesce around a common goal. This phenomenon had occurred before in the history of America, and it is a blessing that such a group has emerged yet again.

Before we came together as a network, many of us believed that we were laboring along, as "voices crying in the wilderness." As we begin to meet and work and pray together, we discovered "unity in numbers."

While each individual in the movement is a leader in his or her own "right," each agrees that there is "strength in unity of purpose." So, this body of warriors is uniquely fitted "for such a time as this," to tackle and attain victory for their common cause.

Many of the 21st century warriors would tell you that their "gathering together" came to be due to mighty and miraculous "acts of God." They all generally agree that faith, hope and love work together in their "group" to bring about a certain "unity of the spirit in the bonds of peace."

Today, this group is known as The National Black Prolife Coalition (*www.blackcoalition.org*). In part, this is our history, which is yet in the making. Below is the original mission statement of the Black Prolife Movement and the current mission statement of the Coalition:

21ST Century Black Prolife Movement

Vision Statement

It is the vision of the National Black Pro-life movement to promote traditional family values and to produce strong and healthy families where babies are safe and able to reach their full potential in life.

Mission Statement

It is the mission of the National Black Pro-Life Movement to promote a culture of life through divine guidance.

Core Values

1. We believe God is the Author of Life and states have the authority to affirm life.
2. We believe children are essential; they are the lifeline to the survival to the human race.
3. We believe the cycle of life is continued through the fundamental marriage of one man and one woman.
4. We believe the community is the visible expression of life.
5. We believe the viability of a nation is connected to the value of human life in all stages.

National Black Prolife Coalition

Who We Are

The National Black Prolife Coalition is a network of prolife and pro-family organizations committed to restoring a culture that celebrates Life and Family cultivating Hope in the black community.

Vision Statement

To end abortion by restoring a culture of Life and the foundation of Family in the black community.

Mission Statement

We will promote traditional family values from a Biblical worldview to produce strong and healthy families where babies are safe and able to reach their full potential in life. Through education and awareness media campaigns, community events, political action, lobbying and coalition building of prolife and pro-family advocacy groups, we will restore Life, Family and Hope in the black community.

Core Values

We believe we are all deliberate creations, of one blood, made in the image of God.

We believe children are essential and deserve protection, personhood, nurture, and love in the womb and throughout childhood.

We believe the foundation of a stable and healthy society is rooted in the marriage of one man and one woman.

We believe the community is the visible expression of life.

We believe the viability of a nation is dependent upon its value of human life in all stages.

Genocide in the Bible

Pharaoh, seeking to abort God's deliverance plan ordered the midwives to kill the babies when the mothers went into labor. This order for partial-birth abortion in Genesis sought to kill all baby boys of Moses' nation to prevent the liberation of a people. The midwives refused to kill or abort the babies, because they feared God! Today, there are battles in the state legislatures to help doctors and nurses make the same choice for life.

Molech and Baal worship: During child sacrifice ceremonies, children were killed or burned alive. God forbade idol worshippers to pass children through the fire. Abortion clinics kill babies and burn them in incinerators today.

When Jesus was born, the king ordered all baby boys up to age two to be killed. Again, this genocide was planned to abort the liberation of a people. Today, Planned Parenthood and other eugenics advocates like Dr. Peter Singer advocate abortion. Singer writes that a baby is not "viable" until age two, leading some to consider post-birth abortion.

Consider! The sexual revolution is a demonic disaster! Fornication, adultery, rape, incest, abortion, same gender cohabitation all lead to a breakdown of the family!

Satan hates virgins, thus a sexual revolution that flies in the face of God!

Behold, a Virgin shall conceive . . . Satan hates virgins and babies, thus genocide, fornication, adultery, homosexual same sex sex, pornography, lust, and incest . . . and all kinds of vile sins.

And yet, procreative marriage, between one man and one woman eliminates all of the above. Jesus is Lord over all! And His Name shall be called Wonderful, Counselor, The Price of Peace, The Everlasting Father, and His Kingdom shall have no end!

Connecting the Dots

1450-1800's—Between 1450 and the end of the nineteenth century, slaves were obtained from along the west coast of Africa with the full and active co-operation of African kings and merchants. (There were occasional military campaigns organized by Europeans to capture slaves, especially by the Portuguese in what is now Angola, but this accounts for only a small percentage of the total.)

In return, the African kings and merchants received various trade goods including beads, cowrie shells (used as money), textiles, brandy, horses, and perhaps most importantly, guns. The guns were used to help expand empires and obtain more slaves until they were finally used against the European colonizers. The export of trade goods from Europe to Africa forms the first side of the *triangular trade*.

Across the Continents, Two Battles Raged

Wilbur Wilberforce was a British politician, a philanthropist and a leader of the movement to abolish the slave trade. In later years, Wilberforce supported the campaign for the complete abolition of slavery, and continued his involvement after 1826, when he resigned from Parliament because of his failing health.

That campaign led to the Slavery Abolition Act 1833, which abolished slavery in most of the British Empire; Wilberforce died just three days after hearing that the passage of the Act through Parliament was assured. He was buried in Westminster Abbey, close to his friend William Pitt.

President Abraham Lincoln and the Civil War championed the abolitionists' movement in America to end slavery. Three-thousand (300,000) "white" soldiers died fighting in the Civil War to end slavery. Blacks sold Blacks to white slave traders. Some Blacks even owned slaves. There were cruel white masters. There were white abolitionists. The battle was not white against black, but good against evil.

Slavery in the United States

Slavery in the U.S. began soon after English colonists first settled Virginia in 1607 and lasted until the passage of the Thirteenth Amendment to the United States Constitution in 1865.

Before the widespread establishment of chattel slavery, much labor was organized under a system of bonded labor known as *indentured servitude*. This typically lasted for several years for white and black alike, and it was a means of using labor to pay the costs of transporting people to the colonies.

By the 18th century, court rulings established the racial basis of the American incarnation of slavery to apply chiefly to Black Africans and people of African descent, and occasionally to Native Americans.

In part, because of the Southern colonies' devotion of resources to tobacco culture, which was labor intensive, by the end of the 17th century they had a higher number and proportion of slaves than in the north.

From 1654 until 1865, slavery for life was legal within the boundaries of the present United States. Most slaves were black and were held by whites, although some Native Americans and free blacks also held slaves. The majority of slaveholding was in the southern United States where most slaves were engaged in an efficient machine-like gang system of agriculture.

According to the 1860 U.S. census, nearly four million slaves were held in a total population of just over 12 million in the 15 states in which slavery was legal.

Of all 1,515,605 families in the 15 slave states, 393,967 held slaves (roughly one in four), amounting to 8% of all American families.

Most slaveholding households, however, had only a few slaves. The majority of slaves was held by planters, defined by historians as those who held 20 or more slaves. The planters achieved wealth and social and political power. Ninety-five percent of black people lived in the South, comprising one-third of the population there, as opposed to 2% of the population of the North.

The wealth of the United States in the first half of the 19th century was greatly enhanced by the labor of African Americans. But with the Union victory in the American Civil War, the slave-labor system was abolished in the South.

This contributed to the decline of the post-bellum Southern economy, though the South also faced significant new competition from foreign cotton producers such as India and Egypt, and the cotton gin had made cotton production less labor-intensive in any case. Northern industry, which had expanded rapidly before and during the war, surged even further ahead of the South's agricultural economy.

Industrialists from northeastern states came to dominate many aspects of the nation's life, including social and some aspects of political affairs. The planter class of the South lost power temporarily. The rapid economic development following the Civil War accelerated the development of the modern U.S. industrial economy.

Twelve million black Africans were shipped to the Americas from the 16th to the 19th centuries. Of these, an estimated 645,000 (5.4% of the total) were brought to what is now the United States. The overwhelming majority were shipped to Brazil. The slave population in the United States had grown to four million by the 1860 Census.

Evil Fruit from a Wicked Tree

There is an ancient enemy to the human family that seeks to divide and conquer among the villages and communities. This enemy wears many different faces, but underneath, the motives are the same—to destroy the human family. From Bible days to the present 21st century, we can see that ancient idolatry and child sacrifices were part of the strategy to destroy the human family.

Genocide remains a major tactic in bringing about the destruction of the human family. Bible examples of such include the idol worship of Molech and the practice of child sacrifice. Another example is Moses who was spared from the partial birth abortion. And during the time of Jesus' birth, baby boys were massacred.

As we enter more modern times, we can see that the western transcontinental modern slave trade where Africans sold Africans to Caucasian slave traders who profiteered from free slave labor is an example of the genocidal strategy to control and in some instances practice population control among the human family. Examples of these include the Dred Scott Decision, Jim Crow Laws, the Eugenics Movements (Hitler, Margaret Sanger, many others), and sterilization and chemical birth-control spearheaded by Planned Parenthood.

In the area of education in the 20th century, the Brown vs. Board of Education decision and the removal of prayer from public schools and the public square weakened our educational system and wounded our family structure. When the free love and sexual revolution movements hit America, the foundation of the natural family structure began to crumble. Secular Humanists' attacks on procreative marriage, family and natural human sexuality continue into the 21st century.

The legalization of abortion with the passage of Roe vs. Wade (spearheaded by our government with Planned Parenthood as the vehicle) started in the mid-20th Century. Its deadly tentacles reach into the 21st century bringing death to over 50 million babies and countless numbers of injuries and harm to women and families.

Add to this other social inhibitors of life, liberty and the pursuit of happiness, including escalating statistics of health problems such as HIV/AIDS and other diseases that are linked to lifestyle decisions. It all proves that there is a real enemy of the human family. Finally, note the imbalance in the justice system in America where African American males are now the highest number in the prison population. Is this what some are calling "late, late term abortions," in that young people who are not aborted in the womb have their dreams "aborted" by invasive and harmful social influences?

One Human Race

Acts 17 teaches that we are all of the same blood, the same human family. Most Americans have "mixed" blood. Examples: Martin Luther King Jr.'s great grandfather was Irish, and his great grandmother was a freed African slave. Many "whites" are mixed with say English and French, or Spanish and English, etc. Nobody is stark Black or White, just shades of pink, brown and ebony. So why does the dictionary define white as good and pure and black as dark and evil? A lie from Satan!

Thank God we have an even stronger blood covenant which is the blood of Jesus. Fourteen million (14) million, 50 million, who's counting? God is counting, and He is calling us to say enough is enough!

In the 20th Century

The first human law sanctioned abortions occurred in New York around 1970. A "birth control clinic" founded by racist eugenicist Margaret Sanger was operating in New York at the time. Abortion would spawn from there.

Voices of compassion, with the spirit of the abolitionist rose in protest to the human tragedy of abortion/baby slaughter that was rising up from New York. African American voices were counted in the numbers of those who wanted to stop abortion.

While America was Sleeping

In the 20th Century, Jesse Jackson and others led the African American community away from their values of the ages. Social injustice arose in the name of abortion rights. In considering the civil rights of all people, we examine how many people end up facing sickness, disease, poverty, incarceration and other undesired outcomes as a result of living in a "consequence-free" society.

Social problems such as the high rate of school drop outs, failing school systems, the fallout from the sexual revolution, teen pregnancy, abortion, the breakdown of the family, unjust justice systems, links to poverty and crime are all connected. *Jesus did not kill the poor, He fed them!* Poverty does not cause sin. Sin causes poverty.

21st Century Black Prolife Facts

- Abortion kills babies, hurts women and robs fathers of their seed and legacies. (*www.silentnomoreawareness.org*)
- Abortion is genocide. Black mothers and babies are targeted by the abortion industry. (*www.blackprolifecoalition.org*)
- Abortion is funded by racists. (*www.maafa21.com*)
- Life is a Civil and Human Right. Abortion is a Civil and Human wrong. (*http://www.civilrightsfoundation.org/founder.html*)
- There is one human race and each life is precious from conception until natural death. (*www.personhoodusa.com*)
- Dr. Martin Luther King, Jr. was pro-life. (*http://www.priestsforlife. org/africanamerican/king-planned-parenthood-1-8.pdf*)

Abortion and the Economy

Since 1973, 50+ million babies have been aborted. Over 15 million of those aborted babies are black. If each baby had a baby, that would be 100 million Americans missing from the economy today.

There are 100 million missing social security accounts, 100 million missing jobs, 100 million missing contributors to the economy. Where are the missing black scientists, doctors, teachers, engineers, etc.? They are gone because of abortion clinics . . . 38 million African Americans are missing in action.

According to *www.blackgenocide.org* reports, the cost of the abortions in the black community alone since 1973 is $4 billion dollars. How many foreclosures could that have stopped? Added to these startling statistics are the costs of pain and suffering of the mothers who are subject to experiencing breast cancer and other illnesses related to post abortion issues.

What Planned Parenthood Won't Tell You

- Abortion is linked to breast cancer, cervical cancer, depression and other health problems for women. (*http://abortionhurts.blogspot. com/2005/06/ptsd-abortion-and-chronic-pain.html*)

- Birth control pills and IUDs also are linked to breast cancer, cervical cancer, and other health problems for women. (*www. abcbreastcancer.com*)
- There have been over 50 million "legal" abortions since 1973 in America. The global numbers are higher. (*http://www. blackprolifecoalition.org/numbers-dont-lie/*)
- Nearly one third of abortions in America are committed on Black women, who are considered the "underserved population." Margaret Sanger, Planned Parenthood's founder, once said "colored people are like weeds and need to be exterminated. We don't want the word to get out . . ." (*www.maafa21.com*)
- Abortion clinics kill babies and hurt women for money. (*http:// liveaction.org/planned-parenthood-racism-project*)
- Abortion supporters lie when they say pregnancy care centers hurt women. Pregnancy care centers offer support, assistance and love to women in crisis and families in need. (*www.care-net.org*) (*www. heartbeatinternational.org*)
- Women die from "legal" abortions just like they died when abortion wasn't "legal." (*http://chastity.com/chastity-qa/birth-control/abortion/ before-abortion-was-legal*)
- Abortion is a surgical or chemical that has many risks. Abortion is not safe. (*www.physiciansforlife.org*) (*www.aaplog.org*)
- Planned Parenthood doesn't want you to know that abortion kills babies and hurts women because they want you to keep paying for abortions. They don't love you, they love your money. (*www. bloodmoneyfilm.com*)
- Anti-life, marriage and family messengers know that sexual purity and marriage between one man and one woman will prevent abortions, sexually transmitted diseases and a host of other social "ills" but they want to continue to lie to us. (*www.teachinglikejesus.org*)
- Abortion was "legalized" in America in 1973 with the passage of Roe vs. Wade, a deceptive piece of federal legislation that was built upon lies that abortion was good for women.

Enter the 21st Century

Near the end of the 20th Century, flowing into the 21st Century, African American voices were raised in protest against "Black Genocide". When

Jesse Jackson and other leaders abandoned the message of life in favor of a "women's right to abortion" message, new prolife messages emerged from within the Black communities.

In this collection, we can only highlight a few of the valiant Black voices of those who fight for Life, Liberty and the Pursuit of Happiness. These warriors support Life, Marriage and Family under the Banner of Jesus Christ.

Is the Womb a Sanctuary or a Tomb?

Often, post-abortive mothers and their assisting caregivers report that surviving children born after their mothers' abortions display such behaviors as extreme anxiety such as screaming or crying when they hear a vacuum cleaner, or excessive crying at times . . . or trauma when they touch the next baby in Mother's tummy . . .

Ask yourself this question: "How would I feel if I had lived 9 months in a violent crime scene?" A sanctuary is a place of refuge and asylum. As we pray for post-abortive healing, let us remember all of the effects, including, but not limited to the links to breast cancer, cervical cancer, depression, substance abuse, and survivors' syndrome. Abortion is a major proponent of the culture of death. Choose life!

Time out for Politics

God is not a Republican or a Democrat! Politicians in both parties have played a part in America's racist practices. God is the answer to our problems, not politics.

Let's be real! One party runs on righteousness, one on justice. Yet, Righteousness and Justice belong together. Life, liberty and justice are universal human issues, universal human rights. We need to encourage all political leaders to support life from conception until natural death.

Give unto Caesar

The government and the justice system should not violate the civil rights of a baby in the womb. LIFE belongs to God. Vote Prolife!

Life, Marriage, Family and Purity Converge

We want parents to have the freedom to raise families. We support good education, good health, and all programs that benefit a safe and blessed quality of life. Many social issues that impact the Black community can be solved and resolved by following God's Word for life.

Working Together and Networking with Others

All of our gifting and callings come from God. Recognizing this, we remain grateful when we are able to work together on projects. We are also blessed to work with other "organizations" and "ministries" to advance the calling of the National Black Prolife Coalition.

In the first decade of the 21st Century, we worked together to advance the message of abundant life in many venues using powerful tools that were granted and inspired by God. Some of our ventures include:

1. **Defund Planned Parenthood:** Working with the Gerard Health Foundation and Students for Life, Live Action Films and others, we were able to promote the early stages of the messaging of how Planned Parenthood is targeting Black communities and hurting women.

2. **Abortion is NOT Healthcare:** Recognizing that abortion and abortion causing drugs and chemical birth control agents are linked to breast cancer and other serious medical conditions, members of the growing Black Prolife Movement came together to host a media campaign regarding defeating the Administration's proposals to continue to fund abortion and its byproducts through federal tax dollars and to advance the message that abortion is *not* health care. We were joined by members of the prolife medical community and pregnancy care center leaders.

3. **MAAFA21.com:** Several members of the NBPC appear in this eye opening film. The release of the film ignited a "viral" media effort. College campuses are being visited. Black ministers and community leaders are being invited to view the film across America. The film has a major impact on the prolife message.

4. **PRENDA—Prenatal Nondiscrimination Act:** Members of NBPC joined author of PRENDA Bill in Washington, DC to host a screening of MAAFA21.

5. **Blood Money:** Members of NBPC are involved in promotional screenings of the enlightening Blood Money film trailer that exposes the heartless and mercenary tactics of the abortion industry.

6. **The Heartbeat Bill:** Taking the lead from ***www.protectingblacklife. org,*** NBPC members coalesced to work in Ohio to advance the message that a baby's beating heart is part of its humanity. From conception/fertilization a human is a human. The beating heart of the baby gives witness to this truth.

7. **I Am Somebody Campaign:** Inspired by the leader of the National Black Prolife Union, this is a major awareness campaign. A baby is a person with a spirit, soul and body. In the womb, the baby cries out, "I am somebody!"

8. **I vote Prolife Campaign:** Inspired by the Founder of King for America and the Founder of the Radiance Foundation, this campaign takes the message of the importance of the prolife vote to a new level. For decades, there has been an ongoing effort to inspire people to vote their values, and to vote prolife. This crusade moves the masses to take ownership of the message and to vote and proclaim, "I am prolife"!

9. **Prolife Freedom Rides:** Inspired by the National Director of Priests for Life, along with the Director of African American Outreach for Priests for Life, this bus tour encompassed southern cities with the message that the Freedom Rides of the 20th Century Civil Rights Movement carry on in the 21st Century as we ride for the babies. Members of the NBPC boarded busses and proclaimed the relevance of the 21st Century Prolife Movement.

10. **National Day of Mourning Campaigns:** Inspired by the founder of The Restoration Project, this national day of prayer mounted a new level of our awareness campaign.

11. **Endangered Species Campaign:** Inspired by the founders of The Radiance Foundation and The Restoration Project, in concert with Georgia Right to Life, this campaign delivers the message that Black babies and their mothers are being targeted by the abortion community. The NBPC helped to advance the message of this powerful billboard campaign.

12. **40 Days for Life:** The NBPC joins ranks with leaders of this impactful prolife Prayer Movement.

13. **Personhood Movement:** A person is a person no matter how small. The NBPC joins the leader of the Issues4Life Foundation and others at the forefront of this Movement. This message is a vital plank of our platform.

14. **Betrayed—*www.abortioninthehood.com*:** Inspired by the founder of The Restoration Project, this billboard campaign delivers the message that contemporary Black pro-abortionists are betraying the Black community.

15. **Numbers Don't Lie Trilogy: (*www.blackprolifecoalition.org*)** This motion graphics series brought to life by the founder of The Radiance Foundation hits home and hits hard about the startling facts of genocide and abortion statistics.

16. **Media Impact**—Including this Anthology, members of the NBPC write articles, blogs, and books, and appear on radio, television, in print media, and on the social network. These contributions to the shifting social and spiritual climate have notable and lasting impact.

What is Personhood?

Personhood is the cultural and legal recognition of the equal and unalienable rights of human beings. When the term "person" is applied to a particular class of human beings, it is an affirmation of their individual rights. In other words, to be a person is to be protected by a series of God-given rights and constitutional guarantees such as life, liberty, and the pursuit of happiness.

Where Do We Go From Here?

At the beginning of this chapter, we spoke of unity of our faith. We spoke of life, liberty and of love. This book is a labor of love from prolife warriors who are carrying forth the message of the sanctity of life, so that the generations to come will be able to carry the banner into their lives. We pray to see abortion end in our lifetime, so that we and our children will live.

Dr. Alveda King, niece of Dr. Martin Luther King, Jr., is Founder of King for America www.kingforamerica.com and Pastoral Associate with Priests for Life www.africanamericanoutreach.com.

CHAPTER 2

Dr. Martin Luther King Jr. and the Civil Rights of the Unborn

Dr. Alveda King

Have I now become your enemy because I am telling you the truth?
Galatians 4:16

My uncle, Dr. Martin Luther King, Jr., is revered throughout our nation—and the world—as a champion of injustice for all who are oppressed. His legacy is one that resonates with his family and is cherished by all. For this reason, it is incumbent upon me to clarify an event that seems to contradict the values Dr. King held so dear with regards to the civil rights of the unborn.

First, some history . . . In 1939, Margaret Sanger, founder of Planned Parenthood outlined a plan to solicit leaders from the Black church to promote a plan that would unwittingly cause the demise of millions of its members. Realizing the importance of the "colored minister" in his community, Sanger considered him to be of more value than any physician. Yet, she despised the faith of Negroes and considered religion to be an exercise in superstition. "They still believe—large numbers of them—that God sends them children," (March 8, 1941).

Pulpit to Pew

Sanger's plan was to enlist the minister to promote Planned Parenthood from the pulpit and impact the listeners in the pew. "The most successful, educational appeal to the Negro is through a religious appeal," she wrote. "We do not want word to go out that we want to exterminate the Negro population, and the minister is the man who can straighten out that idea if it ever occurs to any of their more rebellious members," (December 10, 1939).

During the 60s, who better to engage to promote what appeared to be a beneficial plan promoting family planning than Dr. Martin Luther King, Jr? His leadership in the community and status worldwide numbered him among a select group of handpicked Negro leaders.

In 1966, Dr. King was presented with the first Planned Parenthood Federation of America Margaret Sanger Award "presented annually to recognize leadership, excellence, and outstanding contributions to the reproductive health and rights movement," (PPFA Margaret Sanger Award Winners). Today, his name heads the list and is prominently displayed on Planned Parenthood's website. By aligning Dr. King with the nations' biggest abortion industry—one that has destroyed over 50 million lives—we view the award in hindsight as nothing more than a wolf in sheep's clothing or worse, a Trojan Horse of gigantic proportions.

Abortion is a violent act against a helpless victim. Dr. King, a man of love, peace, and non-violence with a solid Christian faith, was assassinated before the truth of Planned Parenthood and their map for genocide was unveiled following the passage of Roe vs. Wade. For a time, many were fooled. History and research has revealed Planned Parenthood's true abortion agenda, and it is in direct conflict with the teachings of Dr. King.

Dr. King did not personally accept the award. His wife, Mrs. Coretta Scott King attended the ceremony and received the award for him. In her speech, she mentioned the benefits of family planning among Negro families and the "kinship" between the Civil Rights Movement and Margaret Sanger's early efforts.

Nowhere in this speech was there a mention of the word, "abortion." And, there is much speculation regarding the real author of the speech. However, it is a well-known fact that during her lifetime, Mrs. King, unlike her husband, supported abortion and personally held a more liberal view on marriage and human sexuality.

Setting the Record Straight

As Dr. King's niece, I want to set the record straight, especially since I understand how it is to be blatantly lied to, deceived and intentionally misled. I accepted the lies of Planned Parenthood until I learned the unfortunate truth of the violence of abortion through my own personal experience. Had I understood Planned Parenthood's agenda I would never have aborted a child.

One need only read the writings of Dr. King to conclude that he would neither agree with the violent violation of the civil rights of the millions of aborted babies nor with Planned Parenthood's chemical and artificial birth control methods that are responsible for the subsequent blitz of women's health problems.

> The Negro cannot win if he is willing to sacrifice the futures of his children for immediate personal comfort and safety. Injustice anywhere is a threat to justice everywhere.—Dr. Martin Luther King, Jr. (1929-1968)

Daddy King

My grandfather, Dr. Martin Luther King, Sr., twice announced, "No one is going to kill a child of mine." The first time Daddy King said this was to my mother who was facing an "inconvenient pregnancy" with me. The second time I was facing an inconvenient pregnancy and told him about my predicament. In both instances, Daddy King said, "No!"

Tragically, two of his grandchildren had already been aborted when he saved the life of his next great-grandson with pro-life statement.

Like Mrs. Laura Bush who in interviews and her book admits she is pro-abortion, Mrs. Coretta Scott King was at odds with her husband's ideology regarding life and human sexuality. These women chose platforms that were not reconciled to the reality of the blessings of procreative reproductive health leading to monogamous healthy marriages between husbands and wives, the birth of healthy babies, and the continuation of God's plan for families nurtured in love and righteousness.

It is ludicrous to suggest that Martin Luther King, Jr. would have endorsed any acts that chemically or surgically dismember and kill babies in the womb and that butcher women under guise of providing "safe abortions." Planned Parenthood and her allies hide the truth that many hysterectomies, breast cancer surgeries and other female reproductive illnesses are the consequences of abortion. They promote death over life and call it Civil Rights.

How can the "Dream" survive if we murder our children? The fate of every baby, helpless in the womb of its mother, is subject to his or her mother's will. She decides whether the child lives or dies—a decision provided by Roe v. Wade to keep the black population at a minimum. How is it that a woman has the right to make the final choice of whether the child lives or dies? Should not that choice be left to God? Would the Giver of Life not ultimately proclaim, "Choose life!"

I, Too, Have a Dream

I, too, have a dream. It's in my genes. As Christians, we must press on in the conviction that we are a colony of heaven called to obey God rather than man. Small in number, we must remain big in commitment. We must be too God intoxicated to be astronomically intimidated. By our effort and example may God use us, imperfect vessels that we are, to bring an end to such ancient evils as infanticide, abortion, racism, and oppression.

Dr. Alveda King, niece of Dr. Martin Luther King, Jr., is Founder of King for America www.kingforamerica.com and Pastoral Associate with Priests for Life www.africanamericanoutreach.com.

REFERENCES

December 10, 1939. Letter from Margaret Sanger to Dr. C. J. Gamble. March 8, 1941. Letter from Margaret Sanger to D. Rose.

PPFA Margaret Sanger award winners. (1966). Retrieved August, 2012 from *http://www.plannedparenthood.org/about-us/newsroom/politics-policy-issues/ppfa-margaret-sanger-award-winners-4840.htm*

CHAPTER 3

We Shall Overcome . . . Abortion

Day Gardner

Throughout the month of February, we take the time—one month out of the year—to remember the tragedies and to celebrate the triumphs of African Americans in history. We celebrate the fact that we are a strong race that survived the horrors and inhumane treatment of an enslaved people, individuals who were presumed by many to be less than human.

We came together in the 1960s facing very difficult times after thousands of African Americans suffered physical torture and sometimes even death simply for wanting to experience the American dream. And their lives were sacrificed because they insisted that we be allowed to experience the freedoms that all American citizens are entitled to under the laws of this great nation.

Big Strides Blind Eyes

Since the 1960s, we have continued to make great strides in breaking down color barriers and overcoming the walls of inequality. We have become doctors, lawyers, educators, movie stars, corporation owners and more. But I worry that many of us in the black community have forgotten what the struggle was all about. In our quest for higher education, bigger houses, better jobs and flashier cars, have we become blind to the fact that more than a thousand of our children die each day by the horrible practice of abortion?

These children are denied their most basic human right—the right to life. This is the very same right for which our ancestors so proudly worked, marched and died.

More than 50 million children have been killed by abortion. Seventeen (17) million of them were black children. Abortion has become the number one killer of black people in this country, killing more African Americans that accidents, heart disease, stroke, crimes, HIV-AIDS and all other deaths combined!

What bothers me is this. We are very quick to recognize racism everywhere else except in the one area that truly affects all of us. Most blacks will agree that racism is still very much alive but they say nothing when abortion facilities are purposefully placed in poor, minority communities.

This is no accident! More than 37 percent of all abortions are performed on black women. In one year, more than 400,000 black babies have been killed by abortion—their little bodies dismembered, necks severed, heads crushed.

We must realize that abortion is a billion dollar a year business that makes most of its money by killing our children. Abortion providers use us to make their blood money. If we as black people say no to abortion the industry will cease to exist.

We must raise our voices like thunder to stop the killing. We are the underground railroad of our time and it's up to us to make the atrocity, which is abortion, a terrible thing of our historical past.

If we stand united in the Word of God against this horrific practice, *I do believe, we shall overcome* this, too.

Day Gardner is President of the National Black Pro-Life Union www.nationalblackprolifeunion.com.

CHAPTER 4

Is Choice a Delusion?

Reverend Levon R. Yuille

Is choice a strong delusion? According to Webster's Dictionary, choice needs two elements to have a real option, and only one element of true choice can prevail in a two-element situation. It also defines equation as a formal expression of the sameness of reference of two expressions. Choice advocates want us to believe that all they are fighting for is a choice between having and not having an abortion.

I believe most of us know we do not need laws to think about doing or not doing something. There is no law against thinking, nor could there be such a silly law. So, are choice folks really fighting for the right to think about an abortion? This is what they would like us to think the choice equation is all about.

The Choice Equation

There must be at least two points of focus before we can equate our decision to that of making a choice. In the choice debate, do we really have two true points of consideration?

If I understand the choice argument correctly, they argue that a woman has a right to do whatever she wishes with her body. Due to my assumption that a woman only has one body, this fact would suggest that a choice person is thinking about doing something to her body.

In the choice equation, is the choice argument indeed only about *one* body? I think not. As a matter of fact, the choice argument is about a mother and a living child, and then we do have the necessary and logical entities that will support the concept of choice. But what is the choice relative to this mother and living, innocent child?

The mother is alive and the child is alive. So the argument most certainly cannot be for life, because life is a given—both entities are alive. So what is there to choose? The choice folks are definitely not fighting for life.

What is the choice equation, and where are the two points of consideration? Life can't be one of the decisions to be made. The living child already eliminates the decision of life, so if life has already started, what is the choice?

Death is Left

Logically, there seems to be only one option, and if life as an option has been eliminated, what's left besides death? Could the only choice in the choice movement be death? Has the living innocent human being been sentenced to death because of choice?

The Bible commands that we not shed innocent blood, "So shalt thou put away the guilt of innocent blood from among you, when thou shalt do that which is right in the sight of the Lord," (Duet 21:9). Is Choice really a choice, or is it a strong delusion that too many people are accepting?

Dr. Levon Yuille is Pastor of The Bible Church in Ypsilanti, MI, Founder of The National Black Prolife Congress and Host of acclaimed radio talk show, Joshua's Trial http://biblechurchypsi.org/introduction.html.

CHAPTER 5

Abortion by the Numbers

Catherine Davis

For thirty nine years now, the arguments for or against abortion have obscured, and most times redirected attention away from abortion's impact on communities of color, especially the black community. For the sake of this discussion, let's set the "for "and "against" arguments aside since they have little to do with abortion by the numbers and would only serve to cloud the issue.

The numbers do not lie, no matter how some may try to manipulate them to support their position on this volatile issue. In the states and cities where we can access abortion data by race, the numbers of abortions on black women are disproportionately high—two, three, sometimes five times their presence in the population. In state after state we see a pattern of black women streaming into America's abortion clinics at 3 times the rate of white women. Something is terribly wrong.

Takes My Breath Away

One example of this is the state of Georgia. In Georgia, black women have had 50% or more of all abortions in the state over the last 15 years (1995-2009). For ten of those years, the black abortion rate exceeded 55%. And, for nine of those years, 25% or more of the viable pregnancies in Georgia's black community ended in abortion.

Georgia has most, if not all, of the incremental laws that were designed to restrict abortion: 24 hour waiting period, Woman's Right to Know, Parental Notification, Ultra Sound and Unborn Victims of Violence Act. Despite these laws, black women consistently have led in the numbers, and in some years, the abortions have almost reached 60% of the state's total. I found these numbers to be staggering and they literally took my breath away!

More Aborted than Born Alive

But New York City numbers actually chilled my bones. In 2011, an article in the New York Post proclaimed that "60 percent of all unborn African-American babies are aborted." Written by Michael Benjamin, a recently retired state representative from the Bronx, the article went on to describe "A strange silence" by those in the city that had failed to react to this astonishing number. Benjamin was reporting on 2009 statics that had just been released by the NYC health department in their annual *Summary of Vital Statistics*.

That report showed that in 2009 there were 68,203 viable pregnancies among black women of child bearing age. Of that number 40,798 ended in abortions—more black babies were aborted than were born alive. Seeing those numbers drove me to find out how long the numbers in New York City had been upside down.

The answer broke my heart because the annual reports revealed that for at least a decade this has been the case. And 2010 brought little change—59.1% of New York City's 65,209 viable pregnancies in that year were aborted (Charlesworth, 2011). Again more aborted than born alive.

Slick Marketing Clouds the Debate

Planned Parenthood, the National Abortion and Reproductive Action League Pro-Choice America (NARAL) and other abortion advocates carefully cloak their rhetoric in the garments of the women's' rights and more recently civil rights movements, obscuring the real intent of their population control agenda. Since its inception, Planned Parenthood has carried the mantle of controlling the black birth rate. Beginning with Margaret Sanger's (Planned Parenthood's founder) Negro Project, they have long sought black faces and voices to promote birth control and now abortion.

Hiring its first black minister "to straighten it out should it ever occur their more rebellious members that we want to exterminate them" in 1939, Planned Parenthood continues to hire black ministers and community leaders to promote their cause among blacks. Today, they include slick media campaigns using black women and black ministers to promote abortion and access to abortion.

They enlist black elected officials, such almost all of the Black Congressional Caucus, to not only promote abortion and birth control, but to ensure little if any legislation comes out of the Congress that would begin to address abortions' disparate impact on blacks. In fact, in 2011, the CBC was willing to allow the government to shut down rather than defund Planned Parenthood, despite Title X, the legislation that funds family planning, prohibiting funds from going to organizations that use abortion as a means of family planning.

Stop It!

The black community must come together to stop the population control agenda of Planned Parenthood and other abortion providers. We must come together to eliminate abortion, the tool being used as the greatest instrument of genocide in America. I pray you join your voice with those working to stop it.

Catherine Davis is President of The Restoration Project based in Stone Mountain, Georgia www.abortioninthehood.com.

REFERENCE

Charlesworth, M. (January 9, 2011). 41% of New York City pregnancies end in abortion. *ABC News*. Retrieved from *http://abclocal.go.com/wabc/ story?section=news/local/new_york&id=7883827*

CHAPTER 6

Abortion: The Robbing of a Heritage

Reverend Johnny Hunter

Abortion is racism in its ugliest form. Because of some very suave planning by abortion supporters and providers, abortionists have eliminated more African-American children than the KKK ever lynched. This is one truth that is very disturbing.

Think about it. From 1973 to 1992, abortionists have snuffed out the lives of over nine million African-American children before their first birthday. Over nine million beautiful black children were prevented from ever having the opportunity to become artists, musicians, doctors, teachers, lawyers, judges, taxi drivers, ambulance drivers, nurses, secretaries, senators, representatives, salesmen, sales clerks, computer programmers, analysts, managers, waitresses, waiters, tellers, leaders, followers, ordinary people, extraordinary people, parents, grandparents, and ancestors.

They were robbed of the most essential of all rights—the right to life. They were robbed of their opportunities, and those of us who remain are robbed of their contributions to humanity.

Abortion Helps Blacks?

When liberal racists defend abortion as a way of helping blacks, I challenge them to show me the bodies of the dead African-American children the abortionists have helped. When a plantation Negro says he supports abortion because he cares about the sisters, mothers and daughters, he is a hypocrite of the lowest order. To deny the next generation of brothers and sisters the right to live is the ultimate self-destructing mechanism in the African-American community.

The legacy and heritage we are leaving is the most important treasure we can give our children. As African-Americans, it is our responsibility to leave a legacy to the next generation, one upon which they may build a better life for themselves. Many great men and women have left us a heritage, but much of our heritage was robbed by slave owners.

Two hundred years ago our African-American heritage was robbed by a group of elitist individuals who intentionally kept us ignorant concerning the devastating effects of slavery. Today, our heritage is being robbed by elitist individuals who have intentionally kept us ignorant concerning the devastating effect of abortion on our race. They are robbing us to profit from the deaths of our sons and daughters.

It is Time

The time has come for people of all races, religions, creeds and nations to stand up on behalf of the next generation of children. It is time to reclaim what is left of a broken legacy of enduring love and strength through faith in God.

It is time to no longer use the excuse of poverty. Who knows whether or not this is the child who will bring his family *out* of poverty?

It is time to no longer use the excuse of having this child later. No man and woman can ever conceive the same child twice.

It is time to insist that no child ever face discrimination because of race or place of residence.

It is time that African-American men and women insist that their children and their children's neighbors are no longer denied the inalienable right to life and the opportunity to appreciate their heritage.

There is an old African proverb which says, "No one knows whose womb holds the chief." Have they killed the chief? I hope not, but I do know that many of the chief's people have been destroyed in a war directed at them in their most defenseless moments.

The Destruction Continues

As a person who values human life, I feel very troubled that the youngest of our race are not guaranteed the opportunity to have their day in the sun. I have joined other Christians and have paid a very light price of time in jails and prisons for trying to save a little one. The destruction continues.

I have spoken to churches in over half the states in the America and have taken the gospel of life to three foreign countries including South Africa. I have seen people weep as they are confronted with the horror of this holocaust. Still, the destruction continues.

I have had personal contact with congressmen and senators on Capitol Hill. I have dined with them and expressed my concern for the consequences that are inevitable. I have even been arrested on Capitol Hill with other men and women of faith for trying to protect Chinese refugees from being returned to China to undergo forced abortion, sterilization and, in many cases, death. Still, the killing continues.

I have prayed at the very gates of hell itself and have been encouraged to see courageous Christians leave their comfort zones to confront imposed death masked as choice. We have received more favorable press recently than in any other period of our pro-life work. Yet, even these improvements, the murder of the innocents continues.

It's not just me. All over this nation, prophets are sounding the alarm. Repent or certain destruction! The warnings of prophetic voices like Erma Craven and Rev. Arthur Colbert are still echoing after their deaths, "Beware of the tactics of eugenics—abortion, poverty and genocide." Still, imposed death continues.

Don't Obey the Death Order

It is time for the women of our nation to become like the mothers and midwives in ancient Egypt who did not obey the death order. It is time for evangelists to step off their well—furnished pulpits and go into the streets to call nations to repentance. It is time for pastors to make use of the shepherd's staff and boldly face the wolves.

Pastors must chase predators out of the pastures so that God's lambs can grow safely and be nurtured. Congregations need to escape from those pastors who invite the wolves into the sanctuary lest on the final day of reckoning, they realize that they were robbed of their souls.

It is time for leaders nationwide to become outraged.
It is time to insist that the killing stop.
It is time to refuse to be ignored!

You are the light of the world.
A city that is set on a hill cannot be hidden.
(Matthew 5:14)

We must emulate the Acts of the Apostles and the Civil Rights Movement in America. As people of faith and action, we must speak up for justice. Let our voices be silent only in death prior to our resurrection. Let us not go silently into the night. Make noise! Wake up our brethren and sisters who are in a deep slumber lest they too be slaughtered.

Join us as we implement new strategies, recruit the compassionate, and educate our people to avoid the various disguises of death. In every local city where we are invited, we will help Christians combat this evil through fervent prayer, skillful praise, the acquiring of knowledge and, above all, in Christian love. Let us love God and keep His commandments.

Reverend Johnny Hunter is an ordained minister with the National Clergy Council and a prolife advocate. www.learninc.org

CHAPTER 7

Persons Not Property

Reverend Walter Hoye

By 1830 slavery, was primarily located in the Southern United States of America, and it existed in many different forms. African Americans were enslaved on small farms, large plantations, in cities and towns, inside homes, out in the fields, and in industry and transportation.

By 1860, on the eve of the Civil War, Historian James L. Huston emphasized the role of slavery as an economic institution. Huston, a leading advocate of secession, placed the value of southern held slaves at $2.8 billion. At about $3 billion in 1860 currency, the economic value of slaves in the U.S. was more than the combined value of all the factories, railroads and banks in the country or about $12 trillion in U.S. dollars today.

Much of the North's economic prosperity derived from what Abraham Lincoln, in his second inaugural address, called "the bondman's two hundred and fifty years of unrequited toil." President Lincoln was asking Americans to consider the obligations created by slavery. The first of those obligations is to acknowledge the full truth.

The Full Truth

The full truth is this: African American Slaves were considered property, and they were property because they were black. Their status was enforced by public policy and reinforced by violence. Slaves throughout the South had to live under a set of laws called the Slave Codes. Codes varied slightly from state to state, but the basic idea was the same—slaves were considered property, not people, and were treated as such.

The killing of a slave was almost never regarded as murder, and the rape of slave women was treated as a form of trespassing. So intolerable were the conditions under which African Americans slaves suffered from day to day that some went as far as committing suicide or mutilating themselves to ruin their property value.

As an African America, I ask how could this be justified. Wasn't it obvious that slaves were living, breathing human beings? Where was the outrage from the American public?

The Language of Oppression Past

Haig Bosmajian, Professor Emeritus in the Speech/Communication Department at the University of Washington, says, "While names, words, and language can be, and are, used to inspire us, to motivate us to humane acts, to liberate us, they can also be used to dehumanize human beings and to 'justify' their suppression and even their extermination," (Bosmajian, 1983).

In order to justify the inhumane treatment of African American slaves and soothe the conscious of the Americans, dehumanizing terminology or the "language of oppression" was established and propagated by way of both "academic" and "legal" opinion at the very highest levels of our educational and legal communities.

From 1815 to 1830, the American Colonization Society: "Free black in our country are . . . a contagion." In 1857 the U.S. Supreme Court decided, "A negro of the African race was regarded . . . as an article of property . . . a subordinate and inferior class of being." In 1858, the Virginia Supreme Court decision declared, "In the eyes of the law . . . the slave is not a person".

- In 1867, Buckner Payne, Publisher, "The Negro is not a human being".
- In 1900, Professor Charles Carroll, "The Negro is . . . one of the lower animals".
- In 1903 Dr. William English, "The negro race is . . . a heritage of organic and psychic debris".
- In 1909, Dr. E. T. Brady, "They [Negroes] are parasites".

The Language of Oppression Present

Today, even while modern medical science clearly and overwhelmingly supports the humanity and personhood of the pre-born child, the same financial motives and oppressive language strategies that were used to oppress African American slaves are being used, right now, to justify killing pre-born children.

For example, in 1973, the U.S. Supreme Court decided, "The Fetus, at most, represents only the potentiality of life." Again, in 1973, the U.S. Supreme Court declared, "The word 'person,' as used in the 14th Amendment does not include the unborn."

- In 1979 Professor Joseph Flectcher said, "Pregnancy when not wanted is a disease . . . in fact, a venereal disease."
- In 1980 Dr. Mariti Kekomaki, agreed that "An aborted baby is just garbage . . . just refuse."
- In 1984, Professor Rosalind Pollack Petchesky declared, "The Fetus is a parasite."
- In 1984, Rabbi Wolfe announced, "A fetus is not a human being."
- In 1985, Dr. Hart Peterson on fetal movement summarized that it was, "Like . . . a primitive animal that's poked with a stick."
- In 1986, Attorney Lori Andrews summed up the abortion argument with this statement, "People's body parts [embryos] are their personal property."

These sentiments are alive and well today. Just a few years ago, the language of oppression was clearly articulated in the words of sitting U.S. Supreme Court Justice Ruth Bader Ginsburg who said in an interview that she was surprised at a 1980 court ruling that prevented the restoration of Medicaid funding for abortions, because, in her opinion, when Roe v. Wade was decided in 1973 "Frankly I had thought that at the time Roe was decided, there was concern about population growth and particularly growth in populations that we don't want to have too many of," (Bazelton, 2009).

Dehumanization

History teaches us, time and time again, that the use of oppressive language to demonize and dehumanize certain segments of the human race is incontestably evil. In Germany, the persistent portrayal of the Jews as, "vermin," "bacilli," "parasites," and "disease," contributed to Adolf Hitler's "Final Solution."

In the antebellum South, the deliberate and systematic labeling of African Americans as "chattel," "property," "beasts," "feebleminded," and "useless eaters," eased the conscious of many and paved the way for the subjugation and suppression of African Americans. From the East coast to the West coast the defining of the American Indian as "non-persons," "savages," and "Satan's partisans" led to the extermination of a significant portion of the American Indian population.

The Jewish holocaust in Germany, African American slavery in the antebellum south, and the death of countless American Indians were despicable events in our human history that were accompanied by the use of dehumanizing language. Similarly, the dismemberment and destruction of the bodies of the most vulnerable among us—the pre-born child—is entirely indefensible.

Persons Are Not Property

Human beings are persons and persons are *not* property. As a civil society we must move beyond the powerful elite's loathsome language of oppression and recognize the inherent, inalienable and self-evident humanity of all human beings. Regardless of the means by which we were procreated, the method of reproduction, age, race, sex, gender, physical well-being, function, or condition of physical or mental dependency and/or disability, all human beings deserve to be protected by love and by law.

When Accepting the Nobel Peace Prize on December 10th, 1964, Dr. Martin Luther King, Jr., said, "I believe that 'unarmed truth' and 'unconditional love' will have the final word in reality. This is why "right, temporarily defeated, is stronger than evil" triumphant." Today, the unarmed truth is that the pre-born child is a person, not property.

- I believe personhood is God-given and not government-granted. It is not offered to the elite and denied to the "least of these."

- I believe personhood, addresses the most important right of all . . . the right to live, without which all other rights are meaningless.
- I believe personhood is right.

The "unconditional love" for the pre-born child is rooted in the love that Christ has for all. While the current conditions may have temporarily defeated the personhood of the pre-born child, I believe the righteousness of personhood is stronger than the evil of pre-natal murder and that it will ultimately prove triumphant.

And, I believe personhood is the final word in reality of the pro-life movement.

Reverend *Walter Hoye is Founder\President of the Issues4Life Foundation www.issues4life.org, the California Civil Rights Foundation www. civilrightsfoundation.org and Founder of the Frederick Douglass Foundation of California www.fdfca.org.*

REFERENCES

Bazelton, E. (July 7, 2009). The place of women on the court. *New York Times Magazine*. Retrieved November 20, 2009 from *http://www. nytimes.com/2009/07/12/magazine/12ginsburg-t.html?pagewanted=all*

Bosmajian, H. A. (1983). *The language of oppression*. Lanham, MD: University Press of America. Retrieved November 20, 2009 from *http:// www.washington.edu/research/showcase/1983a.html*

CHAPTER 8

Abortion: The Sin of Idolatry

Dr. La Verne Tolbert

For you shall worship no other god, for the LORD,
whose name is Jealous, is a jealous God.
Exodus 24:14

God is jealous. His jealousy is often misunderstood. It's easy to understand why.

Most equate God's jealousy with the unstable emotions of an insecure boyfriend or girlfriend whose poor personality development results in an overwhelming need to control. This need is fear-based and produces inappropriate responses that are ugly, pathetic, pitiful, and wholly unattractive.

God's jealousy is different. He is not jealous *of* us. He is jealous *for* us. God is jealous about idolatry—worship of false gods. Why? He is protecting us, because worship of false gods leads to death.

The Old Testament is replete with examples of God's disobedient children worshipping foreign gods, the idols of their neighbors. Idolatry was not just about bowing and praying to a false god. These idols demanded sacrifice—the lives of children. Why?

The demonic powers hate babies because they hate Jesus. When they destroy "the lease of these" (Matt. 25:40, 45), the most vulnerable among us, they're destroying a picture of Jesus himself, of the child delivered by the woman who crushes their head (Gen. 3:15). (Moore, 2009, p. 64)

Idolatry continues to demand the lives of children today through abortion. Let's examine the ancient rites. Are there any similarities?

Abominations of the Nations

As the children of Israel prepared to enter the land which the Lord God had given them, they did so with this warning, "When you come into the land which the LORD your God is giving you, you shall not learn to follow the abominations of those nations," (Deut 18: 9). Burning children as an offering to an idol during pagan worship rites leads the list of abominations. Gross sexual immorality, including orgies and prostitution, often accompanied these occult practices.

Israel was quite familiar with Amon, the god of the Egyptians, who was the god of fertility (Comay & Brownrigg, 1980). As they conquered nations en route to the Promised Land, they would also become familiar with Chemosh, the abomination of Moab, and Molech, the abomination of Ammon (Wood, 1970).

Chemosh and Molech

Chemosh required human sacrifice, and 2 Kings 3: 27 describes the shocking account of the King of Moab who offered his oldest son by burning him on a wall. Molech was also worshipped by "offering up human sacrifices," usually a child from the family (Comay & Brownrigg, 1980, p. 268).

Imagine placing children into the enormous belly of these idols—a blazing furnace—and watching them burn alive while participating in a drunken orgy! What could be more tortuous?

Our God forbids Israel from offering their children to Molech, a demon-god who demands the violent sacrifice of human babies (Lev. 20: 1-8). Indeed, he denounces Molech by name. He further warns that he will cut off from the people of God not only the one who practiced such sacrifice but also all who "at all close their eyes to that man when he gives one of his children to Molech" (Lev. 20:4). Behind Molech, God recognizes, there is one who is a "murderer from the beginning" (John 8:44). (Moore, 2009, p. 66)

Our true God is protective. He wants to keep His children from practices that result in the slaughter of innocents. This is why He demands worship of no other god except God the Father through the Lord Jesus Christ. Children are supposed to live.

Abortion's Cruelty

Abortion is as cruel as the idol worship of Chemosh and Molech. The saline salt solution burns babies alive in the womb. Many are born still breathing, and Planned Parenthood places these children in plastic bags and smothers them until they die.

In New York City, the Department of Health required that a death certificate be issued for every baby who was aborted. Al Moran, Planned Parenthood's board chair, fought hard to have this rule overturned. Now, death certificates are only required if the baby "takes a breath before it dies," (Tolbert, 2007, p. 91).

The spirit of Molech is at work among us even now. Even as you read this page, there are bones of babies being ground to unrecognizable bits, perhaps even a few short miles from where you 're sitting. There are babies lying in garbage receptacles, waiting to be taken away as "medical waste." (Moore, 2009, p. 66)

Because of sexual immorality, which worships man by placing that boyfriend or girlfriend on the throne above God's throne (Romans 1), a so-called unwanted pregnancy results. It's inconvenient. So why not sacrifice the baby to the god of self-love?

Many claim that abortion isn't murder. But if a woman is pregnant, it means that she is going to have a baby. If she has an abortion, she is no longer going to have a baby. What happened to the baby?

Where is the humanity? Where is the decency, the noble character of America when it advocates the destruction of the preborn under the guise of "freedom of choice"? This is a great country, the greatest nation on earth. Surely there's a better, more humane solution to the threat of poverty than abortion.

As a nation, we are guilty of the sin of idolatry. As a nation, we must repent.

Spiritual and Moral Decline

Like Solomon, America started well. But also like Solomon, America did not remain faithful to her God. She became influenced by the humanistic philosophies that at heart deny the very existence of God. This once great nation now wallows miserably in the spiritual and moral decline that is characterized by the sin of compromise.

Just as Solomon allowed the "thinking and customs of other nations to influence his decisions and manner of living" (Wood, 1970, p. 299) resulting in syncretism—worshipping God along with anything or anyone else—America has allowed pagan influences to champion worship of *any* god except God the Father through Jesus Christ.

Christians and Abortion

So who is having these abortions? We are. According to the Alan Guttmacher Institute, the research arm of Planned Parenthood:

The highest proportion (43%) identified themselves as Protestant. Twenty-seven percent (27%) of women having an abortion identified themselves as Catholic, and 8% as a member of another religion; 22% reported no religious affiliation. Thirteen percent (13%) identified themselves as "born-again" or evangelical three-fourths of whom were Protestant. (Jones, Darroch, & Henshaw, 2002).

Those who claim to know Jesus and who protest against abortion the most account for nearly 80% of all abortions. Something is wrong with this picture.

Some Good News

There's light in this tunnel, and it's because of our teenagers. In this same Guttmacher study, there's good news about those who are *not* having abortions. Between 1994 and 2000, adolescent abortions declined 39%, "in large part because many adolescents aged 15-17 have not had sex," (Jones, Darroch, & Henshaw, 2002). Who says abstinence doesn't work?

Perhaps Christians can learn from our youth. We complain about abortion, but do we expect those who aren't Christians to obey Jesus Christ if we don't? If Protestants, Catholics, and Evangelicals obey God, we will shut down every abortion mill in our communities.

> *If My people who are called by My name will humble themselves, and pray and seek My face, and turn from their wicked ways, then I will hear from heaven, and will forgive their sin and heal their land.* (2 Chronicles 7:14)

La Verne Tolbert, Ph.D., is a former board member of Planned Parenthood, New York City, from 1975 to 1980 where she learned the truth about abortion detailed in her book, Keeping You & Your Kids Sexually Pure. She is founder/ CEO of Teaching Like Jesus Ministries, a parachurch ministry that equips leaders in the local church www.teachinglikejesus.org.

REFERENCES

Comay, J. and Brownrigg, R. (1980). Who's who in the Old Testament. New York: Bonanza Books.

Jones, R., Darroch, J., and Henshaw, S. (September/October 2002). Patterns in the socioeconomic characteristics of women obtaining abortions in 2000-2001.

Moore, R. D. (2009). Adopted for life: The priority of adoption for Christian families & churches. Wheaton: Crossway.

Perspectives on Sexual and Reproductive Health. Volume 34, 5. Retrieved January 21, 2011 from *http://www.guttmacher.org/pubs/ journals/3422602.html*

Tolbert, L. (2007). Keeping you & your kids sexually pure: A how-to guide for parents, pastors, youth workers, and teachers (originally published by Zondervan). *www.xlibris.com*

Wood, L. (1970). *A survey of Israel's history.* Grand Rapids: Zondervan.

CHAPTER 9

Planned Parenthood, Eugenics, & the Black Abortion Rate

Pastor Stephen Broden

The scourge of abortion is having a direct impact on the demographics of our nation. Most demographers tell us that it takes 2.1 children for a family to replace itself. The 2000 census reported 1.86 children per family, below replacement when the number of immigrants, both legal and illegal, is not included. As of this writing, the latest replacement population data (2010) is not yet available.

America is trending toward depopulation, most dramatically among black Americans. This is readily apparent upon examining abortion and demographics in the black community.

Abortion in the Black Community

Black Americans represent 12% of the total population of the United States but currently account for 36% of all abortions. The percentage has been even higher in the past.

The Alan Guttmacher reports that 1.21 million abortions were performed in 2005. It further shows that black women were nearly 5 times as likely as non-Hispanic white women to have an abortion, and Hispanic women were nearly 3 times as likely to abort their pre-born babies, (Guttmacher, 2011). This equates to 683,294 black babies aborted in 2005, or 56% of all legal abortions that year.

According to population data provided by the U.S. Census Bureau, aborting those nearly 700,000 black babies is the equivalent of killing more than five times the entire black population of Oakland, CA, or killing more than the entire black population of Washington, D.C., Atlanta, GA, and Oakland combined! In total, since 1973, there have been more than 15 million black children aborted in America among the 53 million who will never be born.

More Black Abortions than Live Births

These statistics are simply breathtaking, and indicative of the success the abortion industry has had with messaging its culture of death into the black community. Recently released 2008 numbers paint an even grimmer trend for the black community in New York City, revealing that there are more abortions than live births. For every 1,000 births, there are 1,489 abortions (Guttmacher, 2011).

It seems that abortion is now birth-control in the black community. But abortion at this rate also spells genocide for the black community.

Why is the Black Abortion Rate So High?

There are many reasons to answer this question, but the most sinister is rarely discussed: the specter of the Eugenics Movement. Eugenics is the study of methods to improve the human race by controlling population. Francis Galton coined the word in 1883, believing that the "proper" evolution of the human race was thwarted by philanthropic outreach to the poor and "inferior."

Galton and his first cousin, Charles Darwin, were heavily influenced by the writings of Thomas Malthus, an 18th century economist, who advocated population control by controlling agricultural production and cutting off charity to the poor and "inferior races." In 1859, Darwin, who admired Malthus, wrote "On the Origin of Species by Means of Natural Selection, or the Preservation of *Favored Races* in the Struggle for Life" (italics added).

But the most notorious eugenicist is Margaret Sanger, founder of Planned Parenthood and the mother of the abortion industry in America. Sanger's views suggest that her efforts to promote birth control demonstrate a desire to "purify" the human race through eugenics, perhaps even to eliminate minority races by placing birth-control clinics in minority neighborhoods.

The mentality of Sanger, Malthus, Galton, and Darwin is still alive today in Planned Parenthood and the American Eugenic Society. In 1970, the Society defined eugenics in this way: "The essence of evolution is natural selection, the essence of eugenics is the replacement of natural selection by conscious, premeditated, or artificial selection in the hope of speeding up the evolution of desirable characteristics and the "elimination of undesirable ones."

Obama Advisors Promote Eugenics

These ideas are dangerous for those who may be designated as "undesirable" or "no longer economically viable." Indeed, within the Obama administration, bureaucrats like Health Care Policy Advisor, Ezekiel Emanuel (who resigned in January 2011), and John Holdren, the Administration's Science Advisor, advocate population control using the rationale originated by Malthus.

In 1977, Holdren authored a book entitled *EcoScience* in which he advocates extreme measures including forced abortions and sterilization to control population. The connection of abortion with the philosophy of eugenics is also evident in Supreme Court Justice Ruth Bader Ginsburg's 2009 revealing statement. In a New York Times interview, Justice Ginsburg said, "Frankly I had thought that at the time Roe was decided there was concern about population growth and particularly growth in population that we don't want to have too many of," (Bazelton, 2009).

WOW! Ginsburg really revealed her heart. It seems Roe was not passed for a woman's right to choose after all, but rather for the purpose of population control, at least in the mind of Justice Ginsburg. And *who* are the "we" in Ginsburg's quote? Could "we" be the eugenicists who are hidden away in high places making policy decisions that impact society and our culture? Or perhaps the "we" is government-run health care with death panels?

Is it any wonder that with 70% of all Planned Parenthood facilities located in black communities with slick marketing and sophisticated messaging the black abortion rate is through the roof? It seems obvious that Planned Parenthood's presence is deliberate targeting within the black community to carry out the eugenic plot encompassed in the distorted desires of Malthus, Galton, Darwin, and Sanger to "control population in order to purify the human race."

Remember, government funding provides about one-third of Planned Parenthood's budget. Is population control through the prism of eugenics how you want your tax dollars to be spent?

Stephen Broden has served as Pastor of Fair Park Bible Fellowship in Dallas, TX for 20 years www.fpbfellowshipchurch.org.

REFERENCES

Bazelton, E. (July 7, 2009). The place of women on the court. *New York Times Magazine*. Retrieved from *http://www.nytimes.com/2009/07/12/magazine/12ginsburg-t.html?pagewanted=all*

Guttmacher. (August, 2011). Facts on induced abortion in United States. Retrieved from *http://www.guttmacher.org/pubs/fb_induced_abortion.html*

CHAPTER 10

The Negro Project 2.0

Pastor Dean Nelson

I distinctly remember the moment that I first wrestled with the problem of abortion. Like many young men of my generation, I had always assumed that if abortion was legal it must be okay. Since Roe v. Wade and Doe v. Bolton—which made it illegal to restrict abortion in any stage of pregnancy—was decided when I was just five years old, I had never really considered the fact that the legality of abortion was relatively new.

By the grace of God, I did not engage in premarital sex, and so it was not an unexpected pregnancy that prompted me to consider the morality of abortion. I grew up in a small country town and was not aware of anyone I knew ever terminating a pregnancy. On occasion women and girls had children out of wedlock, of course, and this I understood to be regrettable.

Yet whether these were children of neighbors, friends or relatives, they were welcomed, doted on, cared for and seemed to turn out as well as those of us who had been born well after our parents' weddings. It would have never occurred to me growing up that children conceived out of wedlock to young mothers would have terrible lives and thus would be better off dead.

A Critical Examination

No, my passive approval of abortion came from a lack of critically examining the issue. I respected women; women, I was told, needed to have the right to decide what to do with their bodies. That seemed good enough for me.

So it was only in college, when I struck up a conversation with some pro-life students that I was forced to reconsider my views. When I mentioned the legality of abortion, a student politely countered that slavery, too, had been legal but that did not make it right.

This point forced me to consider: what if abortion was *not* okay? Did this mean anything for America? What about black Americans?

The more I learned of the history of the abortion rights movement in the United States and abroad, the more uncomfortable I became. I learned that there was a time not too long ago when black women had proportionately fewer abortions than white women and on average gave birth to more children.

This disparity worried women like Planned Parenthood founder Margaret Sanger, who considered blacks "unfit" and was concerned about their numbers becoming overwhelming. She launched The Negro Project, an initiative to use black leaders and ministers in particular as community advocates for her eugenics strategy to open up birth control clinics in black neighborhoods. Sanger's primary goal was to reduce the number of babies born to black women.

Where the Clinics Are

While few today would overtly espouse such beliefs, the overwhelming majority of abortion clinics stand in minority neighborhoods. This coupled with the view that the third child of a poor black woman is somehow less of a blessing than the first child of a wealthy white woman, showed me that Sanger's convictions lived on, albeit in a muted, politically correct form.

Nowhere is Sanger's legacy more apparent than in the disproportionate attention abortion advocates pay to urban areas. The National Abortion and Reproductive Action League Pro-Choice America (NARAL), one of the nation's leading abortion-rights advocates, launched their Urban Initiative in the fall of 2008.

Interestingly, the goal of this initiative was the scrutiny and increased regulation of pregnancy help centers in urban areas working with urban leaders, mostly elected officials. These centers provide free pregnancy testing, ultrasounds, pre-natal nutrition classes, counseling, and referrals to social service agencies for women facing unplanned pregnancies.

Nine out of ten women who visit a pregnancy help center will decide to carry their pregnancy to term. If they feel unable to care for the child themselves, they are connected with adoption services. For those who choose to abort, such centers provide post-abortive counseling for women who need it.

NARAL is Strange

There are two very strange things about NARAL's urban initiative. First, in no other context has NARAL expressed interest in the hundreds of suburban pregnancy help centers that service mostly white women. As of this writing, 60% of black pregnancies in New York are aborted;[1] clearly black women have access to abortion.

Yet NARAL is most concerned with the 40% of women who may have visited a pregnancy help center and carried their babies to term. Second, as NARAL tries to increase restrictions on pregnancy help centers, they are simultaneously lobbying for relaxed regulation on abortion clinics. Such proposals include allowing non-physicians to perform surgical abortions and making it impossible to sue an abortion provider for malpractice, even if the mother dies during the procedure.

If they are truly concerned with women getting the best care, why wouldn't they want to hold abortion providers accountable for malpractice? Clearly, we are witnessing The Negro Project 2.0.

Reducing Abortion?

In theory, almost everyone agrees that abortion is not a good thing. Even some abortion advocates will state the desire to reduce the number of abortions. We are often told that the only way to reduce abortion is to increase the availability of contraception, in the same way we were told that the availability of abortion was the only way to reduce out of wedlock births. Yet we have more birth control today than we did forty years ago, and we have more abortions *and* more out of wedlock births.

The sad truth is that there are powerful organizations at work in America who do not want to see abortions reduced, particularly among black Americans. They do not believe that all babies are blessings, and they aggressively seek out pregnant black women and tell them that the babies they carry will ruin their lives. Abortion not only brings hundreds of millions of dollars to these organizations, (The Abortion Industry,

2008) but it also reinforces their view that childbearing should be reserved primarily for the middle and upper classes.

Adoption Waiting Lists

In fact there is right now in this country a waiting list of families waiting to adopt infants, and specifically black infants. There is no reason that any woman should fear that a baby she is unprepared to care for will not end up in a loving family that has been waiting, hoping and praying for her child. It is my prayer that these women will find the help and support they need.

Pastor Dean Nelson is the Vice President for underserved outreach of Care Net, and the Chairman of the Frederick Douglass Foundation www.frederickdouglassfoundation.com.

REFERENCE

McDermott, G. & Swain, M. (March 26, 2008). The abortion industry. *The Washington Times.* Retrieved from *http://www.washingtontimes. com/news/2008/mar/26/the-abortion-industry/*

CHAPTER 11

The Language of Oppression

Reverend Walter Hoye

Haig Bosmajian, Speech/Communication Professor Emeritus at the University of Washington says, "While names, words, and language can be, and are, used to inspire us, to motivate us to humane acts, to liberate us, they can also be used to dehumanize human beings and to 'justify' their suppression and even their extermination."[2] In order to justify the inhumane treatment of African American slaves and soothe the conscious of the Americans, dehumanizing terminology or the "language of oppression" was established and propagated by way of both "academic" and "legal" opinion at the very highest levels of our educational and legal communities.

The Language of Oppression Past

From 1815 to 1830, the American Colonization Society reported, "Free blacks in our country are . . . a contagion." In 1857 the U.S. Supreme Court decided, "A negro of the African race was regarded . . . as an article of property . . . a subordinate and inferior class of being." In 1858, the Virginia Supreme Court decision declared, "In the eyes of the law . . . the slave is not a person."

In 1867, Buckner Payne, Publisher wrote, "The Negro is not a human being." In 1900, Professor Charles Carroll affirmed, "The Negro is . . . one of the lower animals." In 1903 Dr. William English declared, "The Negro race is . . . a heritage of organic and psychic debris." In 1909, Dr. E. T. Brady announced, "They [Negroes] are parasites." In 1973, the U.S. Supreme Court decided, "The Fetus, at most, represents only the potentiality of life." Again, in 1973, the U.S. Supreme Court declared, "The word 'person,' as used in the 14th Amendment does not include the unborn."

The Language of Oppression Present

In 1979 Professor Joseph Flectcher affirmed, "Pregnancy when not wanted is a disease . . . in fact, a venereal disease." In 1980 Dr. Mariti Kekomaki answered, "An aborted baby is just garbage . . . just refuse."

In the Sunday, July 12th, 2009, edition of the New York Times Magazine, the power of the language of oppression to corrupt our conscious was revealed in the words of sitting U.S. Supreme Court Justice Ruth Bader Ginsburg, who said in an interview that she was surprised at a 1980 court ruling that prevented the restoration of Medicaid funding for abortions, because, in her opinion, when Roe v. Wade was decided in 1973 "there was concern about population growth and particularly growth in populations that we don't want to have too many of," (Bazelton, 2009).

Leadership and Eternal Truth

History teaches us, time and time again, that the use of oppressive language to demonize and dehumanize certain segments of the human race is incontestably evil. True leadership holds the resonance of eternal truth bound by the conviction to stand up for the truth.

When one's convictions are compromised for the promise of comfort or power, perpetuating lies in the desire to attain or maintain status is the rule of the day. Such a leader or organization cannot proclaim service to God or man.

Brothers, we really need to talk.

Reverend Walter Hoye is Founder\President of the Issues4Life Foundation www.issues4life.org, the California Civil Rights Foundation www. civilrightsfoundation.org and Founder of the Frederick Douglass Foundation of California www.fdfca.org.

REFERENCE

Bazelton, E. (July 7, 2009). The place of women on the court. *New York Times Magazine*. Retrieved from *http://www.nytimes.com/2009/07/12/magazine/12ginsburg-t.html?pagewanted=all*

CHAPTER 12

Influencing the NAACP Towards Life

Reverend Arnold Culbreath

The National Association for the Advancement of Colored People (NAACP), founded in 1909, remains the nation's oldest and largest civil rights organization. As it approaches its 102nd anniversary, the NAACP continues to work toward the betterment of the lives of African Americans and others. Suffice it to say, the NAACP is considered by many to be a very influential organization.

The national NAACP website's Health Advocacy & Issues page states, "African Americans continue to have the highest incidence, prevalence and mortality rates from chronic diseases like cardiovascular disease, diabetes and obesity. Additionally issues like HIV and infant mortality have continued to overwhelm the Black community."

Although each of these issues needs to be addressed, reduced and eventually eliminated, the Centers for Disease Control documents that abortion remains the leading cause of death in the African American community, eclipsing all other causes of death combined. However, the issue of abortion remains absent from the NAACP's educational and advocacy efforts.

Startling Statistics

- Fifteen million (15,000,000) black babies have died by abortion in the US since 1973. That's 363,705 black babies dying by abortion per year (approx. 996 per day).
- Over 60% of Planned Parenthood's abortion mills are strategically located in black communities.
- Black women have 37% of the abortions, while making up only 13% of the US female population.

These statistics should cause every black pastor, every black leader, every black person and every organization focused on outreach and advocacy to the black community to be outraged.

However, this is not the case, largely because they are unaware of this problem. And in other cases they may be aware of the problem but unwilling to deal with it. This is why I am partnering with other national black prolife leaders and organizations to educate, motivate and activate the African American community. I believe education and the dialogue generated as a result of it is a key place to start in reducing and eventually eradicating abortion from our community.

A Pro-Abortion Past and Present

I believe groups like the National Association for the Advancement of Colored People (NAACP) should use their influence to significantly address this problem by informing its members of this critical information. As leaders within the black pro-life movement and I seek to save precious pre-born lives, we are discussing this issue with the leaders of the NAACP at the national, state and local levels. Considering the grave statistics above, we are saddened to know that, according to the organization, "the NAACP does not currently have a position on abortion."

One old adage says, "If you're not part of the solution, then you're part of the problem." Several black pro-life leaders and I have become members of the organization to provide a pro-life presence from within and to influence the organization toward life.

The NAACP

In 2004, the NAACP went public with several bold pro-abortion statements in its *1992-2003 Health Policies and Resolutions* document, announcing support of the *March Against Fear* (a march by pro-abortion activists) in Washington, D.C. In this document, the NAACP stated:

> **WHEREAS**, the NAACP has supported equal access to family planning materials and information since 1968 and;
> **WHEREAS**, more than eight decades ago, the NAACP's most distinguished founder, Dr. W.E.B DuBois understood that making birth control available to poor women helped them gain control over their lives. Every woman, he wrote in 1920, must have the right of procreation 'at her own discretion,' and;
> **WHEREAS**, today, women of color seek abortion at rates higher than their percentage in the population, and overwhelmingly describe themselves as pro-choice in public opinion surveys, and **WHEREAS**, on April 25, 2004, thousands of pro-choice supporters will gather in Washington, D.C. for the March Against Fear to demonstrate their support for the right to choice, and **WHEREAS**, a woman denied the right to control her own body is denied equal protection of the law, a fight the NAACP has fought for and defended for nearly 100 years, and **WHEREAS**, many other organizations of women of color have endorsed the March, **THEREFORE, BE IT RESOLVED,** that the NAACP adds its endorsement and support for the March Against Fear and urges all who believe in equal rights to attend on April 25, 2004 in Washington, D.C.

In response to this official statement, two pro-life resolutions were introduced in 2004 and again in 2007. A pro-life resolution was crafted by a local NAACP chapter in Macon, Georgia requesting that the NAACP renounce their pro-abortion position and become involved in educating the black community about this problem.

In 2004 and again in 2007, this pro-life resolution was approved by both the local Macon chapter and the Georgia State Chapter, but failed to pass the national resolution committee. Although the NAACP did not agree to assist in educating the black community about the abortion problem, it did reduce its position to a so-called "no policy" on abortion.

The national NAACP office said the resolution was "filled with errors, and simply inaccurate," but could not tell me what the alleged errors were. A woman I spoke to at the NAACP national office stated that the Macon chapter would receive a letter from the national office, informing them why the resolution was not approved. However, at the time this chapter was written, the Macon, Georgia chapter has still received no such letter.

A Prolife Education

Several black prolife leaders and I attended the 98th NAACP National Convention in Detroit, MI in July 2007. Although the prolife resolution was not approved by the resolution committee, thus preventing it from being read at the convention, several of us were successful in educating many members of the NAACP.

We personally placed copies of the prolife resolution into the hands of Julian Bond, Chairman of the Board and Dennis Hayes, Interim President and CEO, who both said they'd look into it. Prolife educational materials were also given to many of the convention attendees. The recipients' responses continually confirmed their lack of awareness of this problem.

Not only are several black prolife leaders and organizations working to persuade the NAACP from within, but also from without. Many have attended the organization's national and local events and have participated in picketing and peaceful prayer initiatives outside these events for a number of years. And much educational literature has been given to those who have attended these events. Because these educational efforts are always done in a peaceful manner, there has never been any significant altercation resulting from them to my knowledge.

Promising Results

As previously stated, I have been a member of the NAACP for several years, collaborating with other national black pro-life leaders in an effort to persuade the NAACP to use its influence to educate its members about abortion's silent annihilation, and our efforts are paying off. Although the national NAACP continues to hold a so-called "no position" on abortion, several local NAACP chapters across the country are creating opportunities for this critical information to be shared with their members.

There are many within our communities who still choose to believe that abortion and a woman's "right to choose" is what's best for our community, but there are many more people who are appalled after hearing the information. They ask "why haven't we heard this before?" "Where has this information been?" "What can we do about it?"

Providing answers to them questions is where we have a great opportunity. Because of educational forums occurring within a number of the organization's local chapters, many women and men are opening up and discussing how abortion has hurt them and are receiving resources to help with their healing.

Although the national organization chooses not to deal with this critical issue which continues to decimate the black American community, many of the local chapter presidents get it and are opening up their doors so their members can be equipped and empowered concerning this taboo topic. Through education, precious lives are being saved and mothers, fathers and families are avoiding the traumatic impact of abortion in their lives.

During the course of my time as an NAACP member, I have built a good relationship and rapport with my own local chapter president. I've watched him move from not wanting to deal with this issue at all, to several years later being deeply moved concerning the disproportionate toll abortion is having on the black community. As a result he has created several educational opportunities during our monthly membership meetings including a recent panel discussion between a handful of African American prolife leaders, including me, versus a couple of non-black representatives from the leading promoter and provider of abortion in the nation, Planned Parenthood. Go figure.

Moving Forward

Do not be confused. I am not suggesting that the NAACP is an organization that advocates for the right to life of the unborn. After all, with a "no position" on abortion, how could it be? But what I am saying is that the NAACP is an influential organization that impacts the lives of large numbers of black Americans. And the NAACP works to educate the black community on a host of issues in order to help us to be better.

With abortion being the leading cause of death in the African American community, and education being important to the NAACP, shouldn't the organization use its influence to inform its members about this atrocity?

Consider joining us in the process of influencing the NAACP toward life. In an effort to reach our community through this historic organization with this critically needed life-affirming information, become a member of the organization. However, let me warn you that it is a long, hard, slow and frequently frustrating process, but one I feel is well worth it.

A friend of mine who views this strategy of attempting to reach key pockets of the black community with the pro-life message through the NAACP as pointless, once said to me, "Arnold, if you see the NAACP as a redeemable organization, continue right on with what you're doing." To which I replied, "My focus is not as much on the NAACP being a redeemable organization as much as it is on the thousands of redeemable people that make up its membership, who need to be reached with the critical and often unknown truth about abortion in the black community."

Reverend Arnold Culbreath serves on the boards of several pro-life organizations. He is the Urban Outreach Director of Life Issues Institute, Inc. www. protectingblacklife.org.

CHAPTER 13

For Every Idle Silence:
America's Voiceless Christian Church

Pastor Caesar I. LeFlore III

One of the most unfortunate observations about the Christian church in America at the dawn of the 21st century is that in many ways—as a whole—it has become a powerless, ineffective, and irresponsible church having almost no impact in pushing back the spiritual darkness hovering over our nation and blocking our seeing, understanding, and pursuing the righteousness of God.

As it concerns the most socially relevant moral issues of the day, the church, through its lack of unified opposition to expanding unrighteousness, has become both complacent and complicit to many of the rapidly declining moral values in America that are dragging us headlong down the path to becoming a completely wicked and unholy nation.

God's church in America is choosing what it believes to be the paths of least resistance on many social issues in order to protect itself from being called intolerant by a post-modern society that rejects absolutes in terms of right and wrong behaviors. As a result, the church's voice has been marginalized and finds that it is rarely able to exert any profound influence at critical points of decision on social issues that have consequential impact on the moral and ethical consciousness of the nation.

Weak Voice on Abortion

Nowhere is this more obvious than when we observe the woefully weak voice the Christian church is raising in opposition to abortion on demand in America. The embarrassingly meager support it offers in the fight to oppose abortion and promote the sanctity of innocent human life throughout this nation and around the world can be summed up as shameful, to say the least.

Never has the weight of Christian influence been more desperately needed but conspicuously absent than during the public discourse concerning the morality of abortion and the consequences its political, legal, and religious acceptance would have on the health of our nation. Abortion kills both physically and spiritually and deserves a different response than what we are seeing from the household of faith.

Where, one might ask, is the moral outcry from the more than 225 million Christians in America in response to the abortion holocaust that has claimed more than 45 million innocent lives in the womb since receiving legal sanction in 1973 from the United States Supreme Court? How is it that the church could so easily accept abortion as "*tolerated evil*" simply because of the legal status afforded it by human courts?

Christians and Compromise

How did Christians of all walks, particularly our religious and political leaders, get caught up in the politics of compromise and tacit consent to abortion at the expense of their Christian integrity and values as defined by the Bible? The church and federal government have both obviously become confused and lost track of the moral foundations taken from scripture upon which our great nation was founded.

During our early years, as this nation struggled with itself over the issue of slavery, Christian activist and abolitionist Fredrick Douglas said:

> I have one great political idea . . . That idea is an old one. The best expression of it I have found in the Bible. It is in substance, 'Righteousness exalted a nation; sin is a reproach to any people.' (Proverbs 14:34). This constitutes my politics—the negative and the positive of my politics, the whole of my politics. I feel it my duty to do all in my power to infuse that idea into the public

mind, that it may be speedily recognized and practiced upon by our people.

When there is no leadership from the church that influences the politics of social issues with spiritual consequences such as slavery and abortion, society turns to public opinion and its courts to get their direction. It is from these institutions that we get court decisions like the Dred Scott decision of 1847 that allowed slavery to continue, and the 1973 Roe V Wade decision that legalized abortion in all states.

Without hearing the prophetic voice of God's people declaring truth and demanding, with the authority of God, that truth be reflected in our politics and social practices, society continues to decline to the point that it accepts and defends evil practices such as abortion based on the fact that unethical people have contrived to make them legal. The church would do well to remember that just because the laws of the land justifies abortion doesn't mean that it's justified in the eyes of God.

The church has been woefully remiss in emphasizing that truth to the American public and therefore is partly complicit in creating an environment that allows abortion to proliferate, children to be slaughtered, and women to be victimized by what has become known as "their choice". There is need for great repentance among the people of God.

The late Honorable Henry Hyde, former Illinois Congressman and staunch pro-life advocate, often quoted 4th century Bishop St Ambrose who said, "Not only for every idle word, but for every idle silence must man render an account." The silence of the protestant church over the years concerning abortion has been deafening, and the consequences more dire than anyone could have ever imagined.

The Sin of Silence

More than 45 million legally aborted children, and the church is silent. More than 15 million black children specifically targeted and eliminated, and the black church is extremely silent. Millions of women and men are emotionally and spiritually scarred after aborting their children, and the church stands idly by.

Without a doubt, there will be a reckoning with the Lord for our silences (omissions) as much as for our sins (commissions) concerning the nations adopted position on abortion, a position that blatantly violates

God's heart concerning the sanctity of human life. God gave authority to governments to enforce social order, but He gave authority to the church to influence society and set the standards by which that order would be developed and maintained. Jesus said:

> I will give you the keys of the kingdom of heaven; whatever you bind on earth will be bound in heaven, and whatever you loose on earth will be loosed in heaven. (Matthew 16:19)

Jesus also said that we would be "salt and light" (Matthew 5:13-14). Being *salt* and *light* is more than a religious notion we derive from the teachings of Christ. It's a literal call for Christians to *illuminate* what is true and to *preserve* what is right according to the values and ideals we live out from the teachings of our faith.

God's Divine Process

More than any other entity or institution, the Christian church should be the most passionately motivated entity to turn back the legalized assault on life in the womb that claims more than one million pre-born children annually. Abortion violates the sanctity of the womb and interrupts God's divine process through which He allows human beings to participate in the miracle of bringing human life into existence.

Think about it! When it comes to birthing children, God allows humans to participate in His wondrous creative process that brings forth new life. God chose to place the embryo in the womb of the mother to host the new life growing in her body.

Who should understand and appreciate the sacred process of life coming through the womb more than the Church of Jesus Christ? Our faith was established upon the belief that our eternal souls were saved by the life of One who came from eternity into the earth through the womb of a woman so that he could die to redeem man from his sins. C.S. Lewis called the incarnation, "The Grand Miracle," and marveled that by a miracle that passes human comprehension, the Creator entered his creation, the Eternal entered time, and God became human—in order to die and rise again for the salvation of all people.

He comes down; down from the heights of absolute being into time and space, down into humanity; down further still, if embryologists are right, to recapitulate in the womb ancient and pre-human phases of life; down to the very roots and sea-bed of the Nature He has created. But He goes down to come up again and bring the whole ruined world up with Him. (Lewis, 1947, p. 111)

Theological and Bio-Ethical Foundations

As Christians, we have both a theological and a bio-ethical foundation for such arguments. We believe that Jesus Christ was God who took on human form for Himself; that incarnation took place in the uterus.

And after being conceived by the Holy Spirit and born through the natural process of the womb, Jesus lived a life that affirmed the worth of every person, whether saint or sinner, and gave His life to redeem every person who would ever be born—redemption that was available from the very second that person was conceived! Nigel M. de S. Cameron, in his writing, *Bethlehem's Bioethics* stated:

> God took human form; and he took it not simply as a baby, but as the tiniest of all human beings, a mere biological speck, so small and so undeveloped that it could be mistaken for a laboratory artifact, a research specimen, an object for human experimentation. But this speck was God; this complete genetic human organism, in its primitive and undeveloped form, was so much "one of us" as to bear the existence of the Creator. He dignified humanity by taking the form of this creature he had made in his image; and he did it at the most inauspicious and feeble point in the human life story. At the heart of the Christmas celebration lies the fact of all facts, that God became a zygote. (Cameron, 2005)

For Christians, there should be no difference between the sanctity of life in the womb or outside of it, because there is no distinction in the eyes of God. It's time for the Christian church as a whole to exert its influence in defense of pre-born children in every way possible and to establish in the heart of society a respect for innocent human life at every stage of its development.

Rev. Martin Luther King, Jr. said, "The only thing necessary for the triumph of evil is for good men to do nothing." As it concerns defeating abortion, which has become the leading cause of death in the black community, the Christian church has done close to nothing as a unified body in opposition to it and millions of lives have been lost as a result. Proverbs 24:11-12 commands us to,

Rescue those being led away to death; hold back those staggering toward slaughter. If you say, "But we knew nothing about this," does not he who weighs the heart perceive it? Does not he who guards your life know it? Will he not repay each person according to what he has done?

Cry Loud, Spare Not

It's time for the church of Jesus Christ to say, "We will be silent no longer. We will cry loud and spare no one while condemning that which is evil and promoting that which is good, without apology." Abortion shouldn't be able to stand a chance against a unified church. Jesus said, "and upon this rock I will build my church; and the gates of hell shall not prevail against it," (Matthew 16:18b).

Christians in America, it's time for you to show up, stand up, and speak up against the evil of abortion. Let's us remember that God is not only going to judge this nation for every wicked deed and idle word; but He is also going to judge us for every idle silence. He spoke to us through His prophet Ezekiel:

When I say to the evil-doer, Death will certainly overtake you; and you say nothing to make clear to the evil-doer the danger of his way; death will overtake that evil man in his evil-doing, but I will make you responsible for his blood. But if you make clear to the evil-doer the danger of his way for the purpose of turning him from it, and he is not turned from his way, death will overtake him in his evil-doing, but your life will be safe.

> *And you, son of man, say to the children of Israel, You say, Our wrongdoing and our sins are on us and we are wasting away in them; how then may we have life? Say to them, By my life, says the Lord, I have no pleasure in the death of the evil-doer; it is more pleasing to me if he is turned from his way and has life: be turned, be turned from your evil ways; why are you looking for death? (Ezekiel 33:8-11)*

Reverend Ceasar I. LeFlore III is the Associate Pastor of Lorimer Baptist Church of Dolton, IL and is the Executive Director of The Beloved Community Development Coalition.

REFERENCES

Cameron, N. (2005). Bethlehem's bioethics. *Christianity Today*. Retrieved from *http://www.christianitytoday.com/ct/2005/decemberweb-only/42.0b. html*

Lewis, C. S. (1947). *Miracles*. New York: Macmillan.

CHAPTER 14

Why I Can't Wait

Reverend Walter Hoye

On more than one occasion it has been suggested to me . . . to wait.

> The cause is just, but wait.
> The cause is worthy, but wait.
> The cause is righteous, but wait.

That is, wait for a more opportune or favorable time to pursue the just, worthy and righteous cause of the California Human Rights Amendment. This suggestion to wait, has come to me by way of men and women:

- Who love me and have proven themselves under trying circumstances to be my friends.
- Whom I highly respect, whose moral credentials are infinitely greater than mine.
- Whose wisdom has been tried, forged in the raging fires of spiritual warfare and found true.
- Whose commitment to our Lord Jesus Christ is beyond question.
- Whose lives reflect the sacred beauty of sacrifice for "love's sake" itself. (Philemon 1:9)

To each and every one of these wonderful saints of God, I want to say thank you for the time you have spent with me. Thank you for your wisdom, for your prayers and for your love. I want you to know that I have taken every word to heart.

Yet, I cannot wait.

With all due respect, I cannot wait for a more opportune or favorable time to pursue the just, worthy and righteous cause of the California Human Rights Amendment.

You see, my people are dying.

Arnold M. Culbreath, the Urban Outreach Director for "Protecting Black Life," reports since 1973, over 14.5 million black babies have been killed by abortion and that 1,200 black babies die by abortion daily.

My people are dying.

According to Alan Guttmacher Institute (AGI), the research arm of Planned Parenthood, black women are nearly five (5) times as likely as non-Hispanic white women to have an abortion.

My people are dying.

According to the U.S. Center for Disease Control (CDC) report entitled, "Abortion Surveillance—United States, 2006," the abortion ratio among black women, defined as the number of abortions per 1,000 live births, is 450 abortions per 1,000 live births. The abortion ratio for black women far exceeds the abortion rate for any other people group.

Considering the fact that abortion is not the only reason a baby in the womb of his or her mother dies, today a black American child has less than a 50% chance of being born. It is safer on the streets for a black child in the worse neighborhoods America has to offer than on the inside of the womb of his or her mother.

My people are dying.

Abortion remains the leading cause of death in the black America. Abortion alone accounts for 3 times more deaths in our community than HIV/AIDS, violent crimes, accidents, cancer, and heart disease combined.

My people are dying.

The U.S. fertility rate is an indicator that shows the potential for population change in the country. A rate below 2.1 indicates populations decreasing in size and growing older. Today, according to the 2006 U.S. Census, our fertility rate is below the replacement level at 1.9. Black America is no longer replacing herself.

My people are dying.

According to the National Vital Statistics Reports, Vol. 48, No. 11, the abortion rate among married black American women is 3 times greater than it is among white women.

My people are dying.

Again, according to the National Vital Statistics Reports, Vol. 58, No. 4, October 14th, 2009, today for every 100 black babies born alive, there are another 77 black babies killed by abortion. Said another way, for every one black baby born alive, practically one black baby is killed by abortion.

My people are dying.

According to the archives at the Tuskegee Institute, between 1882 and 1968, 3,446 Negroes were lynched by the Klu Klux Klan (KKK) in the United States of America. Today, abortion in the black community kills more black Americans in less than 3 days than the Klu Klux Klan could kill in 86 years.

My people are dying.

According to the U.S. Center for Disease Control (CDC) and the Alan Guttmacher Institute (AGI), since 1973 (i.e., the year abortion was legalized in the U.S.) more black American babies have been killed by abortion than the total number of black American deaths from all other causes combined.

My people are dying.

If we were to ask the average high-school student how many U.S. soldiers died in the Vietnam War, the most probable answer would be roughly 58,000. This is the number of American military personnel deaths. Today more black babies are killed in less than 2 months from abortion than the total number of American military personnel that died in the Vietnam War.

My people are dying.

According to a study in the Journal of American Physicians and Surgeons, Volume 13 Number 4, Winter 2008, entitled "Does Induced Abortion Account for Racial Disparity in Preterm Births, and Violate the Nuremberg Code?" Black American women have 3 times the risk of suffering an early preterm birth (EPB, birth under 32 weeks) and 4 times the risk of an extremely preterm birth (XPB, birth under 28 weeks).

This report, authored by Brent Rooney, M.Sc., Byron C. Calhoun, M.D., M.B.A. and Lisa E. Roche, J.D., reports a "statistically significant" increase in the risk of EBP or XPB in women who have a history of induced abortion (IA) when compared to women with no history of induced abortion.

When one considers the fact that XPB babies have a 129 times higher risk of being born with the horribly debilitating effects of cerebral palsy and that according to Rooney, Calhoun and Roche, "about 43% of pregnancies in black American women end in induced abortion" alone, and when you understand that these numbers describe a rate of death in the black community that only reflects the impact of induced abortion, you are at a point where you are beginning to understand that . . .

My people are dying.

The targeting of black America by eugenics minded, pro-abortion forces is easy to see when you consider that black Americans make up about 12% of the population of the United States of America and yet according to Planned Parenthood's Alan Guttmacher Institute, 37% of all abortions in the country are performed on Black American women and their preborn children.

In other words, 12% of the population of this country, black Americans, is responsible for 37% of all abortions in the United States of America.

If you consider about half of black America is female then you're looking at around 6% of the population of this country being responsible for 37% of all abortions in the United States of America.

If you consider child bearing age from 15 to 44 then you're looking at around 3% of the population of this country, black Americans, being responsible for 37% of all abortions in the United States of America. Tony Perkins, the President of the Family Research Council says, "Preliminary data currently being compiled on all abortion facilities in the U.S. shows that over 20 states have abortion facilities in areas where the African-American population is 50% or higher." He continues, "In fact, 10 states and Washington, D.C. have abortion centers located *exclusively* in minority areas," (Hoste, 2010).

I cannot wait, my people are dying.

Abortion is the Darfur of the Black American community.

If nothing changes.

If America does not become more efficient at killing babies in the womb of their mothers in the future, if we do not take into consideration the number of chemical abortions, if the rate of death, due solely to the impact of induced abortion in the Black community, remains constant and does not increase or decrease over time, black America will face the very real possibility of being an endangered species by the year of our Lord Jesus Christ two thousand one hundred (2100).

That is, I said, if nothing changes . . .

However, everything is changing.

If President Obama is successful in his efforts to install his health care vision for America, the numbers of Black babies killed by abortion will skyrocket.

Alveda King, the niece of Dr. Martin Luther King, Jr. has said, "Those of us who care about the civil rights of all Americans, born and unborn, oppose Obamacare because we oppose the expansion of the most racist industry in America—the abortion industry."

Frankly, time for my people is running out. The time for me to act is now.

I simply cannot wait.

Perhaps others can afford to wait.

Nevertheless, I cannot wait because the abortion numbers are higher in my community, among my people than in any other people group.

Perhaps others can tell the future. However, I do not have the power to tell the future. I can only tell you about the One who holds the future.

Perhaps others are wiser than I am. After all there are "certain political realities" at work in our world today and the mere presence of such realities surely calls for an experienced hand.

While I am sure others are wiser, have more experience and know how to come in and go out, I still cannot wait.

I cannot wait for . . .

- Public opinion to favor me,
- Political equity or capital necessary to guarantee victory to be voted into office, or
- Proper funding required to meet the surely inevitable challenges that will come.

America is changing, my people are dying and I cannot wait.

I believe faith in Christ along with a repentant heart will allow us to receive His forgiveness and boldly face the wickedness in high places that walks among us today.

I believe such faith in Christ will allow His Body and Bride to perform the works of life that will overcome the works of death.

I believe the California Human Rights Amendment, by embracing the issue of "Personhood," addresses the most profound and the most serious ethical dilemma this country has ever faced.

I believe the California Human Rights Amendment offers all of us an unprecedented opportunity for dialogue centered on the core issue of the abortion debate, the "humanity" of us all.

Imagine the power of Christ at work in us as we engage the culture for His sake by asking such questions as:

What does it mean . . .

- To be made in the image of God?
- To be fearfully and wonderfully made?
- To be respected as a person?

Dr. Martin Luther King, Jr., in defense of his belief in "Nonviolence" said:

> Nonviolence is a powerful and just weapon. It is a weapon unique in history, which cuts without wounding and ennobles the man who wields it. It is a sword that heals. Both a practical and a moral answer to the Negro's cry for justice, nonviolent direct action proved that it could win victories without losing wars, and so became the triumphant tactic of the Negro Revolution of 1963. (King, 1964)

I believe the California Human Rights Amendment today is what nonviolent direct action was to the Civil Rights movement of the 1960's. It is a powerful, just and righteous weapon.

I believe the California Human Rights Amendment "ennobles the man who wields it." It is the kind of weapon that God favors and will honor as His people engage the world around them in dialogue for Christ's sake.

I believe the California Human Rights Amendment is both a practical and moral answer to the preborn's cry for justice, for righteousness and for life itself.

I believe, on this side of heaven, it is never too late to start doing right.

Maybe you believe in God the same way I do and/or maybe you see the same divinely inspired opportunity that is set before us today, as I do? If you can, then help me today, because you cannot wait either.

Brothers, we really need to talk.

Reverend Walter Hoye is Founder\President of the Issues4Life Foundation www.issues4life.org, the California Civil Rights Foundation www. civilrightsfoundation.org and Founder of the Frederick Douglass Foundation of California www.fdfca.org.

REFERENCES

King, M. (December 11, 1964). Nobel Peace Prize Lecture: The quest for peace and justice. Retrieved from *http://www.nobelprize.org/nobel_ prizes/peace/laureates/1964/king-lecture.html*

Hoste, R. (April 6, 2010). Blacks and Abortion. Retrieved from *http:// www.alternativeright.com/main/blogs/hbd-human-biodiversity/ blacks-and-abortion/*

CHAPTER 15

My Abortion Testimony

Chaplain Ayesha Kreutz

I am the mother of 6 children—one by forced abortion when I was 14, one who died as a result of a miscarriage a few years after my abortion, one as the result of an ectopic pregnancy, probably because of the morning after pill I had taken, and 3 living (one was so very close to being aborted). I remember the first time I heard someone say, "Having an abortion didn't make me any less pregnant; it just made me a murderer too."

Oh how that ripped at my soul and still does as it made me come to the understanding that I am the mother of a dead child. The abortion didn't turn back time and it didn't make me less pregnant either. It just made me the murderer of my child and it made me a mother to a dead baby. In those moments I had to hang my head in shame and admit, as ugly as this may sound, it is true: I killed my own flesh and blood and killed off generations of a bloodline. And that's why I chose to become outspoken and pro-life.

Pain and Terror

Where do I start? Do I talk about my abortion, the pain and the terror that followed, or do I talk about the life of abuse and pain which led up to the decision to abort, or do I talk about the abortion I almost had after I had healed and turned "pro-life"?

I will share with you the last in that long series of life's trials. I am not sure that you realize what causes one to consider and then too often follow through with the killing of their child. Yes, we do understand by instinct that it is a life, otherwise we as woman would not agonize so much over the decision to abort.

The idea that "it is just a blog of flesh" is ludicrous. If that were so, it would not be such an agonizing decision. There would not be tears shed, and there would be no deadening of our feelings in the decision-making process of "The Choice." So I will tell you, in case you don't know, it *is* sin and hopelessness that drives one to consider an abortion, and, in too many cases, actually go through with it.

I was no different. There are many excuses to justify the decision, but it always, when being honest with ourselves, comes down to being in a place where we feel as though we have "No other choice."

I knew the Lord when I got pregnant out-of-wedlock for the 6th time. I didn't have a strong foundation, but I did have a personal relationship with Christ that I was developing and was well aware of God's Word and will. I had been studying and growing in the Lord for about 6 years by this time, so I was no dummy.

I had no excuses for succumbing to the sin of my flesh. I knew in my heart, God was just going to forgive me in the end no matter what I did or was about to do. He's a forgiving God, and I would just repent afterwards. I had it all figured out. Even so, in my finite mind I told myself, "I will give God an opportunity to change my mind."

I had just moved back to Rochester, New York. I didn't know I was pregnant, but within the first couple weeks, I realized I needed to take a pregnancy test. I was living with my best friend, Tiffany, in her 3-bedroom house, with her husband and their 3 kids, in her unfinished basement with my two kids. And here I was with the nerve to be pregnant! I had nothing, nothing at all but Tiffany and my Love for God.

My Planned Parenthood Appointment

That next Sunday, I wasn't going to attend church with Tiffany because I had set up an appointment to murder my baby the next day at Planned Parenthood. I knew it was wrong but saw no other way out.

I had just had a baby! I had superficially "repented," and then boom . . . straight away again I fell into the temptation of my flesh and the need to feel loved. In the end, to keep up appearances so Tiffany didn't get suspicious—she knew me very well—I went to church knowing there was nothing God could say or do at this point to change my mind.

I knew I could have an abortion, then repent, and God would forgive me. And I knew that in the end that was best for me (so that nobody would know of my mistake, again), for my other two kids (I could barely take care of them as it was, needing state assistance with my life just a mess), and for those who looked up to me as a person and as a spiritual guide.

I was afraid that I would be causing them to turn away from God, to say, "Look at her! If that is what it means to be Christian, why bother with it anyway?" And so hopelessness was my muse. The whispers of Satan grew and festered, and I had no one I could talk to. I would not and could not even dare to tell my best friend. I was too embarrassed and ashamed. Nor did I tell the father of my child with whom I would never want to raise a kid. But that is another story all to itself.

Towards the end of the service, I walked right up to the Pastor Ron Domina and said to him, with my ego still intact, "Listen, I have scheduled an appointment tomorrow for an abortion . . ." He didn't know me from Adam, mind you, as this was just my second visit to this large church called Bethel Christian Fellowship. But I continued, "So if you know somebody that might be able to tell me something that would, you know, not have me do it, then, fine."

Scrambling for Help

He looked at me wide-eyed like, "What?" I have to chuckle a bit here thinking back on it, and Pastor Ron said, "Hold on, hold on. Let me get you someone else to talk to you. I am sure we can find someone." He went off purposefully scrambling.

Through the grace and power of God, I was introduced to Terry and Jerry via Bethel Christian Fellowship and Candy Giles. I cannot imagine a world without faithful servants of the Lord like Terry and Jerry. What if people really did just give up on the whole abortion issue and left people like me to our own devices and hopelessness? What if no one was on the front lines, no one willing to be the hands and feet of God who consider it worth the time and effort? That's a bleak world that I'm glad I don't have to live in anymore.

Terry and Jerry Crawford met with me the next day . . . the day of my scheduled abortion. Now, I did have a plan. I figured I would meet with them and then go to Planned Parenthood for my appointment. Planned parenthood, by the way, had told me that they have a pill I could take now and have the abortion in the privacy of my home now, so no one has to know. It is like forcing your body to have a miscarriage, they said, and I was like "WHAT? Really?" That had solidified it for me. "Ok I can do this. This will be easy," I thought.

As I sat across the Crawford's at Bill Gray's restaurant with my young infant in tow, they started sharing with me something I had not been hearing. They started sharing with me love, encouragement, compassion and hope, with no sides of condemnation! It was the finest meal I'd had in years.

I told them I had no choice and that their efforts were in vain. Yet they pressed on, like good salesmen, reading me and letting me know that it was ok. And you know, having been raised in an atheist hippy home and being influenced by the liberal media all the time, I thought we Christians were condemning and mean.

I did not expect the compassion and understanding that I experienced. As Christians, they would be ashamed of me or so I thought. And God would not be able to use my family and me for His purpose if I let the world see my dirty sins.

Look at King David

And they said, "No, not only can God still use you, but look at King David and all He did. There are people who will help you, who will let you and your two children live with them so that you can disappear from everything while you are pregnant and have the baby. Afterwards, they will keep the baby (as an open or closed adoption), and no one would have to know you were ever pregnant if that is what you want."

"What? Really? No way!" I thought that this is just stuff from the movies, but it's not real life. Why would someone support me and my children just to have me keep my baby and/or to adopt my baby, especially if they already had kids of their own?

It blew my mind, but Terry and Jerry explained that this is so because God has a plan for your child. God loves that baby, and that baby deserves a future.

A Future?

I wondered at that. Terry and Jerry made me realize that God had entrusted me with this baby, and that if God believes in me, it changes everything. God spoke to me: "Don't give up on me, Trust me. I have a plan. Just own up to what you did and do not sin again. Don't use a lie to cover up a lie. Just let me be your guide and your path. I will work it out."

When God speaks, I listen, or at least I did at that point in my life which I now consider to be a knot in my life line. There is a period of time before the knot and one after the knot, and as every day passes, the part before the knot becomes smaller and less painful than the period after the knot.

Adoption, Maybe

Now, I was not going to keep the baby, but I had decided that giving her up for adoption was her best chance at having a real family and that that would also be best for my other two children and for me. In the end though, I kept her. But that is another story entirely.

I did indeed live with Terry and Jerry's friends after the birth. They were all incredibly supportive in my decision to keep the baby, and I remain close friends with them all to this day.

Today as I watch her grow up, I think always of Rescue Rochester, Terry and Jerry and how God is perfect. I also think about how the enemy is a liar who comes to steal from us and cheat us. He cheats these children out of a future and a destiny. Life is not just about me, but also about all those around me. God is faithful and true, and He loves at all times.

Today, because of who God is and because of the bold and resolved prolife people like those who run Rescue Rochester who have answered His call, my child Shalom Ari-Ella Bet-el Maxine is 5-years old and has a destiny. In a way, she is my redemption. I am thankful. God has faith in me enough to give me the privilege to raise one of His.

God, through those who want to cultivate a culture of life and acceptance instead of death and rejection, held me steady and breathed life into my hopeless spirit. Today, I am not just a sinner saved by grace, but I am a saint of the Living God. I am a child of the Most High, and that makes me a prophet, more than a conqueror through Christ, marching in a triumphant procession, overcoming the devil by the blood of the Lamb and the word of my testimony. And I know, I have been bought with a price, and I am redeemed by Jesus Christ.

Married Now

I am also married now to a wonderful man who loves and adores my children as much as he does me. After living through this, I decided I could be silent no longer. God welled up in me a passion so great that I could no longer be silent. I had to speak out and be a voice for the voiceless.

Chaplain Ayesha Kreutz is a Bible-believing Christian striving to be a servant to those around her by acting as the willing hands and feet of God http://blackgop.ning.com/profile/ChaplainAyeshaKreutz.

CHAPTER 16

A New Trojan Horse for Abortion

Dr. Eric Wallace

Have you ever marveled at how fiction so often parallels real life? A few weeks ago, I had the pleasure of watching one of my all-time favorite movies, Troy. It was the 2004 version of Homer's epic poem the Iliad. The film captures in about two hours the epic battles between the Trojans and an array of Greek city-state warriors lead by King Agamemnon and the great warrior Achilles. They are battling over the infidelity of Helen who left Agamemnon's brother for Hector's brother Paris.

In all actuality, the infidelity is just an excuse for King Agamemnon to try to consolidate his power. Thus, the Greeks lay siege to the fortified city of Troy for 10 years without success until Odysseus comes up with the ploy of the "Trojan Horse".

A Goodwill Gift?

Unable to defeat the Trojan defenses, the Greeks devised their own plans to get inside the city without having to shoot an arrow, swing a sword or even throw a rock. They will be welcomed in under the guise of a "gift" in the shape of a horse. The Trojans, now thinking the Greeks have brought them a goodwill token after forfeiting the battle, bring the huge statue right in the midst of their city (of course they'd soon find the horse is hollow and filled with angry Greeks).

At this point, the citizens of Troy, after partying all night, believe they've won the war and fall asleep. The Greeks disembark from the horse, open the city gates and sack the city. Unfortunately, unbeknownst to the Trojans, this "gift" was not a gift at all, but a well-orchestrated rouse used to defeat their city.

The interesting thing is, every time I watch this movie I'm hoping the Trojans will just simply "wake up." I want Hector to defeat Achilles in what is the best battle scene of the movie. I want the Trojans to burn that wooden horse. But regrettably, the outcome is always the same.

The lessons from this story for our modern-day fight to save the unborn are uncanny. Pro-abortion forces have been using various methods to push their agenda forward for more than 37 years. They hide behind the name of Planned Parenthood and are now trying to be included in the health care (Obamacare) debate under the name or idea of "reproductive rights," "reproductive health," and "reproductive justice."

The Stupak Amendment

At the writing of this article the pro-abortion forces, who would love to see abortion covered in the proposed mandated health care legislation, have been thwarted by the House of Representatives Stupak-Pitts Amendment, which was written by Democratic Rep. Bart Stupak of Michigan and Republican Rep. Joseph R. Pitts of Pennsylvania, as an amendment to the Affordable Health Care for America Act. The amendment actually enforces the Hyde Amendment, which has been in place since 1977 to prohibit the use of federal funds for abortions. The amendment was later modified to allow for federal funding of abortions in rare cases when the life of the mother is in jeopardy and in cases of rape.

Stupak-Pitts does not evoke new legislation but ensures that the Hyde Amendment is enforced in this new health care legislation. Here, from the Congressional Record, are Rep. Stupak's own words:

> Mr. Speaker, our amendment does one very simple thing:
> It applies the Hyde Amendment, which bars federal funding for
> abortion except in the case of rape, incest, or life of the mother
> to the health care reform bill. The Hyde Amendment has been
> law in federal funding of abortion since 1977 and applies to all
> other federally funded health care programs, including SCHIP,

Medicare, Medicaid, Indian Health Services, Veterans health, military health care programs and the Federal Employees Health Benefits Program.

More specifically, our amendment applies the Hyde Amendment to the public health insurance option and private policies purchased using affordability credits. I am not writing a new federal abortion policy. The Hyde Amendment already prohibits Federal funding of abortion and the use of Federal dollars to pay for health care policies that cover abortion. This policy currently applies to the 8 million Americans, including members of Congress, covered under the Federal Employees Health Benefits Program, and should apply in this bill. (Stupak, 2009)

The language and intent of the Stupak-Pitts Amendment makes it clear that no federal monies will be used for abortion. Unfortunately, the Senate health care proposal is not that cut and dry.

Sen. Ben Nelson of Nebraska, a pro-life Democrat, threatened to withhold a critical 60th vote for the bill unless restrictions on abortion funding were tightened. There was a compromise that Nelson believed was satisfactory. A press release put out by Nelson's office states that the provisions:

(1) ensure that no public funds will be used for abortion; (2) mandate that every state provide an insurance plan option that does not cover abortion; and (3) gives each state the right to pass a law barring insurance coverage for abortion within state borders. (Nelson, 2009)

Sen. Nelson also stated, "My values and principles have required me to fight hard to prevent tax dollars from being used to subsidize abortions." He continued, "I believe we have accomplished that goal."

But there are many on both sides of this debate who would disagree with Nelson's assessment. Needless to say, the pro-abortion advocates think it is too constraining while pro-life advocates find the language unclear and full of loopholes.

According to an AP report, "Sen. Tom Coburn, R-Okla., who has been waging an all-out battle to derail the Democratic bill, said Reid's language "throws the unborn under the bus." Rep. Bart Stupak, originator of the

Stupak-Pitts Amendment in the House, in his own press release stated that, "While I appreciate the efforts of all the parties involved, especially Senator Ben Nelson, the Senate abortion language is not acceptable. I will continue to work with my colleagues on this issue as the process moves forward," (AP News, 2009).

Add to the debate, the pro-life groups who also take issue with the language in the bill and you have the Trojans and the Greeks arrayed for battle all over again.

When the Senate and the House reconvene together in conference to try to combine legislation for these bills, the stage will be set for an epic battle like the one between Hector and Achilles who fought to the death. I am only afraid that like in the movie the one with true honor (Hector) will end up losing.

Another Trojan Horse

Though, rest assured even as this battle continues to rage, it is far from over. Even if the Stupak-Pitts language prevails there awaits yet another "Trojan horse." They call it "global warming" or "climate change" and they swear that it is anthropogenic (man-made).

Thus, lurking within its mandates are proposals for another kind-of—population control. Since humans cause global warming, we will need to limit the human birth rate to save the planet. Population control to save the planet will be the next Trojan horse to gain government support for abortions.

The "Greeks" are building their horse. The United Nations, Sierra Club and others have already written papers about slowing down our population growth. Here is a statement taken from the Sierra Club's Web site as it addresses population growth and global warming:

> We must also work to slow population growth by increasing access to voluntary family *planning* and *reproductive health* programs so that families are better able to choose the number and spacing of their children. The Sierra Club's Global Population and Environment Program supports efforts to *empower women* and families through education about responsible reproductive health and natural resource use vital components of the global

goal to secure a healthier environmental future. [Italics mine to highlight the code language for abortion]

Actually, we need only look to President Obama's Science Czar, John Holdren, who co-authored *Ecoscience* in 1977 with his colleagues Paul Ehrlich and Anne Ehrlich. In the book they advocate for:

- Compulsory abortions which could be sustained under the constitution;
- Adding a sterilant to drinking water or staple foods;
- Forced adoptions, abortions and sterilization ("reproductive responsibility");
- Government dictating family size number of children.

Holdren, an eco-alarmist who believes climate change is anthropogenic, will suggest that draconian measures be used to protect the planet.

So, we need to be aware that a "gift" from the climate change people is coming to a fortified city gate near you! They will try to infiltrate our legislative process and argue for government imposed "reproductive health." I strongly suggest (this time) that we burn the horse to the ground lest we find our society destroyed from within by people who only care about their own agendas.

Their selfishness and hubris is only out done by their ungodly devises. Heaven help us if we fail to recognize this attack before it is fully implemented. Unlike the city of Troy, may we recognize—before it's too late—that the battle for life is never over. No matter the outcome in Washington, we cannot let down our guard nor rest in small victories. Then, maybe this time the good guys will win.

Eric M. Wallace, Ph.D., is the founder and Publisher of Freedom's Journal Magazine. He has been in publishing for over 15 years and in ministry over 30 years www.freedomsjournal.net.

REFERENCES

AP News. (December 19, 2009). Abortion coverage battle on health bill continues. *http://townhall.com/news/politics-elections/2009/12/19/ abortion_coverage_battle_on_health_bill_continues/page/full/*

Nelson, B. (2009). Nelson to support health care bill: Delay would hurt Nebraska families, workers and employers. Press Release. *http://www. bennelson.senate.gov/press/press_releases/121909-01.cfm?renderforprint=1*

Stupak, B. (November 7, 2009). Affordable health care for America act. Recorded statement/transcript. *http://www.c-spanvideo.org/ appearance/595085772*

CHAPTER 17

Is There Not a Cause?

Minister Emmanuel Boose

The year, 1973 was the beginning of one of the darkest times in American history. The Supreme Court legalized abortion with its Roe vs. Wade decision. Since then, over 54 million unborn helpless infants have been massacred right here on American soil. As followers of Jesus Christ, we must arise again as a people and a nation. In the words of the late Rev. Dr. Martin Luther King Jr., "We must stand up for truth, stand up for justice and stand up for righteousness."

The Bible says, says, "What have you done? The voice of your brother's blood cries out to Me from the ground," (Genesis 4:10). I ask you, my brothers and my sisters, "What have you done?"

I hear the voices of over 54 million of our brothers' and sisters' blood crying out! I can also hear Revelations 6:10 saying, "And they cried with a loud voice, saying, 'How long, O Lord, holy and true, until You judge and avenge our blood on those who dwell on the earth?'" How long my brothers and sisters? Not long!

Slaying the Innocent

Deuteronomy 27:25 says, "Cursed is the one who takes a bribe to slay an innocent person. And all the people shall say, 'Amen!'" I want you to think about who you voted for. Are they pro-life or pro-choice? If you voted for someone who was pro-choice because somehow it would be an economic benefit for you, then you have just taken a bribe to slay the innocent.

Worldwide, over 126,000 children are massacred daily on American soil and over 3,700 innocent babies are massacred every day using our tax dollars. About 3% of all abortion is due to the mother's health predicament; 1% due to fetal abnormalities; 1% due to rape or incest and 95% of abortions are done as a mean of birth control. Approximately, 53 out of 100 African American children are aborted, or should I call it what it really is, "genocide", which is defined as the deliberant and systematic destruction of a racial or political group.

Unity Ends the Atrocity

Unity is the key to ending this heinous atrocity. They're using our tax dollars to fund the execution of helpless infants? Do they not deserve due process, which is a violation of the 14th amendment rights? This states "No state shall deprive any person of life, liberty or property without due process of law." This is the greatest civil rights violation in American History.

You might ask, "What can I do?" David, a little shepherd boy, took a rock and a rag and slayed Goliath. We have the same God on our side. Take your vote, and let's slay the giant of abortion in our nation.

Minister Emanuel Boose is the co-host of the Chicago-based "Change Your Community" radio broadcast www.cycbroadcast.

CHAPTER 18

A Letter to Honorable John Boehner, Speaker of the House of Representatives

Dr. Timothy Johnson

February 8, 2012
The Honorable John Boehner
Speaker of the House of Representatives
Washington, D.C. 20515

Dear Mr. Speaker:

I would like to take this opportunity to restate the position of The Frederick Douglass Foundation as it pertains to the Susan B. Anthony and Frederick Douglass Prenatal Nondiscrimination Act (H.R. 3541) sponsored by Arizona Congressman Trent Franks.

On the eve of Frederick Douglass' 194th Birthday, it is sad to know there are members of the 112th Congress who are benefactors from the struggles of the 1950-60's and now like to parade themselves as modern day civil rights leaders yet have proven themselves not to be concerned about the unborn children killed every year in this country. More striking is the fact that these same so-called leaders are promoting and supporting the complete elimination of the Black community in the United States which they themselves are members of. And finally what is very offensive today is their desire to strike the name of Frederick Douglass from H.R. 3541 on the grounds that the inclusion of Frederick Douglass's name is serving some other purpose.

It is time the American people learn the true history of both Frederick Douglas and Susan B. Anthony. While Frederick Douglass was a strong advocate for women's rights, he was equally a strong advocate for the Declaration of the United States and especially believed,

> We hold these truths to be self-evident, that all men are created equal, that they are **endowed by their Creator** with certain unalienable Rights, that among these are Life, Liberty and the pursuit of Happiness . . .

As a Lay Preacher, there is absolutely no way he would have accepted or tolerated the Pro Choice agenda currently operating in this country. Furthermore, his writings suggest even after the Roe vs. Wade decision was handed down, he would have been appalled to know the Black American community is headed toward total extinction and other groups of people are slowly heading in the same direction.

Please keep the name of H.R. 3541-Susan B. Anthony and Frederick Douglass Prenatal Nondiscrimination Act. There is no better way to honor both of these original American Civil Rights heroes.

On behalf of the Frederick Douglass Foundation, we would like the record to show that we applauds the work Congressman Trent Franks and the other co-sponsors of this bill who have worked so tirelessly to ensure that abortion cannot be used as a tool of discrimination in this great nation.

If you require additional information from the Frederick Douglass Foundation, please know we stand ready to support the efforts to pass H.R. 3541, immediately. For additional information, feel free to contact me directly at tfjohnson@tfdf.org or call (202) 241-8333.

Sincerely,

Timothy F. Johnson
Founder and President
The Frederick Douglass Foundation

CHAPTER 19

Planned Parenthood is NOT Your Friend: Why Planned Parenthood Targets the Inner City

Dr. La Verne Tolbert

*If you see the poor oppressed in a district, and justice and rights
denied, do not be surprised at such things; for one official is eyed by
a higher one, and over them both are others higher still.*
Ecclesiastes 5:8

Planned Parenthood, the nation's primary abortion provider, has clinics in inner-city neighborhoods throughout America. On one corner, there may be a Planned Parenthood Comprehensive Clinic, and within just a few short blocks, another clinic. This time it's Planned Parenthood *Express*.

To service African American (and Hispanic) minors, clinics are either located directly on school grounds or within short walking distances of schools. The question begs to be asked: Why does Planned Parenthood target the inner-city?

Margaret Sanger's Negro Project

An exploration of Planned Parenthood's founder, Margaret Sanger (1879-1966) and her philosophy may provide a clue. In her autobiography, she expresses disdain for the poor whom she calls the wretched of humanity.

Eugenics—the improvement of the race through controlled breeding—identifies certain ethnic groups as dysgenic, meaning they are biologically defective or deficient and therefore unworthy of procreation. Sanger's mission was to prevent the multiplication of the unfit for race betterment to guarantee a cleaner race (Sanger, 1938). "Birth-control," said Sanger, "is nothing more or less than the facilitation of the process of weeding out the unfit, or preventing the birth of defectives, or of those who will become defectives," (Sanger, 1920).

Her 1939 Negro Project provides further rationale for the proliferation of Planned Parenthood clinics throughout inner-cities. The proposal, which called for hiring Colored ministers and selecting a Negro Advisory Council who would *appear* to run a family planning campaign, was to popularize family planning in southern black communities using community people as spokespersons (Grant, 1988).

Sanger decried the fact that blacks believed "that God sends them children," (March 8, 1941). But, she believed that the best educational approach was through religion. "We do not want the word to get out that we want to exterminate the Negro population, and the Minister is the man who can straighten out that idea if it ever occurs to any of their more rebellious members," (December 10, 1939).

Has her tactic of working in communities and through churches been so successful that clinics abound in our neighborhoods? Although these combined reasons may provide a backdrop for discussion, the answer is *No*.

The Role of the United States Government

Sanger's personal mission alone did not propel Planned Parenthood to such national status. Planned Parenthood is in black neighborhoods because of strategic planning, a shared goal, multiple committed partnerships, and the sustained dedication of financial resources—a monumental effort that only the United States government could achieve.

As an organization, Planned Parenthood met opportunity. What began with Sanger's Birth Control Federation in 1916 had, by 1960, become a national movement. Renamed Planned Parenthood Federation of America (PPFA), popularizing birth-control for the poor had a three-fold purpose—controlling the growth of the population to preserve a quality of life (Hellman, 1971); (2) producing children of higher intelligence in keeping with the ideals of the Eugenics philosophy (Valenza, 1985); and

(3) controlling population growth through the Malthusian strategy of monitoring one's own fertility (Malthus, 1812).

The organization in place, opportunity surfaced when African American women, who were perceived to be particularly fecund or fertile, became the focus of the government's national family planning efforts (Farley, 1970). Reducing the size of traditionally large black families was a priority that eventually would impact other minorities as well.

Population Growth and the American Future

In July, 1969, President Nixon asked Congress to create a Commission on Population Growth and the American Future to study population growth and its effect on federal, state, and local governments (Scheyer, 1970). A few months later, in October, the National Center for Family Planning Services was established in the Health Services and Mental Health Administration (HSMHA) of the Department of Health, Education, and Welfare (DHEW now the Department of Health and Human Services or DHHS).

The federal government bemoaned that it was quite late in doing so, but finally there was a shared commitment in assuming a "responsible role in family planning efforts," (Scheyer, 1970, p. 24). This would be achieved by developing a "meaningful federal and private partnership among all interested groups" to address "this area of great social need;" grants and contracts would be awarded to support services which encouraged "consumer participation and consent," (Scheyer, 1970, p. 24).

> In a country of 200 million, a growth rate of one percent per year produces enough additional people to populate a new Washington metropolitan area every year. And we are feeling the impact—in the crowding of cities, the sprawl of suburbia, the vanishing wilderness, the trespass of pollution. Every one of us feels it where it hurts most—in the quality of our lives . . . .
> And what is most tragic and most ironic is that we, who need it least, have readily accessible to us and to our wives the means of deciding how many children shall share our large and well-spaced houses and our trips to the beach. Those who lack our ways of buffering the pressure of population on their lives also lack the means to decide how many shall share their lot. (Scheyer, 1970, p. 22)

DHHS Hires Planned Parenthood

Planned Parenthood is now a government agency. With the DHEW (DHHS) task of developing family planning programs and coordinating with other federal and private efforts to assure community family planning services, the HSMHA hired or subcontracted Planned Parenthood to provide comprehensive services for the low-income population. The National Center for Family Planning Services in the HSMHA established "a meaningful federal and private partnership" by officially incorporating Planned Parenthood into the federal government under the umbrella of DHEW (DHHS) (Scheyer, 1970, p. 24).

Through the Family Planning Services and Population Research Act of 1970—commonly referred to as Title X—Planned Parenthood receives federally-funded grants and contracts to provide a "radically simplified delivery system" by establishing free or low-cost non-medical, walk-in clinics in poor, inner-city neighborhoods for women who are high risk of pregnancy (Gobble, Vincent, Cochrane, & Lock, 1969; Planned Parenthood of New York City, 1970, p. 25).

A pilot program in Forsyth County, North Carolina convinced researchers that walk-in clinics attracted the poor to utilize their services (Gobble et al, 1969). Autonomous clinics were to be entities that were separate from hospitals to service the immediate target—the five million women in this country who are in need of subsidized services (Scheyer, 1970).

Five million *Negro* women . . .

Of this population, three critical age groups were identified: teenagers and young adults 15-22 years old, women in their middle and late twenties, and those 28-30. Scheyer (1970) noted that "reduction in population growth achieved as a by-product of the enrichment of individual and family living can enrich the lives of every one of us," notably, those who considered themselves to be among the elite (p. 25).

A Catchy Phrase

"Equal opportunities for the poor" became the media-magic catch-phrase to market Planned Parenthood's services to minority women (Hellman, 1971). "Skill, tact, and innovation" were necessary so that clinics would be appealing and non-threatening (p. 40).

In other words, black women must be encouraged to view Planned Parenthood as their *friend*. And who to better communicate this message than . . . a black woman? She was being groomed for this task and would soon assume a leadership role.

Go to Schools

But black women were still hesitant to go to these new facilities. Low clinic utilization in New York caused Planned Parenthood to reexamine its strategy. More drastic solutions, such as the decentralization of public schools to accommodate "school-based family planning information and education programs," were recommended (PPNYC 1970, p. 28).

Comprehensive sex education went hand-in-hand with providing contraceptive and birth-control services for teenagers. So in 1970, Mary Calderone, medical director of Planned Parenthood, resigned her post to establish the Sex Information and Education Council of the United States (SIECUS). The role of SIECUS is to serve as a national clearinghouse for sex education curricula for all public schools throughout the United States (Guttmacher & Pilpel, 1970).

The biggest challenge was still ahead—the amendment of parental notification and consent laws to provide services to minors of any age (Pilpel & Wechsler, 1971). But the Supreme Court would soon adhere to the Commission's recommendations by reversing parental rights.

The Final Report

In 1972, the Commission, chaired by John D. Rockefeller 3rd, issued its final report noting that "small differences in family size will make big differences in the demands placed on our society," (*Population and the American Future*, 1972, p. 45). It was determined that over-population contributed to the crisis of environmental deterioration, racial antagonisms, the plight of the cities, and the international situation. Perspectives for addressing the population were to: (1) slow growth by freedom from unwanted childbearing; (2) include minorities and women into the mainstream of America; and (3) recast American values toward the ecology system.

> The time has come to challenge the tradition that population growth is desirable: What was unintended may turn out to be unwanted, in the society as in the family. (Population, 1972, p. 7)

Goals to improve the quality of life included slowing and eventually halting U.S. population growth by promoting an average of two children per family. For white women, the Commission recommended passing the Equal Rights Amendment so that women would find meaningful work outside of the home. Stereotypical roles and low-status jobs were "unlikely to compete effectively with childbearing" while attractive work and rewarding employment "may compete successfully with childbearing beyond the first child" (*Population and the American Future*, 1972, p. 154).

To address the "crisis of overpopulation" among blacks, the government committed to the "full support of all health services related to fertility," and to "an extension of government family planning project grant programs," (*Population and the American Future*, 1972, p. 167). Stating that the task for fertility-related services was too important to be left to voluntary organizations or to private efforts, the government assumed leadership responsibility for an extensive information and education component in addition to the mass provision of services.

The Commission mandated generous federal funding of Planned Parenthood, a commitment that continues today. It recommended that Planned Parenthood be financed through Title X grants—$225 million in fiscal year 1973, $275 million in fiscal year 1974, $325 million in fiscal year 1975, and $400 million each year thereafter.

Schools and Curriculum

The Commission recommended that states eliminate legal restrictions regarding access to contraceptives for minors. States should make contraceptives available to minors in settings considered to be appropriate for them—their schools.

Schools were to assume the responsibility of teaching family planning, population control, and sexuality education which would be financed through DHEW/DHHS. Teachers and school administrators were to receive training and curriculum integrated with family planning information (*Population and the American Future*, 1972).

With oversight from the DHEW (DHHS) and the National Institute of Mental Health, sex education would be made available to all teenagers in combination with "community efforts sponsored by youth-oriented groups, Planned Parenthood centers, and similar groups," (*Population and the American Future*, 1972, p. 134). California Senator Alan Cranston objected.

> I do not believe the Commission has placed sufficient stress on the role and responsibilities of parents regarding the provision of birth-control information and services . . . Society and schools should make every effort to encourage child and parent to discuss these matters honestly and openly. Our educational programs should stress this.
>
> I have similar concerns about medical authorities providing contraceptive services to unemancipated teenagers without parental consent or knowledge. I strongly believe that it should be the obligation of the health professional to counsel the unemancipated teenage patient to raise this issue with his or her parents. (*Population and the American Future*, 1972, p. 269)

Despite additional passionate arguments, the majority vote carried. Now, legal statutes on parental rights had to be changed accordingly. "To implement this policy, the Commission urges that organizations, such as the Council on State Governments, the American Law Institute, and the American Bar Association, formulate appropriate model statutes," (*Population and the American Future*, 1972, p. 170).

And they did.

Condoms and Clinics

With a common national agenda, attention now turned to deciding which contraception was most effective for teenagers. Condoms were the solution (Harvey, 1972).

African American teenagers from single-parent homes were identified as children who were at high-risk of illegitimate conception and therefore in need of specialized services through school-based clinics (SBCs) (Abernethy, 1974). Researchers also documented that since whites managed to avoid illegitimacy, African American adolescents who were given social rewards for motherhood (Sklar & Berkov, 1974) were to be the primary focus of fertility-related services (Morris, 1974; Zelnik & Kantner, 1974).

The SBC or school-based health clinic was seen as the best hope of reducing the incidence of the "unwed mother syndrome" among inner-city children (Edwards, Steinman & Hakanson, 1977). Schools were encouraged to prevent unwanted births by publicizing the location of contraceptive services for teenagers (Goldsmith et al., 1972).

Parents Object

By 1973, there were two SBCs operating on school grounds. The first clinic opened quietly in a Dallas high school in 1970, (Kirby, 1989; Kirby, Waszak & Ziegler, 1989) but opening the second in 1973 in a junior/senior high school in St. Paul, Minnesota proved problematic. Objections from parents, teachers, and community leaders forced a 2-year delay, but the Board of Education finally granted its approval with the stipulation that contraceptives not be distributed on school grounds (Dryfoos, 1985; Edwards et al., 1980).

Clinic enrollment remained low until a range of additional services were added to boost students' participation—athletic, job and college physicals, immunizations, and a weight-control program. For "specialized procedures, tests, and consultations," it was "arranged" that students be transported to nearby hospitals (Edwards, Steinman, & Hakanson, p. 765).

Lower the Voting Age

With the legalization of abortion nationwide in 1973, laws regarding parental notification and consent continued to be a stumbling block for Planned Parenthood. The voting age had been lowered from 21 to 18 but not to grant teens the privilege of voting at a younger age. With the right to vote, an 18 year-old was now recognized as an adult, which meant she could receive contraceptive services without asking permission from her parents (Paul, Pilpel, & Wechsler, 1974).

In 1977, the *Carey v. Population Services International* Supreme Court decision reversed parental consent laws. The Supreme Court ruled that contraceptives were to be made available to all minors without parental notification or consent (Paul & Pilpel, 1979).

Abortions in the Morning

This cleared the way for SBC staff to remove a girl from school for an abortion without informing her parents. Here's how it works.

In the morning, SBC nurses drive the student from her school to a nearby Planned Parenthood facility where the abortion is performed. The student is transported back to school in the afternoon (Feroli et al., 1992). Parents do not have to be informed by the school or by Planned Parenthood nurses and clinic staff that their child has had major surgery.

Additionally, Planned Parenthood instructs the "woman"—she is not to be called a "girl" no matter her age—that she does *not* have to inform her parents about the abortion. Girls and boys may also opt for sterilization, again without parental notification or consent. While the regular school nurse may not give a child an aspirin without her parent's consent, SBC nurses may perform pelvic examinations and prescribe medications right in the school (Tolbert, 2007).

Negro Project Failure

In 1975, I was invited to become a board member of Planned Parenthood New York City. I attended my first board meeting filled with anticipation. The bus ride from the mid-town office where I worked as an editor over to the Margaret Sanger Clinic was a short one. Over time, I noticed that several of the board members arrived in chauffeured limousines.

Once in the building, I walked past the clinic that serviced primarily African American and Latino girls. The elevator took me upstairs to a rather imposingly large boardroom, and I took my seat with the striking observation that I was the only person of color in the room. The majority of board members were male, and the handful of women appeared to be much older than my 27 years.

During the course of my five-year tenure, we received a lot of literature. Most discussed population control and the concern for the growing number of people in the world—poor people in the United States and in developing countries. As the population grew, natural resources were shrinking—air, water, food. I soon understood why the full name for this organization was Planned Parenthood World Population.

I struggled with the question, "Which population are they trying to control?" As a black woman, the boomerang kept coming back to me. I wondered why abortion was more necessary for my ethnic group, why this organization fought so hard to give us this particular "right" when the rights for better education, better jobs, and better housing were so paramount.

Early in my volunteer service on the board, I learned about the biggest challenge that Planned Parenthood New York City faced. For every abortion that was performed, a death certificate had to be issued by the Department of Health.

Death Certificates

Death certificates? Does that mean that the babies were *alive*? I, along with millions of other Americans, debated about when life really begins. When is the fetus viable? When can it live on its own? Abortion could not be murder if, indeed, all that was aborted was a mass of tissue.

I considered resigning from the board. Now that I understood what was really involved, I wanted no part in this abortion business. But the question, "Who will speak up if I leave?" kept me in a quandary. Eventually deciding to remain, I determined to be a thorn in their side and was often the lone "No!" vote on the board.

A Friendly Face

From 1978 to 1992, Faye Wattleton was President of Planned Parenthood Federation of America succeeding Margaret Sanger (Lewis). With religious parents—Watttleton's mother was a Church of God in Christ preacher—here was the *perfect* Negro Project.

Tall, articulate, and attractive with a masters' degree in maternal and infant care, Wattleton propelled the agenda of Planned Parenthood to the front lines of the American debate. To convince black women that abortion was their right, she preferred on-screen face-to-face encounters with Catholic priests—preferably white males wearing clergy collars.

The visual message worked! What black woman wanted a white man telling her what she should or should not do with her body? As she successfully championed abortion, Wattleton also lobbied to bring the morning-after pill, RU 486, to the United States.

Black women were convinced that they had a friend in Planned Parenthood. Clinics were popping up everywhere throughout the inner-city. And in keeping with the Commission's recommended strategy, more schools began to embrace Planned Parenthood's comprehensive reproductive health-care services.

Don't Mention Abortions!

To address opposition to new clinics from parents, clergy, and the community, clinic staff was advised not to dispense contraceptives during the first year of operation. The Center for Population Options offered technical and advisory support to promote SBCs and in 1994, seeking a less controversial name for itself, was recast as Advocates for Youth (CPO, 1986; Kirby, 1986).

This "how to set up a school-based clinic" organization generates reports to maintain generous federal funding and expansion of clinics. One way to prove that clinics are necessary is for clinic staff to cite poverty statistics and the number of poor children who don't have medical coverage as rationale for SBC services (Lovick, 1987).

Advocates also advise clinic staff to de-emphasize abortion, birth-control, and contraceptive services. Instead emphasize other medical services like weight-control or immunizations which are more palatable to parents and principals.

Sexual Activity Increases

The HIV/AIDS pandemic swung the door wide open for comprehensive "safe sex education" in public schools. To "protect" students, more schools needed to distribute condoms to kids. But with condom availability, sexual activity increased (National School Boards Association, 1990).

By 1986, there were 60 SBCs throughout the United States (Kirby, 1986). By 1988, there were over 150 SBCs (Dryfoos, 1988; Kirby, Waszak, & Ziegler, 1989). Expanding clinics in schools was surprising since researchers recognized that SBCs were unsuccessful in impacting pregnancy rates (Dryfoos, 1988).

Pregnancies Increase

Although some researchers warned that where there are clinics, there is an increase of 120 pregnancies per 1,000 among 15—to-19 year olds (Olsen & Weed, 1987), this did not stop their expansion. By 1991, there were 239 SBCs and SLCs—school-linked clinics (clinics located near school grounds) (Waszak & Neidell, 1991). By 1995, there were 607 (Schlitt et al, 1995).

Lawsuits challenged condom distribution based on parental rights in New York, Massachusetts, Pennsylvania, and Washington. Where laws could not be broadly interpreted, the recommendation was to change laws because of the large number of dysfunctional families in which parents do not act in the best interests of their children (English, 1993).

Expensive Operations

School-based clinics are expensive operations. Costs for services, primarily for salaries, range from $90,000 to over $300,000 per clinic (Dryfoos, 1980; Kirby, 1985; School-Based Clinics that Work, 1993).

Even with substantial Title X monies plus state grants, Medicaid, and social services along with funding from private foundations, the cost-effectiveness of SBCs was not proven (Dryfoos, 1985, Warren, 1987). Still, by 1985 there were 13 clinics identified as comprehensive, multiservice units providing abortions. Researchers cited success by reporting 85.3 fewer live births at clinic schools (Ralph & Edgington, 1983).

Are SBCs Successful?

With condoms in classrooms and bathrooms, is contraceptive use among teenagers increasing? In other words, are SBCs successful in reducing pregnancy and increasing condom use?

An evaluation of 4 SBCs in California demonstrates that the availability of contraceptives on site, "which has been thought to be an important convenience factor contributing to positive contraceptive adoption," was not found to be significant (Brindis et al., 1994, p. 163).

Contraceptive use is not related to whether contraceptives are dispensed on site, whether health education and counseling are provided by a health educator, whether contraceptive services are part of a comprehensive array of services that include medical or counseling services, or whether a family planning visit results in the dispensing of contraceptives or a prescription for contraceptives. (Brindis et al, 1994, p. 160)

Clinics in . . . Kindergarten?

Despite these findings, there is urgency to open a clinic in every public school—elementary through high (The Comprehensive School-Health Education Workshop, 1993). Although African Americans are only 13% of the population, SBCs are primarily concentrated in schools that are attended by black children (Lear, 2007).

By 2005, there were 869 school-based health centers (SBHCs) as they are more favorably labeled. New York has the largest number of clinics in schools K-5 with a total of 195. California, with 140, has the second-largest concentration of SBCs, 35% of which are located in elementary schools (Lear, 2007). In all, pregnancy testing (76%) is a primary service.

By 2011, there were 2,000 school-based health centers nationwide providing so-called affordable health care for children (School-Based Health Centers). But evaluation of SBCs demonstrates little evidence that school-based comprehensive sex education strategies are effective (Weed, 2009).

Encouraging Sexual Activity

Some studies indicate that clinics on school grounds may result in a sexually permissive environment that encourages sexual activity. Condom availability may send social cues to males that they are expected to have sexual intercourse, and that sexual activity is acceptable. And, sexual activity may increase since more female virgins may transition to non-virgin status in clinic schools (Tolbert, 1996).

It's understandable why teens report that their school environment encourages them to have sex. In health classes, presentations by SBC nurses desensitize teens by exposing them to explicit comprehensive sex education.

For example, students play games like "The Condom Race" where they sit in groups blindfolded and race to roll and unroll candy colored condoms on anatomically correct, erect penises. The group that wins receives . . . more condoms (Hayden, 1993).

Bible is *Just* Media

Planned Parenthood teachers and nurses don't limit their instruction to safe sex. From an authoritative pulpit, humanist indoctrination occurs—teaching that counters parental values and contradicts basic Christian beliefs.

In one class, students were told that there's no difference between having anal sex or vaginal sex because the anus is as sensitive as the vagina. When some students protested that homosexual sex is against what the Bible teaches, they were told that the Bible is just another form of media like the newspaper, television, books, or the Internet. People simply make different choices about where to get their information.

Even though parents read through the 3-page form with tiny print and signed to opt out students from this instruction, students were not excused. Why? Because Planned Parenthood's sessions are considered research, and students may not opt out of research. Of course, parents have no idea that when they send their children to public school, they are being sabotaged (Caldwell, personal communication).

Abstinence Education

Abstinence education is not a focal point for black children because social science researchers deem it unrealistic (Pittman et al, 1992). However, self-control, self-respect, delayed gratification, planning for the future, building healthy friendships and other values essential to abstinence education are necessary for every area of life, not just in the delay of sexual activity (Tolbert, 1998). Teenagers' future orientation, educational goals, religiosity, and the presence of both parents in the home are factors which reduce the risk of early coitus (Benson & Donahue, 1989).

Years of abstinence education may be responsible for the dramatic decrease in the number of abortions in the United States. In 1986, there were 416,170 abortions per 1,000 women. By 2006, that number had decreased more than half—206,880. Sexual activity rates also declined (Guttmacher, 2010).

Abortion—an enterprise that targets minority communities where blacks reside—is big business in America. School administrators lack funds to procure lab equipment or computers or fix crumbling buildings (Kozol, 1991), but there's ample federal and foundation dollars for clinics and for abortions.

Recent studies demonstrate that students who are taught comprehensive sex education, also called Comprehensive Risk Reduction, are more likely to become pregnant (Weed, 2012). When will common sense prevail?

La Verne Tolbert, Ph.D., is a former board member of Planned Parenthood, New York City, from 1975 to 1980 where she learned the truth about abortion detailed in her book, Keeping You & Your Kids Sexually Pure. She is founder/ CEO of Teaching Like Jesus Ministries, a parachurch ministry that equips leaders in the local church www.teachinglikejesus.org.

Portions of this chapter adapted from Tolbert, L. (1996 Ed.D. dissertation; Ph.D. subsequently awarded). Condom availability through school-based clinics and teenagers' attitudes regarding premarital sexual Activity. (Doctoral dissertation, Talbot School of Theology/Biola University, 1996). *Dissertation Abstracts International, 57/08A,* 3409.

REFERENCES

Abernethy, V. (1974). Illegitimate conception among teenagers. *American Journal of Public Health, 64,* 662-665.

Benson, P. L., & Donahue, M. J. (1989). Ten-year trends in at-risk behaviors: A national study of Black adolescents. *Journal of Adolescent Research, 4,* 125-139.

Brindis, C., Starbuck-Morales, S., Wolfe, A. L., & McCarter, V. (1994). Characteristics associated with contraceptive use among adolescent females in school-based family planning programs. *Family Planning Perspectives, 26,* 160-164. p. 163.

Caldwell, R., Pastor Calvary Chapel Crenshaw. (February 27, 2012). Personal Communication.

Center for Population Options/Advocates for Youth. (1986). *School-based clinic policy initiatives around the country: 1986* [Report]. Washington, DC: Author

Commission on Population Growth and the American Future (1971). Population growth and America's future. *Family Planning Perspectives,* 3(2), 45-52.

December 10, 1939 letter from Margaret Sanger to Dr. C. J. Gamble.

Dryfoos, J. (1980). School-based health clinics: A new approach to preventing adolescent pregnancy? *Family Planning Perspectives, 17,* 70-75

Dryfoos, J. (1985). School-based health clinics: A new approach to preventing adolescent pregnancy? *Family Planning Perspectives, 17,* 70-75

Dryfoos, J. G. (1988) School-based health clinics: Three years of experience. *Family Planning Perspectives, 20,* 193-200

Edwards, L. E., Steinman, M. E., Arnold, K. A., & Hakanson, E. Y. (1980). Adolescent pregnancy prevention services in high school clinics. *Family Planning Perspectives, 12,* 6-14.

Edwards, L. E., Steinman, M. E., Hakanson, E. Y. (1977). An experimental high school clinic. *American Journal of Public Health, 67,* 765-766. p. 765.

English, A. (1993). Condom distribution in the schools. *Journal of Adolescent Health, 14,* 562-564.

Farley, R. (1970). *Growth of the Black population.* Chicago: Markham Publishing.

Feroli, K. L., Hobson, S. K., Miola, E. S., Scott, P. N., & Waterfield, G. D. (1992). School-based clinics: The Baltimore experience. *Journal of Pediatric Health Care, 6,* 127-131.

Gobble, F. L., Vincent, C. E., Cochrane, C. M., & Lock, F. R. (1969). A nonmedical approach to fertility reduction. *Obstetrics and Gynecology, 34,* 888-891.

Goldsmith, S., Gabrielson, M. O., Gabrielson, I., Mathews, V., & Potts, L. (1972). Teenagers, sex and contraception. *Family Planning Perspectives,* 4(1), 32-38.

Grant, G. (1988) *Grand Illusions: The Legacy of Planned Parenthood.* Wolgemuth & Hyatt: Brentwood, TN. p. 93.

Guttmacher Institute. (January 2010). U.S. Teenage Pregnancies, Births and Abortions: National and State Trends and Trends by Race and Ethnicity.

Guttmacher, A. F., & Pilpel, H, (1970). Abortion and the unwanted child. *Family Planning Perspectives*, *2*(2), 16-24.

Harvey, P. D. (1972). Condoms—A new look. *Family Planning Perspectives*, *4*(4), 27-30.

Hayden, J. (1993). The condom race. *Journal of American College Health*, *42*, 133-136.

Hellman, L. M. (1971). Five-year plan for population research and family planning services. *Family Planning Perspectives*, *3*(4), 35-40.

Hellman, L. M. (1971). Five-year plan for population research and family planning services. *Family Planning Perspectives*, *3*(4), 35-40. p. 37.

Kirby, D. (1985). *School-based health clinics: An emerging approach to improving adolescent health and addressing teenage pregnancy* [Report]. Washington, DC: Center for Population Options/Advocates for Youth. (ERIC Document Reproduction Service No. ED 277 955)

Kirby, D. (1986). Comprehensive school-based health clinics: A growing movement to improve adolescent health and reduce teen-age pregnancy [Commentary]. *Journal of School Health, 56*, 289-291.

Kirby, D. (1989). *School-based clinics enter the 90s: Update evaluation and future challenges* [Report]. Washington, DC: Center for Population Options/Advocates for Youth. (ERIC Document Reproduction Service No. ED 320 209)

Kirby, D., Waszak, C., & Ziegler, J. (1989). Executive summary: Utilization, impact, and potential of school-based clinics. In P. Donovan, (Ed.), *An assessment of six school-based clinics: Service, impact and potential*. Washington, DC: Center for Population Options/Advocates for Youth. (ERIC Document Reproduction Service No. ED 320 207)

Kozol, J. (1991). *Savage inequalities: Children in America's schools*. New York: HarperCollins.

Lear, J. G. (October, 2007). It's elementary: Expanding the use of school-based clinics. *California Health Care Foundation*.

Lewis, J. Faye Wattleton. Retrieved February 28, 2012 from About.com Women's History *http://womenshistory.about.com/od/birthcontrol/p/faye_wattleton.htm*

Lovick, S. R. (1987). *The school-based clinic update 1987* [Report]. Washington, DC: Center for Population Options/Advocates for Youth. (ERIC Document Reproduction Service No. ED 328 950)

Malthus, T. (1812): Malthusian—of or relating to Malthus or to his theory that population tends to increase at a faster rate than its means of subsistence and that unless it is checked by moral restraint or by disease, famine, war, or other disaster widespread poverty and degradation inevitably result. Webster's Ninth New Collegiate Dictionary (1985). p. 721.

March 8, 1941 letter from Margaret Sanger to D. Rose.

Margaret Sanger: An autobiography (1938), NY: W. W. Norton, p. 375.

Morris, L. (1974). Estimating the need for family planning services among unwed teenagers. *Family Planning Perspectives, 6,* 91-97

National School Boards Association. (1990, February). *HIV prevention education in the nation's public schools* [Report]. Alexandria, VA: Author. (ERIC Document Reproduction Service No. ED 320 308).

Olsen, J. A., & Weed, S. E. (1987). Effects of family-planning programs for teenagers on adolescent birth and pregnancy rates. *Family Perspective, 20,* 153-195.

Paul, E. W., & Pilpel, H. F. (1979). Teenagers and pregnancy: The law in 1979. *Family Planning Perspectives, 11,* 297-301.

Paul, E. W., Pilpel, H. F., & Wechsler, N. F. (1974). Pregnancy, teenagers and the law, 1974. *Family Planning Perspectives, 6,* 142-147.

Pilpel, H. F., & Wechsler, N. F. (1971). Birth-control, teen-agers and the law: A new look, 1971. *Family Planning Perspectives, 3*(3), 37-45.

Pittman, K. J., Wilson, P. M., Adams-Taylor, S., & Randolph, S. (1992). Making sexuality education and prevention programs relevant for African-American youth. *Journal of School Health, 62,* 339-344.

Planned Parenthood of New York City (1970). Family planning in New York City: Recommendations for action. *Family Planning Perspectives, 2*(4), 25-31.

Population and the American future. (1972). New York: Signet. p. 7.

Ralph, N., & Edgington, A. (1983). An evaluation of an adolescent family planning program. *Journal of Adolescent Health Care, 4,* 158-162.

Sanger, M. (1920) *Women and the new race.* Project Gutenberg. p. 229.

Scheyer, S. C. (1970). DHEW's new center: The national commitment to family planning. *Family Planning Perspectives, 2*(1), 22-24.

Schlitt, J. J., Rickett, K. D., Montgomery, L. L., & Lear, J. G. (1995). State initiatives to support school-based health centers: A national survey. *Journal of Adolescent Health, 17,* 68-76.

School-based clinics that work [Report]. (June, 1993). Rockville, MD: Public Health Services, U. S. Department of Health and Human Services. (ERIC Document Reproduction Service No. ED 359 189)

School-based health centers. Retrieved February 28, 2012 from *http://www. hrsa.gov/ourstories/schoolhealthcenters/*

Sklar, J., & Berkov, B. (1974). Teenage family formation in postwar America. *Family Planning Perspectives, 6,* 80-90.

The comprehensive school-health education workshop [Special issue]. (1993, January). *Journal of School Health, 63.*

Tolbert, L. (1996). Condom availability through school-based clinics and teenagers attitudes regarding premarital sexual activity. (Doctoral dissertation, Talbot School of Theology, 1996). *Dissertation Abstracts International, 57/08A,* 3409

Tolbert, L. (1998). Teaching Abstinence: Legislators Just Said No. [Essay]. *Los Angeles Times.* p. B7.

Tolbert, L. (2007). *Keeping You & Your Kids Sexually Pure: A How-To Guide for Parents, Pastors, Youth Workers, and Teachers. www.xlibris.com*

Valenza, C. (1985). Was Margaret Sanger a racist? *Family Planning Perspectives, 17,* 44-46.

Warren, C. (1987). *Improving student's access to health care: School-based health clinics. A briefing paper for policy makers.* New York: Center for Public Advocacy Research, Ford Foundation. (ERIC Document Reproduction Service No. ED 295 072)

Waszak, C. & Neidell, S. (1991). *School-based and school-linked clinics: Update 1991.* Washington, DC: Center for Population Options/Advocates for Youth. (ERIC Document Reproduction Service No. 341 899)

Weed, S. (2009). Another look at the evidence: Abstinence and comprehensive sex education in our schools. *The Institute for Research & Evaluation.* Salt Lake City, UT.

Weed, S. (2012). Sex education for schools still in question. *American Journal of Preventive Medicine,* 42(3), 313-315.

Zelnik, M., & Kantner, J. F. (1974). The resolution of teenage first pregnancies. *Family Planning Perspectives, 6,* 74-80.

CHAPTER 20

Worry About Children Later

Tegra Little

For we are God's masterpiece. He has created us anew in Christ
Jesus, so we can do the good things he planned for us long ago.
Ephesians 2:10 NLT

I was born in Los Angeles into a middle working class family, raised by my biological mom and my step-father, the eldest of four children, and the only one with a different father. I loved attending church and accepted Christ at nine years old. My childhood years in church were spent at Crenshaw Christian Center. I never remember anyone in the church or in my family teaching me about sex or holiness. As I look back over my life I can clearly see how God gifted me with the Spirit of discernment at an early age.

While growing up I was not fortunate to observe a healthy godly marriage filled with love between my mom and step-dad. Instead I lived in fear not knowing what to expect from a step-father who would come home drunk a couple of days a month after midnight with bloodshot eyes. It was like clockwork. He would stumble into the house around one or two o'clock in the morning and I would over hear my parents having a simple disagreement or misunderstanding, but soon it escalated into harsh words and yelling or screaming. He was verbally abusive to my mother and my younger brother.

Violated at 5-Years-Old

At the tender age of five I awakened one morning frightened and scared. My step-father was kneeled beside my bed and his hand was inside my underwear. I instinctively knew I was being violated. He instantly rushed out of my bedroom.

While getting dressed for school the next morning and lathering my legs with lotion, I innocently blurted out in front of my parents and siblings "Daddy was in my room last night and he had his hand inside my panties." He called me a liar. No one ever told me that my body was special and no one should touch me in my private areas. I just knew it was wrong. The next time he inappropriately touched me was when I was thirteen, he tried to fondle my breast. I was mortified and could not believe what was happening.

I developed a deep sense of hatred and resentment toward my step-father. He wore the public mask of a kind and gentle husband and father on the outside but he lacked integrity behind closed doors. From the age of five to eleven I would secretly tell myself he was not my father because I intuitively knew something was wrong.

What father touches his child inappropriately? A few months before matriculating from elementary school I found out he was not my biological father. I changed my last name to my biological father's name and I wanted nothing to do with my step-father. My mom and step-father eventually divorced when I was fifteen years old.

The Father Void

I was thirteen years old when I decided to take swimming lessons with my siblings and cousins at a local neighborhood park in Inglewood, CA. My mom would often go with us but eventually she decided we could walk.

I received a lot of attention from an older twenty-two year old lifeguard. He always complimented me on my swimming ability, told me I was beautiful and smart. The attention from him replaced the void of not having a father. This older man made me feel special, and I felt loved.

I responded to his pressure to have sexual intercourse but I didn't know that his having sex with me was a crime. If I had told someone, he would have gone to prison for a very long time because I was a minor and he was an adult. Young girls are *victims* when they are tricked by grown men to have sex.

This victimization continued throughout that summer. The role of a lifeguard is to safeguard other swimmers, but I was drowning and didn't even know it. This opened the door to me becoming a sexually active teenager throughout middle school, high school and well into college. As long as I continued to excel in school in my advance placement classes and extra curricula activities, no one in my immediate family would ever think I was having sex.

STD and Pregnancy

I was nineteen and in my first year of college I was infected with an STD, Trichomoniasis. The Centers for Disease Control (CDC) describes Trichomoniasis as the most common curable STD in young, sexually active women. An estimated 7.4 million new cases occur each year in women and men. [1]

During my second year of college I found out I was pregnant. I knew I could not keep the baby. I was in school and had my future all mapped out. I believed the lie "it's just a blob of tissue". Believing the lie was an effort to suppress what I knew did not quite seem right in the back of mind, and it was enough to get me to Planned Parenthood.

I found their services in the Yellow Pages. Clearly, it was all about me and what I wanted. My behavior was narcissistic and since I really did not value my own life what made me think I would value the life of my baby in my womb? My life was spiraling out of control. I had religion and no relationship with Christ, and it was evident that a Christian worldview was absent from my life.

At the time I never told anyone about my pregnancy except my mother. I asked her to take me to the abortion clinic since I needed someone to drive me home after the procedure. She did what I asked.

Planned Parenthood

We walked into the clinic and the lobby was empty. I approached the receptionist window and a woman handed me paperwork to complete. A little while later a black woman called my name and she escorted me into her office. She looked over my paperwork and told me I was still young, in school and I could worry about kids later.

This was the only advice and counsel I was given. She certainly did not try and persuade me into waiting a day or two to think about my decision. It was clear in her mind that what was about to take place was not a big deal and she wanted to make sure I grabbed hold of that same mindset. She then moved me into another room and performed an ultra sound.

I asked her if I could see the screen and she said, "No." I asked, "Why not?" She said, "It's against our policy." Then she told me "there's nothing to see, it's just tissue." In that moment I should have put my clothes on and walked out. She never talked with me about fetal development, the baby's heartbeat or adoption.

Before I knew it I was quickly swept into a sterile bright white room, greeted by a Pilipino woman who asked me to climb onto the table. When the doctor came in, he had a mask on and I could only see his eyes. He told me to relax, I would receive a sedative, and I wouldn't feel anything and the procedure would not take long. It did seem as if the entire procedure was less than an hour.

I remember walking into the locker room and seeing at least ten women sitting next to one another on a long bench. We all looked like zombies. I was shocked to see all of the ladies particularly since I did not see any of them in the lobby. Someone came in the room and offered us juice and cookies. I remember thanking the person and in my comatose state I said, "You guys are really nice in here, you are treating us so well."

I was deceived, delusional and out of my mind. I was in the lion's den and didn't even know it.

I put my clothes on and walked into the lobby to meet my mom. She was between smiles as she greeted me and asked me if I was okay. There was silence in the car all the way home. I felt numb. Two days later I was back to my usual routine with school, work, partying, one foot in the church and one foot in the world. My life was pathetic! I continued to operate in darkness; still not understanding my birthright as a citizen of heaven.

Eight months later I was on a new college campus, before I decided to transfer, auditioning models for a fashion show. There I met a man who would become my husband eight years later. We received wise counsel and abstained from sex two years before our marriage. God had me on a new path.

Infertility

I was thirty-four when I had my first molar/ectopic pregnancy. My OBGYN told me I also had a lot of scar tissue in my fallopian tubes. Two years later at thirty-six I had a miscarriage, followed by another molar pregnancy at thirty-seven. At thirty-eight I had a partial hysterectomy.

My Oncologist did not see a problem with us having our own biological children. Since I still had my ovaries, we could sign-up with a surrogacy agency and pay a whopping fee for a gestational surrogate to carry the child for us. I was absolutely devastated.

The woman from Planned Parenthood was right about one thing when she said, "You can worry about kids later." Worry was now the operative word.

My husband never knew I was post-abortive. We really wanted to become parents but the journey was not easy, in fact it was brutal. I thought for sure I had accepted God's forgiveness for murdering my child but feelings of guilt consumed me.

I truly believed God was punishing me for murdering my innocent child. I was alone with my pain, agony, guilt and shame. I refused to release my secret to my husband and I was boiling with anger because my mother did not try and stop me. She was my mother, why didn't she protect me?

In November 2004, the Holy Spirit whispered to me and said, "I am taking you into a season of loneliness." I was depressed throughout 2005-I was grieving the loss of my aborted child and grieving the fact that I would never be able to carry another child in my womb. At the top of 2006 I knew I needed wise godly counsel for my pain. "For by wise counsel I would wage my own war, and in a multitude of counselors I would be safe," (Proverbs 24:6).

After two months of solid biblical counseling with a great Christian therapist I finally had the courage to talk to my mom about how I was feeling. The conversation brought us even closer together. I was able to release this secret to my husband and he laid his hands on me and prayed over me like never before. He is without a doubt the man who treats me like Jesus.

My child is safe in the arms of my Father and I will be with him one day in Heaven. God turned my mourning into dancing. Jesus set me free and I am free indeed!

I am thankful and grateful to God for His patience with me while I was steeped in a lifestyle of sin. There were consequences to the bad choices

I made and if I could turn back the clock I would do things differently. Sexual abuse, pre-marital sex, STD's, abortion, and infertility are all part of Satan's playground. Pre-marital sex and abortion are outside of God's will. As a true disciple of Christ I refuse to remain silent on issues that are antithetical to the Kingdom of God.

No Longer Bound

Through my pain and deliverance, I answered the call from God to start No Longer Bound-Abortion Recovery Ministry. The ministry launched in January 2010 to help bring healing to women and men who have been suffering with the pain, guilt and shame of a past abortion/s.

Jesus is setting the captives free, healing the broken-hearted, giving recovery of sight to the blind and setting at liberty those who are oppressed as promised in Luke 4:18. By grace alone through faith alone, I am His masterpiece because of the perfect masterpiece He painted on the cross, not just for me but for you.

Tegra Little is Founder/CEO of the No Longer Bound Abortion Recovery Ministry. http://www.facebook.com/pages/No-Longer-Bound-Abortion-Recovery-Ministry/186670624685612

CHAPTER 21

How Can the Dream Survive if We Murder Our Children?

Dr. Alveda King

In this great country of ours, no one should be forced to pray or read any religious documents, and a woman should have the right to decide what to do with her own body. Thank God for the Constitution of the United States!

This Constitution, though, guarantees freedom *of* religion . . . not freedom *from* religion. The so-called doctrine of "separation of church and state" does not appear in our Constitution. Nothing in our Constitution forbids the free exercise of religion in the public square.

Inherent in our Constitutional as an ingredient of the "right to life, liberty and the pursuit of happiness" is the "right to know." Every woman deserves the right to know the serious consequences of making a decision to abort her child.

Oh, God! What would my uncle, Dr. Martin Luther King, Jr., do if he'd lived to see the contents of thousands of children's skulls emptied into the garbage cans of the abortionists' bottomless pits? He dreamed that his four children—and everyone else's—would be judged by the content of their characters, not just the color of their skin. What would he say if he knew that because of the color of our skin, our babies are judged to be worthless and targeted for murder through abortion?

If Only I Knew

Today, I live with a repentant, heavy heart and pray each day for the Lord's forgiveness and blessing. I am a mother of six living children and I am also a grandmother. But I am also regrettably a post-abortive mother. I offer a tearful prayer that sharing the painful tragedy of my life-altering experiences will help save the life of a child yet unborn. If only I knew . . .

In the early 1970's, even though some Black voices were protesting against forced sterilization, artificial chemical birth-control methods and abortion, there were many who were fooled and misled by propaganda that promoted these advances. I was among those who were duped. As a result, I suffered one involuntary and one voluntary "legal" abortion.

My involuntary abortion was performed just prior to the passage of Roe v. Wade by my private pro-abortion physician without my consent. I had gone to the doctor to ask why my cycle had not resumed after the birth of my son. I did not ask for, nor did I want an abortion.

The doctor said, "You don't need to be pregnant, let's see." Without asking for my permission, he proceeded to perform a painful examination which resulted in a gush of blood and tissue emanating from my womb. Afterwards, this doctor explained that he had performed an abortion that he referred to as a simple procedure, a "local D and C."

Like Having a Tooth Removed

Soon after the Roe v. Wade decision, I was again pregnant. There was adverse pressure and beyond this, a threat of violence from the baby's father. The ease and convenience afforded through Roe v. Wade make it all too easy for me to make the fateful and fatal decision to abort our child. I went to a Planned Parenthood sanctioned doctor and was advised that the procedure would hurt no more than "having a tooth removed."

The next day, I was admitted to the hospital, and our baby was aborted. My medical insurance paid for the procedure. As soon as I woke up, I knew that something was very wrong. I felt very ill, and very empty. I asked the doctor and nurses about the way I was feeling but they reassured me, "It will all go away in a few days. You will be fine."

They lied.

Over the next few years, I experienced medical problems. I had trouble bonding with my son and his five siblings who were born after the

abortions. I suffered from eating disorders, depression, nightmares, sexual
dysfunctions and a host of other issues related to the abortion that I chose
to have. I felt angry about both the involuntary and voluntary abortion.
And I experienced uncontrollable waves of guilt over the abortion I chose
to have. The guilt made me very ill.

Praying for Deliverance

I pray often for deliverance from the pain caused by my decision to abort
my baby. I suffered the threat of cervical and breast cancer and experienced
the pain of empty arms after the baby was gone. Truly, for me as well as
for countless abortive mothers nothing on earth can fully restore what has
been lost, only Jesus can.

My children have all suffered from knowing that they have a brother or
sister that their mother chose to abort. "You killed our baby." Often they
ask if I ever thought about aborting them . . .

This has been, and still is, very painful for all of us. My mother and
grandparents were very sad to learn about the loss of the baby. The aborted
child's father also regrets the abortions. If only I knew . . .

Sharing a Birthday

Had it not been for Roe v. Wade, I would never have had that second
abortion. My birthday is January 22, and each year this special day is
marred by the fact that it is also the anniversary of Roe v. Wade—and the
anniversary of the death of millions of babies.

I and my deceased children are victims of abortion. The Roe v. Wade
decision has adversely and negatively impacted me, the lives of my children
and entire family. Where is the right to know?

Silent No More

I join the voices of thousands across America, who are Silent No More
(*http://www.silentnomoreawareness.org/*). We can no longer sit idly by and
allow this horrible spirit of murder to cut down, cut out, and cut away our

unborn children. We cannot allow this spirit of murder to destroy the lives of our mothers.

Abortion kills babies. Abortion hurts mothers. Abortion sometimes kills mothers. Our babies and mothers must live!

As a born again Christian, I am very grateful to God for the spirit of repentance that is sweeping our land. In this there is healing. In the name of Jesus, we must humble ourselves and pray, and turn from our wicked ways so that God will hear from Heaven, forgive our sins and heal our land.

It is time for America, the most blessed nation on earth, to lead the world in repentance and in restoration of life. We must carry the freedom of repentance to its fullest potential by affirming life. We must allow light and life back into our lives and society!

Let us end injustice anywhere by championing justice everywhere, including in the womb. May God, by His grace, have mercy on us all!

Dr. Alveda King, niece of Dr. Martin Luther King, Jr., is Founder of King for America www.kingforamerica.com and Pastoral Associate with Priests for Life www.africanamericanoutreach.com.

State Representative Alveda King 1982

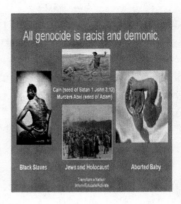

20th Century Prolife Leaders: W. Allen, E. Craven, C. Fisher,
D. Grier, M. Jefferson, G . Keath, G. Lucas, E. Marino,
G. Martin, J. Parker, R. Ross, M. Tulin, C. Upshur,
S. Walton, M. Weiner

W. Hoye, A. Culbreath, B. Fullmore, C. Davis,
S. Broden, A. King, L. Tolbert

A.   Culbreath, S. Broden, C. Davis, W. Hoye,
G. Nadal, C. Childress, V. Hernandez, A. King,
L. Tolbert

J. Hunter, D. Gardner, A. King, B. Fullmore,
S. Mosteller

Catherine Davis

Dr. Day Gardner, Bishop Harry Jackson

Dr. Alveda King, Rev. Dean Nelson

Rev, Arnold Culbreath

Silent No More Awareness Campaign

Dearly and Beloved Departed Mentor
Dr. Mildred Jefferson

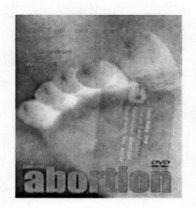

"Latter Rain" Music Video

Image from "WE'VE BEEN GUTTMACHER'D" courtesy of The Radiance Foundation & NBPC

WE ARE PRO FAMILY

And he will go on before the Lord, in the spirit and power of Elijah, to turn the hearts of the fathers to their children and the disobedient to the wisdom of the righteous—to make ready a people prepared for the Lord.
Luke 1: 17

CHAPTER 22

Traditional Values

Elder Levon Yuille

Because someone fails to climb the mountain, this failure does not diminish the beauty or height of the mountain. The climber must simply do what's necessary to ultimately climb the mountain.

There is a great and beautiful mountain that many of us in America are trying to recapture. It is the mountain of Traditional Values. Yes, as corny as it may sound these values made this nation of ours, one of the greatest nations of all times. A nation built by individuals who publicly proclaimed faith in God this nation which has been called the "bread basket of the world" and Champion of Democracy.

There are those who are enemies of the traditional God-centered values that made this nation so great. They have loaded their weapons of anti-traditional values, with ammunition from Darwin's theories, Marx's misguided concepts, Freud's surrender to passion, Wellhausen's so called modernism and Russell, who told us why he did not believe in God. But in the midst of the anti-traditionalist arsenal, they have the ultimate weapon; the mountain climber that failed to reach the top of the mountain.

The anti-traditionalist with glee, point to Jimmy Swaggart, Jim Baker and other high profile traditionalists who failed in their climb. And they use these failures as an attempt to diminish the lofty height and beautiful mountain of Traditional Values. They use these fallen climbers as a method to diminish the mountain and to exalt their concepts of relativism, situational ethics and Marxism.

God-Centered Values

The anti-traditionalist readily ignores the fact that many of America's great institutions, such as, United Way, the Red Cross, Salvation Army, and at least six of our Ivy League colleges are the end results of Christians or Christian organizations. Cities such as Hartford, Connecticut and Zion, Illinois are the products of traditional God-centered values.

We, who believe in traditional values, know that many of us have failed in our climb, but this in no way diminishes the mountain we are trying to climb. The sixties, seventies, and eighties, represent a time of great failings. But the nineties are demanding with its too often failed educational system, decrease productivity, rising crime rate, yes and even failed religious community, that everyone of us with renewed strength, start our climb again to God-centered Traditional Values.

We need to support the party and people that stand for what we believe is morally and ethically right, not only in the sight of man, but more importantly the God of the Judeo-Christian faith. It is the time for all fallen climbers to rise and take America back up the mountain of Traditional Values.

Handfuls of Barley and Pieces of Bread

In the book of Jeremiah we find words similar to the ones we find in Ezekiel.

> *Because with lies ye have made the heart of the righteous sad, whom I have not made sad; and strengthened the hands of the wicked, that he should not return from his wicked way, by promising him life:*

> *And will ye pollute me among my people for handfuls of barely and for pieces of bread, to slay the souls that should not die and should save the souls alive that should not live.* (Ezekiel 13:17-23)

In both of these passages it is noted that the people of God were aiding and abetting individuals who were practicing things contrary to the will of God and these activities were being sorely rebuked by God. The Lord's cause for annoyance was that by His people supporting the very things He was against. This caused evil and wrong to continue rather than stop, for the good of all.

In these days when so many people are complaining about government and the people serving, the words I heard recently come to mind, "We get the government we deserve." It is quite amazing to me how many Christians think their faith has nothing to do with their politics; nothing could be further from the truth.

Matter of fact it was the Christian faith in the hearts of the Pilgrims and Puritans that brought this nation into being. Along with this, it is interesting to note that there have been in the past Supreme Court decisions that said America was indeed a Christian nation (Church of the Holy Trinity v. United States).

Secular America

I think many of our founding fathers would be shocked at the idea of a secular America. Especially since the word secular comes from a Latin word which means worldly or *pagan*. God deliver us from becoming a pagan nation.

The Bible also teaches that Christians should not be in partnership (2 Cor 7:14) with the works of darkness, such as partial birth abortion, along with such initiatives as the homosexual assimilation movement, which is the effort of the homosexual community to make homosexuality no morally different than heterosexual marriages. Because the Bible has spoken so strongly against these behaviors, for Christians to be in partnership with politicians who promote these causes is distressing because we are strengthening things that are contrary to God's law.

Some Christians justify voting for causes they don't believe in because they say they are not a one-issue voter. Regrettably that was the same logic used by the pro-slavery movement advocates. And there are those who because they are influenced by the need for a favorable consideration regarding certain kinds of funding or job opportunities will support those candidates who represent moral issues they don't support. This is most certainly sad because Ezekiel said that means we are betraying God for a handful of barley and pieces of bread.

Anti-Christian Agenda

It is disturbing to note that my community which seems to have more churches than any other community in America. It is described as among the most religious, by their vote the strongest supporters of the most anti-Christian agenda in the history of this nation.

This blind devotion is often justified by the numerous government handouts that have come our way, which is simply saying our loyalty to God is secondary to those with corrupt agenda's that give us something. In other words we have betrayed God for a handful of barely and pieces of bread.

Hopefully all Christian Americans will remember prosperity is not the essence of our faith righteousness is. And with this in mind, we will not vote for those candidates who have chosen to stand against our moral heritage, but will vote our God's righteous standard. Let us not forget that God is not pleased with those who will betray their faith for handfuls of barley and pieces of bread.

Elder Levon Yuille is Pastor of The Bible Church in Ypsilanti, MI, Founder of The National Black Prolife Congress and Host of acclaimed radio talk show, Joshua's Trial. http://biblechurchypsi.org/introduction.html

REFERENCE

Church of the Holy Trinity v. United States, 143 US 457-458, 465-471, 36 Led 226-February 29,1892.

CHAPTER 23

Keeping Your Home a Sex-Safe Place

Drs. Richard and Renée Durfield

In a conversation with a hotel manager, I learned that the most adult-rated movies ordered in a single evening occurred during a time when his hotel was filled with guests, most of whom were attending a large Christian event. If this is true, not only does it dishonor the name of Christ, but it also signals a spiritual epidemic among those who are called by His name.

The Body of Christ is experiencing a head-on assault by what might be the most powerful spirits ever unleashed from the gates of hell. If ministers are to be "wise as serpents," as Jesus commanded, they cannot assume that God will protect their children in spite of their negligence or failure to design effective safeguards to shield them—even in their homes.

Parenting can be a formidable task, but God has promised to empower His people with grace that abounds above prevailing sin. Psalm 127:3 declares that children are God's heritage. Parents must believe that God will grant them the wisdom needed to be effective in executing their responsibility to be faithful stewards of that heritage.

The Challenge

Effective parenting has always been challenging. Even preachers' kids can suffer from what we call *the P.K. syndrome*. Preachers' kids sometimes exhibit the worst kinds of behavior as they react to the constant pressure to conform to parental and biblical expectations. They feel they must act out to not stand out.

Parents can remedy this problem by building a strong sense of godly self-esteem in their children during their formative years. Children must feel they, too, are called and are an important part of their parent's ministry. They must be allowed to partake in and enjoy the benefits of the ministry, in addition to the sacrifices associated with living in a fishbowl environment.

Parents in ministry must earn the trust and respect of their children or face a possible backlash of rebellion, especially when they are entering adolescence. Only teens who have developed a personality marked by a strong sense of self-esteem and virtuous behavior are able to withstand negative peer pressure and the downward pull of their own human nature.

External and Internal Pressure

In our book, *Raising Pure Kids in an Impure World*, we relate the story of the tragedy experienced by the crew of the American nuclear submarine *USS Thresher.*

On April 10, 1963, the *USS Thresher* disappeared about 220 miles off the coast of Boston. Radio contact was lost while the vessel underwent deep submergence tests. The ensuing attempts to contact and then locate the *Thresher* were all in vain.

What happened? Apparently the submarine had gone to a greater depth than it was able to withstand. The water pressure on the outside exceeded the cabin pressure on the inside, and the vessel's walls collapsed. As a result, 16 officers, 96 enlisted men, and 17 civilian technicians were lost.

Our children—and even mom and dad—are like that submarine. The external pressures never let up and only increase as America's culture descends deeper and deeper into immorality. If a person's internal pressure is unequal to the culture's external pressure—if one's character is not strong enough to resist temptation—then he too will collapse. If a teen does not have self-control, the combined weight of hormones, media messages, and peer pressure will simply overwhelm him.

Many of the intrusions that pose the greatest threats are invited into the home. The most insidious intruders can almost always be traced to either unwise or inappropriate behavior within two major categories: marriage and family relationships and family leisure activities.

Family Role Modeling

God requires His people to exhibit the virtues of the gospel in the home as well as outside the home. It is imperative that parents model the behavior they desire in their children. When parents model appropriate behavior, it empowers children. Children should be able to view their homes as peaceful havens where they can build confidence and self-esteem.

It is the primary responsibility of parents to create a peaceful atmosphere in the home. Parents need to make sure each family member is treated with equal respect. Foul language, out-of-control arguments, and conversations marked by screaming and/or shouting should never be allowed. Families must relate to one another as though they were relating to Christ. They must acknowledge that Christ is the unseen guest in every room and live accordingly.

So-called adult entertainment must be considered off-limits for the entire household; including mom and dad. Isn't soft-porn or questionable entertainment that's questionable for children also inappropriate for adult family members? The Scriptures declare, "A little leaven leavens the whole lump," (I Corinthians 5:6 & Galatians 5:9 KJV). In other words, whatever parents allow in part will eventually influence everyone as a whole.

Parental Advocates

Jesus promised His disciples that He would send the comforter to be with them in His absence. The Greek word translated *comforter* is *paraclete* and means someone called alongside to help.

Today, a *paraclete* is known as an advocate. Jesus knew that after His departure His disciples would face a formidable enemy whom they could not conquer without the help of a divine advocate (See John 14:16; 16:7).

Parents are to be advocates for their children. They have the responsibility of emulating the love and care of the Heavenly Father in their role as parents. They should be able to say to their children, "Follow me as I follow Christ." Parents have the awesome opportunity to listen to, advise, guard, correct, and be available to their children regardless of their situation or circumstance.

The parents' role as advocates is of particular importance during their children's formative years, but that role does not diminish when their children reach their teens. Adolescence brings with it physical, emotional and spiritual challenges that are frequently frightening and even painful—not the least of these is their awakening sexuality.

While they are experiencing the personal fears and emotions associated with this tremendous time of transition, they are also confronted with the vicious whirlwind of today's secular youth culture that adds confusion as well as conflicting voices and values.

In Anne Ortlund's book, *Children Are Wet Cement,* she emphasizes the importance of influencing one's children and placing a protective wall around them in their wet cement years. The goal of good parenting is the successful emancipation of one's children.

Good parenting prepares children to develop into responsible adults who have the ability to make independent and responsible decisions. Parents must remember that the cement hardens as children grow (Ortlund, 1995).

The apostle Paul instructed the church at Ephesus to be "imitators of God" (Ephesians 5:1). That admonition could not be more appropriate today.

Parental involvement

A community's outrage arising from the story of a parent reading an elementary school library book to her child made the news. Initially, it appeared to be an innocent story about a prince who was searching throughout his kingdom for one true love. However, the story ends with the prince rejecting all of the young maidens and choosing one of the squires.

We must guard against books that promote gay and lesbian lifestyles. Check your child's in-class assignments as well as their homework and make sure that children aren't being exposed to texts that you would normally censor. One of the best ways to make home a sex-safe place is to be involved in selecting the books children read, the movies they watch, and the music they listen to.

Parents often arrive home exhausted from work and the hour or more they just spent on a crowded freeway. It is easy to relax a few moments while the children are in their rooms entertaining themselves with their favorite activities. During these moments, however, families may be the most vulnerable.

The time between a child's arrival home from school and mom or dad's arrival home from work can be particularly threatening. A protective structure must be in place so parents are relatively certain of what each child is doing in their absence. Depending on the age of the child, a few options for accomplishing this might include:

1. Scheduled reading or homework;
2. Previously screened and approved videos and/or TV programs;
3. Involvement in after-school activities such as band or sports;
4. Involvement in church programs designed specifically for latchkey children;
5. Involvement in a mentoring program sponsored by a church or other reputable organization.

Watch Who's Watching the Kids

A critical element in each of these options is the parent's reasonable confidence in the safety and integrity of the activity and in the individuals with whom the child is interacting. Parents must conduct a thorough examination to ensure the activities, and those involved, are beneficial and not harmful.

Unfortunately, some members of the extended family who may seem trustworthy often inflict the greatest harm. Jesus commanded His disciples, "Be wise as serpents, and harmless as doves" (Matthew 10:16 NKJV). This is particularly true when providing safeguards for one's children.

Parents cannot afford to entrust their children's care to anyone with unproven integrity. Only those who are considered trustworthy—including baby-sitters, friends, and even family members—should be given such responsibility. If possible, parents should arrange for their children to contact them at predetermined intervals so parents are assured they are safe.

This point can be illustrated by the following series of events that changed a young man's life. When he was 7, his parents entrusted him to the care of a much-loved uncle who was also a Boy Scout leader. Little did his parents know that the uncle was not trustworthy and was responsible for committing multiple sexual assaults on the child for at least 5 years! At age 12, this troubled youth wrapped himself in a blanket, poured lighter fluid over it, and set it ablaze. Years of skin grafts and counseling have brought a measure of healing, but he is hopelessly ensnared in a life of confusion and homosexuality.

When children are left unguarded, they become susceptible to a wide variety of evils and tremendous stress. According to Dr. Kevin Leman in *Keeping Your Family Together When the World is Falling Apart,* a teenager's "life is full of pressures that add up to unbearable stress, so unbearable that between 500,000 and 600,000 of them attempt suicide every year, and some 5,000 succeed, "(Leman, 1993, p. 242).

> There is a widespread use of drugs, alcohol, and TV. Yes, I equate TV with drugs because so many youths, not to mention adults, are hooked on this habit-forming electronic escape hatch, which brainwashes them daily with materialism, hedonism, narcissism, and violence. Between the ages of 6 and 18, the average American youth spends 16,000 hours in front of a TV set and witnesses some 18,000 dramatized murders. (Leman, 1993, p. 243)

Safeguard Leisure Time

Safeguards must also be in place to protect children from threats posed by the evils made possible through modern technology. The internet has presented unprecedented opportunities as well as unprecedented challenges to individuals and families.

Since children are able to navigate various websites and programs with greater ease than many adults, the Internet should be of particular concern because it contains a widespread proliferation of unsolicited filth. Internet filters prevent access to inappropriate sites, limit the time children spend online, and also prevent them from revealing private information via e-mail. Keep the computer in a public place such as the kitchen or living room so that you can monitor the activity.

Also available are personal remote TV changers that allow children to only access preselected channels and/or programs. Parents must also be aware that many video games and music videos focus on violence, sex, and murder. Elementary-aged children should be protected from dolls and cartoon characters that expose them to sexually explicit clothes and themes.

Young people should be discouraged from emulating the behavior and dress of many rock stars and other Hollywood personalities. Exposed midriffs, belly button ornaments, and tattoos signal detrimental trends. Despite a child's push for independence, parents need to encourage strong, healthy ties to the family by:

- Inviting friends of like moral values to group and same-sex activities;
- Making your home a magnet for your children's friends;
- Helping children choose appropriate companions;
- Limiting a child's circle of companions to people within 2 years of their age.

It is critical that parents be aware of how significant their influence is during a child's formative years. Parents need to learn effective parenting styles to build family relationships defined by love and respect. Most important, families must make Christ the center of their personal lives and relationships.

Richard Durifield, Ph.D., teaches at Azusa Pacific University in the School for Adult & Professional Studies. Renée Durfield, D.D., is Executive Director of All About Marriage. Portions of this chapter originally appeared in Enrichment Journal, (2005) 10, 112-115.

REFERENCES

Ortlund, A, (1995). *Children are wet cement.* Grand Rapids: Fleming H. Revell.

Leman, K. (1993). *Keeping your family together when the world is falling apart.* Colorado Springs: Focus on the Family Publishing.

CHAPTER 24

The Racialization of Adoption

Ryan Scott Bomberger, M.A.

Adoption is powerful and emotional for the birth mother and the prospective parents. Relinquishing a child and taking in a child who is not biologically related is an incredible act of love and of sacrifice.

We need to foster an environment where people pursue adoption. We accomplish this when the public is educated with stories that typify the adoption experience. This is part of the mission of The Radiance Foundation and its public awareness initiative through TooManyAborted. com.

Negative Media Highlights

Unfortunately, rather than focusing on the millions of positive adoption stories, the media highlights the negative mishaps of adoption and generalizes these instances as the norm. Other myths exist. Many are unaware that adoption is not an expensive process. Depending on the ethnicity of the child and the type of adoption, costs range from $0—to $40,000 (Costs of Adopting, 2010).

It is true that private adoptions of Caucasian infants and international adoptions may be quite costly. Adopting African-American children and children of other races costs less by *tens* of thousands of dollars. African American children are disproportionately represented in the foster care system, and many are waiting for permanent families. They may be adopted at no cost to the prospective parent(s).

With adoption, parents continue to receive monthly benefits—similar to the amount of benefits that foster parents receive—to help care for the child until he or she is 18 years of age. When parents adopt children who have special needs, they receive higher benefits. According to the Georgia Division of Child and Family Services (2010), being African American is one of the factors that qualify as a special needs adoption.

Too Many in the System

Not only are African-American children disproportionately represented in the foster care system, but they also remain in foster care for longer periods of time than do children of other races. The Government Accountability Office, or GAO, reports that 27% of those entering foster care are Black, even though Black children comprise only 15% of the U.S. child population (2007).

There are a number of factors that influence this, but the primary factor is ethnicity. We are a nation still so uncomfortable with the hue of our skin that we miss out on the ultimate act of true racial reconciliation—loving a child simply because he or she deserves to be loved. All adoptions are beautiful, and so are mixed-race adoptions.

With every diatribe about racial healing and better cultural understanding, battle lines have been drawn around adoption. As long as we are human, the evil of racism will always exist. But this should never stop us from endeavoring to eradicate racism especially when it harms the most vulnerable among us—our children. We are all guilty of having our own prejudices, our firmly held stereotypes, our unwillingness to be proactive or more culturally competent (understanding others' cultures), and more tragically, the inability to admit these truths to ourselves.

Foster care offers hope and healing to hundreds of thousands of children who have been removed from their birth families because of abuse, abandonment, or neglect. The Department of Health and Human Services reports that in 2010 there were 408,000 children in the foster care system. More than half, 254,000 exited the system to be reunited with their biological families. Of the 107,000 available for adoption, 53,000 were united with forever families. As many as 54,000 children are waiting to be adopted (DHHS, 2010).

Raising Awareness

There is an acute lack of awareness surrounding the act and process of adoption which is effectively addressed through multi-pronged educational efforts. Life-affirming organizations seek to accomplish this through community events, conferences and media campaigns. The goal is to raise the level of awareness of the need for adoption as well as to encourage more families, especially those in the church, to become involved.

The expectation isn't that every adult should adopt. However, each one of us can play a role in fostering an environment to encourage adoption through our financial contributions, volunteering at pregnancy resource centers, supporting birth mothers, and addressing the causes of poverty, both financially and spiritually.

While adopting children from overseas continues to be popular, especially by high profile celebrities, there remains societal resistance to trans-racial domestic adoption of Black children—a phenomena that has persisted for decades. This politicization needs to be exposed. Groups such as the National Association of Black Social Workers (NABSW) who are rooted in Black Nationalist ideology declared:

> The National Association of Black Social Workers has taken a vehement stand against the placement of Black children in white homes for any reason. We affirm the inviolable position of Black children in Black families where they belong physically, psychologically and culturally in order that they receive the total sense of themselves and develop a sound projection of their future. (Brenner, 1974)

Unfortunately, this outdated Position Statement was reinforced in 1994. Transracial adoptions are acceptable, but only as a last resort if a same-race adoption fails (NABSW, 2003). They oppose the provision in the 1996 InterEthnic Placement Act that eliminates using race as a factor in adoption and foster care placement (Hollinger, 1998). Such advocacy that places a stumbling block in out-of-home permanency is not in the best interest of children who long for parents, no matter the color.

More Transracial Adoptions

Despite the caution to adopt Black children, transracial adoptions from foster care have increased from 17.2% of all adoptions in 1996 to 20.1% in 2003. Although this is good news, the racial disparities in placement outcomes continues (Smith, 2008). Researcher and esteemed scholar, Rita Simon, conducted one of the most cited, in-depth longitudinal studies on the issue. According to Simon, 80% of transracial adoptees *disagree* with groups like the National Association of Black Social Workers.

> The evidence from empirical studies indicates uniformly that transracial adoptees do as well on measures of psychological and social adjustment as Black children raised in-racially in relatively similar socio-economic circumstances. The evidence also indicates that transracial adoptees develop comparably strong senses of Black identity. They see themselves as Black and they think well of Blackness. The difference is that they feel more comfortable with the white community than Blacks raised in-racially. (Simon, 2000, p. 31)

Kinship Care

Instead of forever families for Black children in foster care, the GAO reports that African-American children languish in foster care 15 months or longer simply because there are not enough same race or qualified homes available for them (GAO, 2007). A new legislative push from large organizations including NABSW, Child Welfare League and its subsidiary, Black Administrators in Child Welfare, focuses on more federal funding for guardianship (Emphasis, 2010). (The latter organization does not advocate any out-of-home placements but prefers kinship care, which is placement with a child's relatives.)

Guardian subsidy provides financial support for a child's relative who has been identified as a guardian by child welfare decision-makers. Kinship care, according to the GAO (2007) report, is one of the major factors responsible for Black children remaining in foster care at rates far higher than any other ethnic group.

Pure Religion

The purest form of religion, according to James 1:27, is taking care of widows and orphans. Jewish followers who converted to Christianity were abandoned by their families leaving these new believers without any means of support. The Church was mandated to care for them, to consider themselves as an extended family.

Today, conversion doesn't necessarily result in disassociation, at least in America! However, we are being decimated by a cultural war of abortion and disregard for traditional family life which results in the abandonment of mothers and children. These are the orphans, both born and unborn.

Ryan Scott Bomberger, M. A., is Founder & Chief Creative Officer of The Radiance Foundation. This research is part of a public awareness campaign through TooManyAborted.com www.toomanyaborted.com.

REFERENCES

The costs of adopting: A fact sheet for families. Retrieved March 1, 2010 from   *http://costs.adoption.com/articles/the-costs-of-adopting-a-factsheet-for-families.html*

Georgia Department of Human Services. (2010). What is the definition of special needs. Retrieved March 3, 2010 from *http://www.dfcs.dhr.georgia.gov/portal/site/DHS*

United States Government Accountability Office. (2007). African American children in foster care. *GAO Publication.* No. ADM 07-816). Washington, DC: U.S. Government Accountability Office.

Department of Health & Human Services. (June 2011). Trends in foster care and adoption—2002-2010. Retrieved July 30, 2011 from *http://www.acf.hhs.gov/programs/cb/stats_research/afcars/trends_june2011.pdf*

Bremner, Robert H. (1974). Children and youth in America: A documentary history (Vol. 3). Cambridge: Harvard University Press.

Preserving families of African Ancestry. (January 2003). Retrieved March 5, 2010, from *http://nabsw.org/mserver/PreservingFamilies.aspx*

Hollinger, Joan Heifetz (1998). A guide to the multiethnic placement act of 1994 as amended by the interethnic adoption provisions of 1996. Retrieved from *http://www.acf.hhs.gov/programs/cb/pubs/mepa94/mepachp2.htm*

Smith, S., McRoy, R., Freundlich, M., & Kroll, J. (2008). Finding families for African-American children: The role of race & law in adoption from foster care. Retrieved February 20, 2010, from *http://www. adoptioninstitute.org/research/2008_05_mepa.php*

Simon, Rita J., & Roorda, Rhonda M. D. (2000). In their own words. New York: Columbia University Press., p. 31

United States Government Accountability Office. (2007). African American children in foster care. *GAO Publication*. No. ADM 07-816. Washington, DC: U.S. Government Accountability Office.

Emphasis on Prevention. (n.d.) Retrieved February 20, 2010, from *http:// www.Blackadministrators.org/about_prevention.cfm*

CHAPTER 25

Orphans Among Us:
Where is the Black Church?

Dr. La Verne Tolbert

This is pure and undefiled religion in the sight of our God and
Father, to visit orphans and widows in their distress, and to keep
oneself unstained by the world.
(James 1:27 NASB)

There is a crisis in America.

Over 500,000 children nationwide are growing up in the foster care system. Many of these children are African American and Hispanic, and some are physically or emotionally disabled.

African American children are significantly over-represented and constitute 40-50% of those in foster care. Although only 12% of the overall United States population is Black, one-third of all foster care children are African American. These are the most difficult children to place in adoptive homes.

As a result, Black children remain in the system longer averaging 10 years or more and represent the largest proportion of children in out-of-home care nationally (Hough et al, 2000; Smith & Devore, 2004). The result: too many African American children grow up institutionalized (Singleton & Roseman, 2004).

* The largest state in the nation, California, has the highest number of children in foster care—approximately 105,000;
* Every day in Los Angeles County, 500 children are immediately in need of an adoptive family. Over 30% of these are African American (Grant, personal interview).

Abandonment, Abuse, Neglect

Why are children in the system? The answer is threefold: abandonment—desertion by a parent or primary caregiver; abuse—physical, sexual, or emotional mistreatment; and neglect—lack of proper food, clothing or shelter by a parent or caretaker who is responsible for the child's welfare (California Kids Connection).

Children who are available for adoption are children in the foster care system whose parents have had their rights severed by the state. This means that these children will never be reunited with their birth families because their parents may be incarcerated, on drugs or otherwise incapable of caring for their children. These children are the orphans among us.

The Baggage of Emancipation

At age 18 foster children are emancipated, which is for most, a frustrating and frightening experience. One emancipated male could not get a job because he did not have any proof of identification such as a birth certificate (Dr. Phil, 2009). Seventy percent (70%) become homeless within 18 months of emancipation.

Upon learning that he was to be emancipated from foster care, an 18 year-old male became so distraught that he attempted suicide by standing in the middle of the railroad tracks. Thankfully, he was rescued and immediately hospitalized (Davis, personal interview).

College tuition for all children in foster care is fully subsidized by the state, but since most foster kids have poor grades—they may have attended as many as 15 different schools by the time they reach 7th grade—most drop out of high school. Only 3% of foster children complete college.

According to researchers, foster youth are at high risk of "rotten outcomes" because once emancipated, they end up homeless, unemployed, welfare dependent, with out-of-wedlock births, alcoholic, drug-addicted, or incarcerated (Iglehart & Becerra, 2002). In California, 70% of the prison population has been in foster care (Dr. Phil, 2009).

Because of these devastating statistics, the age of emancipation has been extended to 21 as of January 2012 in many states. This means that youth continue to receive financial assistance instead of being handed a check and their clothes in a brown paper bag. Now, as non-minor dependents youth will be able to live in supervised independent placements. In Los Angeles, that's 1,500 adolescents!

Even with this change, there's little that's encouraging. Surprisingly, the research I uncovered pointed to a long history of faith-based involvement in ministering to the needs of the orphan.

History of Church Involvement

Prior to the Industrial Revolution, there were segregated orphanages that were started by Protestant activists. Following the Civil War, these institutions—Black and white alike—were considered failures because of the emphasis on discipline and regimentation. Children were housed in overcrowded facilities and suffered poor nutrition.

By the late 19th Century, Settlement Houses spread from London to the United States. These facilities housed families and sported pools, gymnasiums, libraries, medical facilities and soup kitchens. By the 20th Century, orphanages began to disappear altogether. Following the Great Depression, public agencies assumed responsibility for delivering child welfare services and churches focused instead on residential treatment such as drug/alcohol abuse (Orr & Spoto, 2004).

This is good news! The Church has been involved. But where is the Black church *today?* Researchers estimate that there may be as many as 8.7 million adults attending predominantly Black churches. How well are we ministering to the children in foster care—children who come from our own communities? Can you imagine what our nation would be if these orphans were raised in Christian homes and became pastors instead of prisoners?

Something is wrong with the Black family that so many children are ending up in institutions. Perhaps instead of church-growth conferences, pastors might equally focus on parenting workshops to equip families to care for their children. Surely, there must be a more proactive response to help these crumbling households. But, why should we care?

Real Religion

James, the brother of Jesus, tells us why. Penned in AD 46, his was one of the first letters written to the church at Jerusalem. Here were Jewish believers who, once converted, were cut off from all financial support by their families. James writes to educate this new body of believers of their responsibility to care for one another, especially the widows and orphans.

Faith, according to James, is both orthodox belief (inner transformation) and orthodox life (outer demonstration). In other words, if a person is truly saved, there ought to be some evidence in the way he or she lives.

> *You have faith, and I have works; Show me your faith without the works, and I will show you my faith by my works.* (James 2:18)

Faith without works or corresponding evidence is dead . . . nonexistent. Earlier in this letter, James clarifies what real religion looks like. This kind of religion—or faith—visits orphans in their distress.

The word, visit, sounds as if it's a cursory term, something one does in passing. But this is *not* the meaning of the word. A literal translation means "to help" (*Vine's Expository Dictionary of New Testament Words*). In other words, pure or real religion *helps* the orphan because this child is distressed—suffering severe pressure of pain or sorrow and anguished with severe bodily or mental pain.

Happily, there are some proactive efforts to address the needs of these children which may spark ideas for interested churches and individuals. Outstanding among these is One Church One Child which began in Chicago in 1979 by Father George Clements, a Black Catholic priest. Thousands of children have been adopted through this partnership with the Department of Children's and Family Services (DCFS). But it seems that the church has become distracted from the real goal of ministry. Have we?

A Seat at the Table

One Sunday morning, I decided to attend a Lutheran church service with a friend. It was quite different from what I'm used to, but it was beautiful to see the entire family, especially the children, participate together as an integral part of the worship service.

At one point, the teacher invited the children to sit on a picnic blanket in the front of the church where they were taught a 10-minute lesson. "Just as each child belongs to a family and has a seat at the dining room table, baptism makes every child a part of God's family and there is also a seat at God's table."

I thought about the orphan. She has no family. He doesn't have a seat at the dining room table. In fact, these children are not even sure where they may be tomorrow or next week or next year. *Family* is key to spiritual development as this example demonstrates. And the church is where family ought to begin.

We *can* do more! We *must* do more! Researchers acknowledge that the African American church has not fully recognized its potential to provide homes and families for Black children. Isn't it time for a change?

Covenants for Kids

"Foster care was never meant to be permanent," says Dr. Edwina Lewis, Supervising Social Worker for DCFS in Los Angeles which recognizes the need for direct help and encouragement from leaders in the faith community. This renewed focus encourages involvement from churches and ministries concerned about helping the orphan.

A new and exciting project—Covenants for Kids: Churches Helping Children in Foster Care—is being launched by Teaching Like Jesus Ministries, Inc., a parachurch ministry in Los Angeles. Covenants for Kids is an intentional effort to involve youth in the congregational life of a local church close to where the foster youth resides.

Here's how it works: Pastors invite Covenants for Kids to introduce the program to their congregants during a Sunday morning service. If time permits, congregants view a video and PowerPoint presentation about the program. After service, volunteers sign up. Once they are DCFS cleared (live-scan fingerprint) and complete a 3 hr. driver's training, they are qualified drive foster youth ages 9-17 to church.

Imagine the simplicity of this project! Volunteers pick up children from their foster homes and bring them to church as often as the youth wants to attend—Sunday services, youth meetings, choir rehearsals, and/or special church outings. Ultimately, the goal is that the child will be introduced to families in the church who may adopt. Or, the child may even be adopted by the mentor. But the important fact is that children are introduced to the Lord through teen ministry, Children's Church or Sunday School.

In the African American setting, Sunday school is a significant context for children's socialization (Haight, 2002). Not only does this introduce a child to Christian faith, but it also helps build relationships with peers and other caring adults. Perhaps the prospect of change that accompanies emancipation may seem less threatening with a network of people to help. Most of all, exposure to a faith-filled environment provides the healing balm that mends these fragmented hearts and revives crushed spirits.

Imparting the Faith

Actively and intentionally mobilizing churches to minister to the needs of children in foster care is as urgent today as it was during biblical times. With Covenants for Kids, even if adoption does not occur, youth will have developed meaningful life-long relationships that will hopefully endure after emancipation from the foster care system.

What a wonderful way to impart the faith to the next generation as we help the orphan. Churches and faith communities—especially the Black church—must hear the cries and address the crisis of orphans. With people of faith the likelihood of successful placements increases. Religiosity is significantly related to the total number of foster/adopted children in the home including and especially African American children (Belanger, Copeland, & Cheung, 2008).

Bennett Chapel

One remarkable example of a Black church that is making a difference in the lives of foster children is Bennett Chapel Missionary Baptist Church in Possum Trot, TX. Since 1998, over 70 African American children have been adopted by church members. They learned of the need for adoptive families from their pastor, Bishop W. C. Martin and his wife, Donna.

Once-a-week for 12 weeks, the Martins drove 120 miles to complete the required classes. First they adopted 2 children and then 2 more. Meanwhile, Bishop Martin preached and preached and preached about the need for and the value of adoption in obedience to scripture. A total of 23 families responded.

Bishop Martin arranged for the state's required classes to be taught locally to save parishioners the tedious drive. Twelve (12) families completed the first set of classes, and then 11 completed a second set of classes. Children now had forever families.

In the words of Donna Martin, the children are "here but not healed," (Belanger, Copeland, Cheung, 2008, p. 100). So this church community depends upon their faith, prayer and the word of God to encourage one another. Overall, the children are thriving.

Potential of the Black Church

Bennett Chapel is another example of the potential within the Black church. Imagine the impact of hundreds of churches like Bennett Chapel. Researchers estimate that 8.7 million adults attend predominantly Black churches but a survey revealed that an overwhelming majority—nearly 96% of respondents—reported that their church's mission statement did not include a focus on the adoption or foster care need for Black children.

Eighty Three (83%) of the ministers reported that they did not address the needs of orphans in their sermons. "The African American church has not fully recognized itself as a potential focus for the efforts in providing for Black children in need of formal adoptive families," (Singleton & Roseman, 2004, p. 84).

With the right tools, projects, and information, pastors can make a tremendous difference. Together, people of faith must aggressively seek creative ways to rescue the orphan, especially older children who are least likely to be adopted or to be permanently placed.

Orphan Jewel

One creative way to help is the newly birthed enterprise, Orphan Jewel, where a portion of jewelry sales is donated to help orphan care ministries *www.orphanjewel.com*. Additionally, the cause and cry of the orphan is shared in venues where the needs of these children might otherwise be unheard. Orphan Jewel is also committed to offering parenting classes and seminars to help all parents, but especially adoptive parents, with their new families.

Orphan Jewel supports Bennett Chapel and responded to the need for funds to assist orphan care ministries in their work because when resources are available, more is accomplished. The ultimate beneficiaries are the children.

It's not a glamour story. It's ministry work. You're taking in children who have been molested . . . children who would eat like animals, down on the floor. You have to train them all over again as if they were one-year-olds. You've gotta be up at odd hours to attend to them when they're crying out in the night. And when you leave for the grocery store, you've gotta deal with their very real fear—a fear that you'll never come back, that you'll leave them all alone again. (Martin, 2007, p. 53-54)

Happily, these children *do* recover. They *do* learn to trust. They learn *not* to be afraid.

They don't have to worry about having food on the table or clothes on their backs. Now they have a place to stay and food to eat. They have a family . . . . If a family is having trouble with a child and needs some help, they don't call Child Protective Services. They call on a neighbor or a nearby relative. Sometimes, that child may stay with someone else for a while till things get straightened out. It's how we relate as family. We're in this together. (Martin, 2007, p. 54)

Doesn't this sound like the heart of Christ? "Jesus took the children in his arms, put His hands on them, and blessed them. Are we ready now to do the same?" (Martin, 2007, p. 106).

La Verne Tolbert, Ph.D. is Founder/President of Teaching Like Jesus Ministries, Pasadena, CA www.teachinglikejesus.org. Their project, Covenants for Kids is in partnership with the Department of Children and Family Services. Teaching Like Jesus Ministries is also ministry partner with Orphan Jewel www. orphanjewel.com.

REFERENCES

Belanger, K. Copeland, S. and Cheung, M. (2008). The role of faith in adoption: Achieving positive adoption outcomes for African American children. In Racial Disproportionality in Child Welfare: A Special Issue. *Child Welfare Journal of Policy, Practice, and Program, p. 99-123.* *http://www.cwla.org/pubs/pubdetails.asp?pubid=J872*

Davis, L. (2009). Olive Crest Transitional Housing Placement Program. Personal communication.

Dr. Phil, May 25, 2009

Grant, S. (June, 2009). Department of Children's and Family Services, Los Angeles, CA.
Personal communication.

Haight, W. L. (2002). *African-American children at church: A sociocultural perspective.* New York: Cambridge University Press.

Hough, R. L., Landsverk, J.A., McCabe, K. M., Yeh, M., Ganger, W.C., & Reynolds, B. J. (2000). Racial and ethnic variations in mental health care utilization among children in foster care. *Children's Service: Social Policy, Research, & Practice. 3*(3), 133-146.

Iglehart, A. & Becerra, R. (2002). Hispanic and African American youth: Life after foster care emancipation. *Journal of Ethnic & Cultural Diversity in Social Work, 11* (1, 2), 79-107.

Martin, WC. (2007). *Small town big miracle.* Focus on the Family. Carol Stream, Ill: Tyndale.

Orr, J., Dryness, G. R., & Spoto, P. W. (2004). Faith-based adoptive/foster services: Faith communities' role in child welfare. *Center for Religion and Civic Culture, University of Southern California,* 3-6. Retrieved from *http://crcc.usc.edu/docs/childwelfare.pdf*

Singleton, S. & Roseman, F. (2004). Minister's perceptions of foster care, adoptions, and the role of the Black church. *Adoption Quarterly.* 7(3), 79-91.

Smith, C. J. & Devore, W. (2004). African American children in the child welfare and kinship system: From exclusion to over inclusion. *Children and Youth Services Review.* 26(5), 427-446.

Vine's Expository Dictionary of New Testament Words. Virginia: Mac Donald Publishing.

California Kids Connection. Retrieved May,2009 from *www. cakidsconnection.com.*

CHAPTER 26

Steve Jobs Changed the World, Adoption Changed His

Ryan Bomberger, M. A.

Millions have experienced the beauty of adoption over this past century. Yet very few people understand the reality of how adoption unleashes the possibility of not just the child, but the family the child becomes a part of. As one who is from a family of 15, I attest to the life-changing effects adoption has on the family and the surrounding community. Sacrifice is at the heart of adoption, and the reward is great.

Steve Jobs

The news hit me in the gut. I couldn't believe I was seeing those few numbers communicating his passing beneath his photo: 1955-2011. Steve Jobs has, literally, changed the world. I'm typing this on my Mac, will check my emails and Twitter status on my iPad, and will stay in touch with everyone I love through my iPhone.

As a creative professional, his visionary work has helped my own visions become reality.

But his vision, his destiny and his ability to affect people, globally, may never have happened. Jobs was adopted as a baby and loved by his parents, Clara and Paul Jobs. The baby they took into their hearts and home had a purpose in life that would be unleashed by the powerful act of adoption.

He began today's revolutionary Apple Company and has departed this world with a professional legacy that is awe-inspiring. The partially bitten apple represents the temptation that millions of us have been unable to avoid . . . waiting in day long lines for shiny objects that proved to us science fiction could be made reality by a creative genius. Jobs' minimalistic approach delivered a multitude of near-perfect electronic devices. From amber screens to full-color high definition, visually we've been changed by the adoption of Apple's technology.

Salvation's Essence

It's amazing to me that, in 2011, especially among Christians, how foreign the concept adoption is. Adoption is the essence of salvation. There is no Christianity without adoption, in the spiritual sense. Yet, in the physical sense, it is rarely considered as an option. For those who are so passionately prolife, it is often the challenge thrown before us in our opposition to abortion, and rightfully so.

We have an opportunity to unleash purpose in a child waiting to be loved. *I was one of those children back in 1971. Steve Jobs was* back in 1955. The beauty of possibility is that we all can play a role in helping to foster and encourage it. Who knows what my children, both adopted and biological, will become? All I know is that loving them, unconditionally, will allow their God-given purpose to flourish.

The *nation's largest abortion chain*, aborting 340 children for every 1 woman that is *referred for adoption*, is the antithesis to this purpose. Planned Parenthood celebrates their founder who said, "We are paying for and even submitting to the dictates of an ever increasing, unceasingly spawning class of human beings who never should have been born at all." Contrary to *Margaret Sanger's warped mentality* that children are "marked when they're born" as "diseased, delinquents, and felons," none of us know the beautiful potential that every life possesses.

We celebrate human triumph over the seemingly insurmountable.

Well-Known and Adopted

There are so many well-known adopted individuals who have impacted many of our lives in one way or another: writer Charles Dickens, inventer

George Washington Carver, singer Nat King Cole, baseball great Babe Ruth, Wendy's founder Dave Thomas, musician/performer Bo Diddley, Olympic Decathlon gold medalist Dan O'Brien, and country singer Faith Hill, just to name a few. Steve Jobs is among this list of infinite possibilities. No matter the perceived worldly success of an adoptee, adoption is a loving act that transforms, not only the life of the child, but the entire family.

And, sometimes, the world!

Ryan Scott Bomberger, M.A., is Founder & Chief Creative Officer of The Radiance Foundation. This research is part of a public awareness campaign through TooManyAborted.com www.toomanyaborted.com.

CHAPTER 27

It's Not Healthcare:
Dangerous Unconstitutional HHS Abortifacient/
Contraceptive/Sterilization Mandate Hurts
Women—

Dr. Alveda King

There are eight law suits addressing the unconstitutionality of the HHS ACS MANDATE. Added to their legal argument is the fact that abortion and it's "cousins" are not health care. Many in the pro-life movement versus anti-life debate are reluctant to make a connection between contraception and abortion. They insist that these are two very different acts—that there is all the difference in the world between contraception, which prevents a life from coming to be and abortion, which takes a life that has already begun.

To the contrary, with some contraceptives there is not only a link with abortion, there is a relationship. Some contraceptives are abortifacients; they work by causing early term abortions. The IUD likely prevents a fertilized egg—a young human being—from implanting in the uterine wall. The pill does not always stop ovulation, but sometimes prevents implantation of the growing embryo. And, of course, the new RU-486 pill works altogether by aborting a new fetus/baby.

Few talk about how abortions and artificial birth control not only kill and/or prevent the birth of babies, but they are also very bad for women's health. Both, for instance, are linked to controversial breast cancer discussions.

A gray area is forced or coerced sterilization. The most visible and classic case of forced sterilization is noted in the testimony of Elaine Riddick in the prolife video, Maafa 21. Her case and those of other women who were sterilized in North Carolina is currently being considered for new litigation.

Breast Cancer Link

Dr. Chris Kahlenborn's book, *Breast Cancer: Its Link to Abortion and the Birth Control Pill*, brings seven years the research, review and analysis of more than 500 studies and related works. It is very timely because of the breast cancer epidemic, which currently threatens every woman. Both abortion and artificial birth control are linked to breast cancer.

Research shows that induced abortion increases the risk of breast cancer for all women with Black women and other minorities having higher rates. Black women number higher and also tend to develop more aggressive cancers. There is also a greater risk in women who have had abortions if they were under age 18 at the time, if they do not have any more children after aborting, or if they have a family history of breast cancer. Family history of breast cancer sometimes also shows family history of abortions.

In 2009, in a study of more than 50,000 African-American women, Boston University epidemiologist Lynn Rosenberg found a 65 percent increase in a particularly aggressive form of breast cancer among those who had ever taken the birth-control pill. The risk doubles for those who had used the contraceptive within the past five years and had taken it for longer than 10 years.

Rosenberg studies black women because they have been underserved in cancer research so far, even though they suffer from higher rates of triple negative breast cancer. Rosenberg's findings linked these cases to the pill. A number of other studies of women of multiple ethnic groups support her research linking the pill to breast cancer, including research done in New England, South Carolina, Long Island, N.Y., and Scandinavia.

For example, in her study, Angela Lanfranchi, M.D. discusses the link between estrogen and breast cancer.

Estrogen also causes breast cancer by directly acting as a carcinogen . . . by directly damaging DNA. The body makes metabolites of estrogen in the course of breaking down the hormone, eliminating its effect. Hormone levels in the body are tightly regulated on a daily as well as monthly cycle basis. One such metabolite of estrogen is catechol estrogen quinone (CE quinone). CE quinone directly damages DNA by pulling purine bases, components of DNA, out of the strands. Women with breast cancer have higher levels of CE quinone in their blood than women without breast cancer.

The primary natural source of estrogen in premenopausal women is the ovaries. A woman whose ovaries have been removed will have a lower risk of breast cancer. This may happen if a woman has her ovaries removed because of disease. There is also a peak of estrogen during the menstrual cycle that causes ovulation. When a woman is under stress, for example during marathon training or by extreme weight loss, she may not ovulate or may miss her cycles altogether reducing her breast cancer risk. During breast feeding a woman may also miss ovulation or cycles reducing breast cancer risk. The primary source of natural post-menopausal estrogen is adipose (fat) tissue. The aromatase enzyme system in adipose cells causes estrogen to be formed from another hormone, androstendione. Therefore postmenopausal obesity also increases risk for breast cancer.

Estrogen can also be had from sources outside the body, usually drugs and sometimes residues found in foods. About 75% of women have taken hormonal birth control in their lives. As explained in a later section on breast lobule maturity, this is especially potent in forming breast cancers when taken by teens or women without children. Most birth control pills contain estrogen and progesterone . . . .

Estrogen has been listed as a carcinogen by the National Toxicology Advisory Panel of the National Cancer Institute since 2001 precisely because they felt women weren't being apprised of their risk of breast cancer sufficiently when hormone replacement therapy and birth control pills were prescribed. (Lanfranchi, 2004, p. 3)

Breast cancer in the U.S. is more prevalent in young black women than in white women of equivalent age, and is the second leading cause of cancer death (after lung cancer) among black women. This may be a consequence of more common hormonal contraceptive use and/or a greater frequency of abortion among young black women. Black women who develop breast cancer generally have more aggressive cancers resulting in a shortened life expectancy.

It has been noted that while Black American's make up approximately 13% or less of America's population, nearly 33% of abortions reported since the passage of Roe v Wade in 1973 have occurred on Black Women. Planned Parenthood, the nation's largest abortion provider, who also distributes free or low cost artificial abortion drugs, has a highly targeted market to Black Women. So, Black women are at a higher risk for abortions and breast cancer and other health related problems as a consequence of being marketed for the causes.

How Abortion Impacts Breast Cancer

At the beginning of pregnancy there are great increases in certain hormone levels (estrogen, progesterone, and HCG) that support pregnancy. In response to these changes, breast cells divide and mature into cells able to produce milk. Abortion causes an abrupt fall in hormone levels, leaving the breast cells in an immature state. These immature cells can more easily become cancer cells.

As of January 1999, 11 out of 12 studies in the United States, and 25 out of 31 studies worldwide, demonstrated that women who experienced an induced abortion had an increased risk of breast cancer. In 1996 Joel Brind, Ph.D., assembled the results of all the studies up to that time. Brind concluded that women who have an abortion before their first full-term pregnancy have a 50% increased risk of developing breast cancer while those who have an abortion after their first full-term pregnancy have a 30% increased risk.

A 50% increased risk means a 50% higher risk than someone would have otherwise. For example, if a person already had a 10% risk of developing breast cancer, then a 50% increase would bring the risk up to 15%. Dr. Lanfranchi concurs:

Most induced abortions occur in normal pregnancies. Studies have shown that the longer a pregnancy exists before an abortion, the higher the risk of breast cancer. This is due to the same mechanism that causes increased breast cancer risk in premature births. After an induced abortion, the mother is left with more Type 1 and 2 lobules where cancers start than before she was pregnant. This causes her to be at increased risk for breast cancer. This is the basis for the independent risk of abortion and breast cancer. (Lanfranchi, 2004, p. 4)

Breast cancer is the worldwide leading cancer in women and is the most common cause of cancer death for U.S. women age 20-59.In the U.S. every year about 175,000 women are diagnosed with breast cancer and more than 43,000 women die from this disease. This means that about one

U.S. woman out of eight will develop breast cancer at some time in her life and about one fourth of such women will die from this disease.

Induced abortion, especially at a young age, markedly increases a woman's risk for developing breast cancer. This risk is increased even further by other breast cancer risk factors such as synthetic hormones (including hormonal contraceptives like the Birth Control Pill, Norplant and Depo-Provera), family history of breast cancer, and others.

Abortion and Fibromyalgia

Psychiatrist and researcher Dr. Philip Ney relates the story of a patient of his who developed fibromyalgia, which causes chronic pain without any apparent cause (Pavone, 2011). He found that she had undergone an abortion just before this pain began, and since then, has developed a theory that in some cases, the pain of fibromyalgia may in fact be caused by chemicals released by the aborted baby's flesh when it is torn apart. These chemicals cross the placenta, and lodge in the mother's nervous system.

In reality, she is feeling not her own pain, but that of her aborted child. We have not yet begun to understand all the implications of abortion, and of how destroying a child in the womb destroys the rest of us. Let's pray that our society may forsake abortion and find healing.

According to counselor and therapist, Dr. Minnie Claiborne, "There are at least 101 post-abortion syndrome (PAS) symptoms. Women are commonly treated for one or more of these symptoms such as depression, but the underlying cause is often never properly identified or treated." Some of the PAS symptoms and side-effects are:

- Sterility—Guilt
- Miscarriages—Suicidal impulses
- Ectopic pregnancies—Mourning/Withdrawal
- Stillbirths—Regret/Remorse
- Bleeding and infections—Loss of confidence
- Shock and comas—Low self-esteem
- Perforated uterus—Preoccupation with death
- Peritonitus—Hostility/Rage
- Fever/Cold sweat—Despair/Helplessness
- Intense pain—Desire to remember birth date
- Loss of body organs—Intense interest in babies

- Crying/Sighing—Thwarted maternal instincts
- Insomnia—Hatred for persons connected with abortion
- Loss of appetite—Desire to end relationship with partner
- Exhaustion—Loss of sexual interest/Frigidity
- Weight loss—Inability to forgive self
- Nervousness—Nightmares
- Decreased work capacity—Seizures and tremors
- Vomiting—Feeling of being exploited
- Gastro-intestinal disturbances—Horror of child abuse

Additional Effects of Harm Caused by certain "reproductive health care" procedures

- Premature Labor and Births due to weakened cervix, scarred and/or perforated uterine walls, etc. (Note: the IUD and surgical abortion procedures have been known to cut or scar the woman's reproductive organs)
- Trauma to Mammary System
- Trauma to Reproductive System
- Exposure to STD germs where failure to properly sterilize instruments occur
- Permanent Sterility (leaving the woman no option to changing her mind later)

Obvious Connection?

It may not be immediately obvious that there is any connection between contraception and abortion, but on further examination, a relationship between the two becomes apparent. Ignoring the issue of contraception leads to a lost opportunity to respect life to the fullest degree.

Neither abortion nor artificial contraception is health care. Consider these connections between contraception and abortion:

1. Many contraceptives can directly cause early abortions.
2. Contraceptive use creates a perceived need for abortion as a "back-up."
3. Contraceptive use causes a devaluation of human life.

4. Both abortions and artificial contraceptives are bad for women's health.

Somehow, for political reasons, selfish gain, lack of knowledge and other variables, there are very obvious solutions that are not on the general or public radar.

BREAKING NEWS!

1. *Women do not have to have unplanned or undesirable pregnancies in most cases. It is a scientific and medical fact that a woman can't become pregnant if she is not ovulating. There are inexpensive ovulation kits on the market that women can obtain and exercise power and control over their right to get pregnant or not. A woman should have the right to say when she will and will not have sex. She should have the right and knowledge to control her reproductive rights.*
2. *There are natural and relatively inexpensive solutions for women who have irregular cycles and ovulation schedules. There is generally no need for invasive measures such as artificial drugs and such in these cases.*
3. *The $365 million a year, $1 million per day that our government tax dollars pay to Planned Parenthood who is the nation's largest abortion provider does not provide information and resources regarding reproductive freedom regarding ovulation and pregnancy choices to women.*
4. *If women do not have sex when they ovulate, there is no reason for them to take harmful chemical and surgical birth control measures, many of which are known to cause heart attacks, strokes, exposure to possibility of cancer and other illnesses.*

So the question is why is it so hard to break through the information barriers surrounding women's health and reproductive rights? Could it be that people on each side of the isle, each side of the arguments have so much vested in their own interests that everyone has forgotten the women and the babies in the midst of the melee?

Dr. Alveda King, niece of Dr. Martin Luther King, Jr., is Founder of King for America www.kingforamerica.com and Pastoral Associate with Priests for Life www.africanamericanoutreach.com.

REFERENCES

Brind J, Chinchilli VM, Severs WB, Summy-Long J (1996). Induced abortion as an independent risk factor for breast cancer: a comprehensive review and meta-analysis. *Journal of epidemiology and community health* 50 (5): 481-96. Retrieved from *doi:10.1136/jech.50.5.481. PMC 1060338. PMID 8944853. http://www.pubmedcentral.nih.gov/ articlerender.fcgi?tool=pmcentrez&artid=1060338*

Claiborne, M. (2012). Personal communication. *www.drminnie.net*

Kahlenborn, C. (2000). *Breast cancer: Its link to abortion and the birth control pill.* Dayton, OH: One More Soul. Retrieved from *http://onemoresoul. com/contraception/risks-consequences/what-a-woman-should-know-about-birth-control.html*

Lanfranchi, A. (2004). The science, studies and sociology of the abortion breast cancer link. *Association for Interdisciplinary Research in Values and Social Change Research Bulletin,18*, 2. Retrieved from *http://www. abortionbreastcancer.com/June2005.pdf*

Pavone, F. (2011). The real pain of abortion. *Priests for Life.* Retrieved from *http://www.priestsforlife.org/blog/index.php/the-real-pain-of-abortion*

Rosenberg, L. (2009). Risk of aggressive breast cancer subtype three times higher for black women. *Psysorg.com.* Retrieved from *http://www. physorg.com/news157184508.html*

CHAPTER 28

Situation Ethics Rears Its Ugly Head and Human Embryos are the Losers

Pastor Stephen Broden

The fundamental tenet of situation ethics is the idea that the end justifies the means. Joseph Fletcher,* who first set forth this idea in 1960, believed "that *there are no absolute laws* other than the law of agape love *and all the other laws were laid down* in order to achieve the greatest amount of this love." Fletcher's argument begins with the idea that there are no absolutes; his worldview removes absolutes in the law of nature, which is the law of God.

Fletcher further believed that "all other laws are only guidelines to how to achieve this love and thus they may be broken if the other cause of action would result in more love." This leads me to ask who determines if the other cause of action equals more love? Essentially what's being stated here is the argument of the greater good. This argument says it's okay to violate a known ethical practice, law or principle for example "thou shall not murder" if by doing so you achieve a greater good.

This, however, begs the question: Who will define what is the greater good? When you remove absolute truth or moral absolutes on what basis do you determine right or wrong? Implied in Fletcher's situation ethics is a prescribed criteria developed by someone, some group or government, who will arbitrarily apply that criteria to trump all other law if they believe a better result can be achieved.

Arbitrary Law

In *How Should We Then Live,* theologian Dr. Francis Schaeffer,** identifies situational ethics as arbitrary law. A close look at what Fletcher contrived in his love scenario reveals that right or wrong is determined by an arbiter who defines a criteria which then determines the appropriateness of an action (means) if it has the potential of producing a result (end) that is greater than ordinary love, agape.

If this makes you a little uncomfortable, then you must feel the same uneasiness with President Obama's recent announcement to lift the ban on "embryonic stem cell research." With the eloquences that can only be compared to that of Mephistopheles when he convinced Adam and Eve to abandon their faith relationship with God, President Obama justified the wholesale murder of human embryos for the unproven potential to benefit others with debilitating injuries and diseases like spinal cord injuries and Parkinson disease and other sicknesses.

Fertilized Embryos Will Die

The President said this research "will ease and end human suffering." What was not said by the President at this his press conference is far more important than what was said. He did not mention that whatever benefit this research yields would be at the expense of life of babies. We must know that these are fertilized human embryos.

A closer examination of what's connected with this decision to lift the ban on embryonic stem cell research reveals a decision sourced in arbitrary law. Moral Absolutes—natural law—is out and the elite few will determine what the greater good is for you, for society, and for me. As Fletcher said, the greater good justifies the means.

At the press conference, President Obama framed his decision to lift the ban in philosophical language that sought to justify an immoral act to kill innocent babies in order to ease "human suffering." Murder by any other name is murder.

Stephen Broden has served as Pastor of Fair Park Bible Fellowship in Dallas, TX for 20 years www.fpbfellowshipchurch.org.

* **Joseph Fletcher** (1905-1991) was an American professor who founded the theory of *situational ethics* in the 1960s, and was a pioneer in the field of *bioethics*. Fletcher was a leading academic involved in the topics of *abortion, infanticide, euthanasia, eugenics,* and *cloning.* Ordained as an *Episcopal* priest, he later identified himself as an *atheist.*

Fletcher was a prolific professor, teaching, participating in symposia, and completing ten books, and hundreds of articles, book reviews, and translations. He taught *Christian Ethics* at *Episcopal Divinity School, Cambridge, Massachusetts,* and at *Harvard Divinity School* from 1944 to 1970. He was the first professor of medical ethics at the *University of Virginia* and co-founded the *Program in Biology and Society* there. He retired from teaching in 1977. In 1974, the *American Humanist Association* named him Humanist of the Year.

He served as president of the Euthanasia Society of America (later renamed the Society for the Right to Die) from 1974 to 1976. He was also a member of the *American Eugenics Society* and the *Association for Voluntary Sterilization. http://en.wikipedia.org/wiki/Joseph_Fletcher*

** **Francis August Schaeffer** (30 January 1912-15 May 1984) was an *American Evangelical Christian theologian, philosopher,* and *Presbyterian* pastor. He is most famous for his writings and his establishment of the *L'Abri community* in *Switzerland.* Opposed to *theological modernism,* Schaeffer promoted a more historic *Protestant* faith and a *presuppositional* approach to *Christian apologetics* which he believed would answer the questions of the age.

A number of Christian leaders, authors, and evangelists credit Schaeffer's ideas with helping spark the rise of the *Christian Right* in the United States and were strongly influenced by him. Among them are *Operation Rescue* founder *Randall Terry, Focus on the Family's James Dobson,* the *700 Club's Pat Robertson, Prison Fellowship's Charles Colson,* columnist *Cal Thomas,* preacher and author *Tim LaHaye,* former Florida Secretary of State *Katherine Harris,* and *Liberty University* and *Moral Majority* founder *Jerry Falwell. http://en.wikipedia.org/wiki/Francis_Schaeffer*

REFERENCES

Fletcher, J. (1966). *Situation ethics: The new morality.* Philadelphia: Westminster Press. Bio Retrieved on February 29, 2012 from *http:// en.wikipedia.org/wiki/Joseph_Fletcher*

Schaeffer, F. (1976). *How should we then live? The rise and decline of western thought and culture.* Wheaton, Illinois: Crossway Books. Bio Retrieved on February 29, 2012 from *http://en.wikipedia.org/wiki/ Francis_Schaeffer*

CHAPTER 29

Homosexuality, Abortion, and Dr. Martin Luther King

Reverend Clenard Childress

One of the more fascinating exchanges in Scripture which depicts the contemporary decorum of debate in our present-day culture is clearly seen when Jesus confronted and debated the pharisaical religious order of His day. John, in the 8th chapter, illuminates the problem when there is debate with those who are in denial of their condition.

The religious elite had no intention of trying to find the truth. These bigots often masqueraded in deception and majored in misinformation deceivimg the uninitiated. Jesus began a discussion about being enslaved to sin and it caused the depth of the problem to surface. Their reply to our Lord's lesson is recorded in John 8:33 when they said, "We have never been in bondage to any man!" Yes, they had become so consumed in their own maliciousness and chicanery, they lost sight of reality and were living in denial believing their own press releases.

The Roman Empire had been occupying and subjugating Israel for multiple years along with the religious elite. They were enslaved to man outwardly and sin inwardly and blind to both. Certainly at that point, Jesus saw the futility of trying to reach that audience with truth, yet out of compassion he persisted.

The elites were determined to twist and malign the facts to accommodate their lifestyle, though in error. They lived in a vacuum of denial refusing to see the obvious. When truth is ignored, or denied, the course often taken by those *in* denial is to first obfuscate, then defame, diminish, and finally denounce the messenger. This crowd resorted to using the "N-word" of that day—Samaritan—and even went so far as declaring that Jesus was the devil.

Sound familiar?

Abortion and Homosexuality

It is similar today, for instead of examining the data, this generation's elites combat truth with ideology, character assassination, deception, and of course, denial. The two defining issues of the day which will determine the course of our culture, and the destiny of our nation, are abortion and homosexuality.

Pro-choice, and homosexual and lesbian activists, all claim their cause is a Civil Rights issue. Yet the "Civil Rights" of the unborn children are being denied, and it is intellectually dishonest to claim a "right" for oneself and by so doing, deny the rights of someone else, especially when that *someone* is an unborn infant.

These individuals are completely wrong because you do not give Civil Rights to sexual orientation because your sexual orientation could be flawed. "Civil Rights" are based on "Birth Rights," and according to the APA, homosexuality and lesbianism is an *acquired* behavior, not something like the color of your skin—something you're born with. You were not born homosexual, so sexual preference is *not* a Civil Right—it's a *preference*.

Dr. Martin Luther King, Jr.

What probably grieves me the most is that they both claim Rev. Dr. Martin Luther King as an icon for their cause, when essentially *nothing* could be further from the truth. Dr. King was a chief facilitator of the Civil Rights Movement, and by his death at the hand of an assassin, he paid the ultimate price for his cause. Freeing African-Americans from centuries of slavery, bigotry and racism, does not equate with sexual preference, and so in some ways, Dr. King's writings are more relevant, imperative, and apropos today than when he first penned them decades ago.

Like any true Prophet of God, he is and was before his time, yet his words—transcending time—speak loudly and clearly to us today. The pimping of Dr. King by the racist abortion industry and by homosexual and lesbian activists, needs to cease.

But since you admire him so much, and like to invoke his name so often, perhaps you might also adhere to his counsel. Below are some excerpts from Dr. King's 1957-1958 monthly advice columns where he answered questions from readers for *Ebony Magazine*. Note his advice on the two defining issues of this present day: Abortion and Homosexuality.

I know there will be those, like the pharisaical religious elite of Jesus' day, who will continue in their state of denial, rejecting the obvious. But for those of you who *objectively* look at this interview, perhaps it will *subjectively* help you decide what is right and what is wrong.

Dr. Martin Luther King On Parenting

QUESTION: I was in a home the other day where a 3-year—old child read the riot act to his mother. The mother took it with a sheepish smile. This, I am told, is permissiveness. It seems to me that what modern children need is a large dose of parental permissiveness applied to their backsides. Do you agree?

MLK: It is quite true that many modern parents go too far in allowing their children to express themselves with hardly a modicum of discipline . . . This **almost "lunatic fringe" of modern child care** has been responsible for most strange and fantastic methods of child rearing in many American homes . . . The child must realize that there are rules of the game which he did not make and that he cannot break with impunity.

Dr. Martin Luther King, Jr. On Premarital Sex

QUESTION: I was raised in a Christian environment. My father placed great stress on premarital virginity. I am 29. Of late, I have begun to doubt the validity of his teaching. Is he right?

MLK: I think you should hold firm to the principle of premarital virginity. The problems created by premarital sex relationships are far greater than the problems created by premarital virginity. The suspicion, fears, and guilt feelings generated by premarital sex relations are contributing factors to the present breakdown of the family. **Real men still respect purity and virginity within women**. If a man breaks a relationship with you because you would not allow him to participate in the sexual act, you can be assured that he did not love you from the beginning.

Dr. Martin Luther King, Jr. On Homosexuality

QUESTION: My problem is different from the ones most people have. I am a boy, but I feel about boys the way I ought to feel about girls. I don't want my parents to know about me. What can I do?

MLK: Your problem is not at all an uncommon one. However, it does require careful attention. **The type of feeling that you have toward boys is probably not an innate tendency, but something that has been culturally acquired** . . . You are already on the right road toward a solution, since you honestly recognize the problem and have a desire to solve it.

Dr. Martin Luther King, Jr. On Abortion

QUESTION: About two years ago, I was going with a young lady who became pregnant. I refused to marry her. As a result, **I was directly responsible for a crime**. It was not until a month later that I realized the awful thing I had done. I begged her to forgive me, to come back, but she has not answered my letters. The thing stays on my mind. What can I do? I have prayed for forgiveness.

MLK: **You have made a mistake** . . . One can never rectify a mistake until he admits that a mistake has been made. Now that you have prayed for forgiveness and acknowledged your mistake, you must turn your vision to the future . . . Now that you have repented, don't concentrate on what you failed to do in the past, but what you are *determined to do in the future.*"

Are You Seeking Truth?

To the seekers of truth in this ongoing debate, I pray you can perceive through his words and feel the spirit of Dr. King and know how he stood on these present-day issues. The iconic use of Dr. King as an advocate for true social justice is as appropriate as the Son speaking on the behalf of his Father. But to attempt to do the same for abortion and homosexual rights, is as using Mahalia Jackson as the voice of hip hop; the fire-breathing abolitionist, John Brown, as the face of the pacifist anti-war movement; proclaiming Marion Anderson mentored Snooki; or portraying Barack Obama, as a Constitutional Conservative.

It's pure deception!

Reverend Childress, Jr. is on the boards of several pro-life organizations.

CHAPTER 30

Why homosexuality is Wrong

Reverend Clenard Childress

The 21st Century offers new challenges to the faith community and to society as a whole. We are faced with social issues which have become increasingly more complex due to ever shifting perceptions of behavior and relationships.

In 1954, Dr. Martin Luther King in his sermon, "Rediscovering Lost Values," warned the country of a disturbing trend called *moral relativism*. Defined, moral relativism is based on individual conscience rather than on established rules or law (Encarta Dictionary). In simple terms, it means that everyone does what is right in his or her own eyes.

During the 60s moral relativism was evident under the guise, "If it feels good, do it! If it doesn't, do it anyway!" During the 70s, "I'm okay; you're okay," became the mantra espousing moral relativism. Today, the chant, "I am loveable and kind!" inculcates this generation. With great prophetic insight, Dr. King believed that if moral relativism was not dealt with, we might lose the nation he had come to love. That was 57 years ago . . .

Moral Relativism and the Book of Judges

The book in the Bible that reflects moral relativism is Judges. It succinctly relates a period in the history of Israel with this astute commentary, " . . . everyone did what was right in his own eyes" (Judges 21:25). As a result, Israel suffered the consequences.

To say something is wrong implies there is a standard or a moral code of ethics or established absolutes that is right and that supersede an individual's desires. But we have forgotten as a nation—and particularly as African Americans—what the champion of the Civil Rights Movement related not so long ago. His tenants were that the Ten Commandments and the principles of the scriptures are *right*, and to deviate from them will cause havoc.

Homosexuality in the Bible

Any cursory search of the Bible regarding homosexuality reveals it is wrong spiritually, physiologically, and socially because it even violates secular natural law (biologically). Leviticus 18:22 clearly warns against men indulging in sexual relationships with other men, and clearly explains God's thoughts about such behavior. "You shall not lie with a man as with a woman; it is an abomination," (Lev. 18:22).

The Apostle Paul in his letter to the Romans warns men and women about the practice of homosexuality and lesbianism underscoring that having sex with someone of the same gender is against nature. We are warned that those who practice such things would suffer terrible consequences.

> *For this reason God gave them over and abandoned them to vile affections and degrading passions. For their women exchanged their natural function for an unnatural and abnormal one; And the men also turned from natural relations with women and were set ablaze (burned out, consumed) with lust for one another, men committing shameful acts with men and suffering in their own bodies and personalities the inevitable consequences and penalty of their wrong doing and going astray, which was [their] fitting retribution.*
> (Romans 1: 26-27 Amplified)

Amazingly enough, and in spite of all the evidence to the contrary, there are clerics today—false prophets, as it were—who say that the Bible does not condemn homosexuality. When Jesus told a group of religious hypocrites that it was going to be worse for them than it was for Sodom, everyone understood that the destruction of Sodom and Gomorrah was by "fire and brimstone," (Matthew 11:23). And, they all knew *why* it was destroyed.

As Christians, should we suppose and can we believe that all of a sudden, God has changed his mind? Jesus said in the last days that it would be as the days of Lot.

The Days of Lot

So, what was it like it the days of Lot? Homosexuality imposed itself upon that society.

> *It was evening when the two angels came to Sodom. Lot was sitting at Sodom's [city] gate. Seeing them, Lot rose up to meet them and bowed to the ground.*
>
> *And he said, My lords, turn aside, I beg of you, into your servant's house and spend the night and bathe your feet. Then you can arise early and go on your way. But they said, No; we will spend the night in the square.*
> *[Lot] entreated and urged them greatly until they yielded and [with him] entered his house. And he made them a dinner (with drinking), and had unleavened bread which he baked; and they ate.*
> *But before they lay down, the men of the city of Sodom, both young and old, all the men from every quarter, surrounded the house.*
> *And they called to Lot and said, 'Where are the men who came to you tonight? Bring them out to us, that we may know [be intimate with] them'.* (Genesis 19: 1-5 Amplified)

In these last days, the homosexual community is demanding that their lifestyle be legitimized and viewed by society as a lifestyle that is right. We are subjected to the distasteful alignment of homosexuality with the "Civil Rights Movement" and with the argument that gay rights should be guaranteed under the Constitution.

These two issues are incompatible. The civil rights of African Americans is not to be lumped with homosexuals who claim they are subject to discrimination because society views their lifestyle as unbiblical and wrong. The same Jesus who condemned Sodom for their lifestyle speaks from the Bible today.

Male Physiology

The physiology of the male body is evidence that it is not designed to be penetrated. Anal sex is the overwhelmingly practice of gay men. Here's a thorough explanation by Dr. John Diggs, an African American doctor who has extensively researched homosexuality.

Anal sex is the sine qua non of sex for many gay men. Yet human physiology makes it clear that the body was not designed to accommodate this activity. The rectum is significantly different than the vagina with regard to suitability for penetration by a penis. The vagina has natural lubricants and is supported by a network of muscles. It is composed of mucus membrane with a multi-layer stratified squamous epithelium that allows it to endure friction without damage and to resist the immunological actions caused by semen and sperm. In contrast, the anus is a delicate mechanism of small muscles that comprise an "exit-only" passage. With repeated trauma, friction and stretching, the sphincter loses its tone and its ability to maintain a tight seal. Consequently anal sex leads to leakage of fecal material that can easily become chronic.

The potential for injury is exacerbated by the fact that the intestine has only a single layer of cells separating it from highly vascular tissue, that is, blood. Therefore any organisms that are introduced into the rectum have a much easier time establishing a foothold for infection than would occur in a vagina. The single layer tissue cannot withstand the friction associated with penile penetration, resulting in traumas that expose both participants to blood, organisms in feces, and a mixing of bodily fluids.

The vagina is the only part of mankind that is designed to receive the components of an ejaculation safely. The anus is not and is subject to an extraordinarily high infection rate. The end result is that the fragility of the anus and rectum, along with the immunosuppressive effect of ejaculate, make anal-genital intercourse a most efficient manner of transmitting HIV and other infections. The only epidemiological studies to date on the life spans of gay men have concluded that homosexual and bisexual men lose up to 20 years of life expectancy. (Diggs, 2002)

Homosexual Marriage

The demand in our present day for homosexual marriage is a threat to the stability of our society and is, without question, a detriment to our children. Laws enacted by Congress during a century of struggle for equal rights for African Americans were intended to eliminate discrimination on the basis of race but never on the basis of an individual's sexual preference, proclivity, or personal behavior. Richard Thompson Ford, a Stanford Law Professor aptly states the problem.

> After all, traditional marriage isn't just analogous to sex discrimination—it is sex discrimination: Only men may marry women, and only women may marry men. Same-sex marriage would transform an institution that currently defines two distinctive sex roles—husband and wife—by replacing those different halves with one sex-neutral role—spouse. Sure, we could call two married men "husbands" and two married women "wives," but the specific role for each sex that now defines marriage would be lost.

Marriage between a man and a woman, the fundamental building block of *all* of societies, not just ours, has stood the test of time for millennia. Monogamy is the expectation in the marriage institution.

Conversely 66% of homosexual couples report having sex outside the relationship within the first year, and 90% after the first five years. Unlike their heterosexual counterparts, 43% of all gay men have had sex with over 500 different male partners during their lifetime. Twenty-eight percent (28%) report having had sex with over 1,000 different male partners. (Diggs, 2002)

Healthy Roles for Children

Children need both parents. As models, both roles are to be lived out before them to assure healthy sexual orientation. To deviate from these norms will dramatically increase flawed orientations and ultimately fan the flame of unnatural sexual preferences.

It is the male component in a heterosexual marriage that brings balance and determines much of the sexual identity of the child. And dad is crucial spiritually in this orientation process. Fathers speak into the psyche of children and ensure their successful orientation.

Boys are edified by the affirmation and care of a father; a daughter is reminded of her beauty and how special she is by her father. Both receive loving hugs of admiration . . . not groping, lustful touching by a predator male seeking to gratify his unnatural sexual urges upon the innocent.

Violating Laws of Nature

Biologically, homosexuality violates secular natural law that is derived from the physical, biological, and behavioral laws of nature as perceived by the human intellect and elaborated through reason. Neither a homosexual male couple nor a female couple has the ability to procreate on their own. Artificial insemination, surrogates, or adoptions are the only ways for parenthood.

Homosexuality is wrong. But we must love the homosexual unconditionally. Loving them does not mean condoning the actions or relinquishing our principles. Dr. King said it best in his address in front of the Lincoln Memorial after the Prayer Pilgrimage for Freedom in 1957.

> What we are witnessing today in so many northern communities is a sort of quasi liberalism which is based on the principle of looking sympathetically at all sides. It is a liberalism so bent on seeing all sides that it fails to be committed to either side. It is a liberalism that is so objectively analytical that it is not subjectively committed. It is a liberalism which is neither hot nor cold.

The biblical reference to the lukewarm, "neither hot nor cold," (Revelation 3: 16) may refer to the passive attitude about moral issues that do not line up with the Word of God. Because this made Jesus disgustingly sick, He will vomit these people out of His mouth.

Some things are right. Some things are wrong. Let us not lose our nation trying to make what is clearly wrong right. No matter how many states pass laws affirming homosexual marriage, it is wrong. Right is right even if everyone is against it, and wrong is wrong even when everyone is for it.

Reverend Childress, Jr. is on the boards of several pro-life organizations.

REFERENCES

Diggs, J. (2002). *The health risks of gay sex.* Corporate Resource Council. Retrieved from *http://www.corporateresourcecouncil.org/white_papers/ Health_Risks.pdf*

Ford, R. T. *http://richardtford.law.stanford.edu/*

CHAPTER 31

Genocide/Suicide of Black America

Dr. Loretto Grier Cudjoe Smith

An aborted education kills the dreams of our youth. A prison sentence aborts the dreams of a young person. Our children, who are not lost/killed in the wash (abortion), are finished in the rinse (school drop outs and incarceration).

Since the legalization of abortion in 1973, Black America has lost 35% of its population with an estimate that over 20+ million Black children have been killed by the abortionists. Of the reported 12% of the population in 1973, some numbers reveal that today Black Americans now constitute only 9% of America's population, with numbers still declining.

The incarceration of Black males at younger and younger ages, often before they have the opportunity finish school or to reproduce; and often remaining incarcerated for longer periods beyond their natural abilities to reproduce and function as healthy parents, is an integral part of the plan to control the birth rate of Blacks in America. This explains why the liberal white racist, who has strongly contributed to promoting harmful social behaviors, releasing social constraints and instigating the overall moral deterioration in our communities leading to the criminalization of young Blacks (who are the victims and scavengers for every human experiment promoted by these social architects), is also the same racist who is strongly pro-abortion and who most recently is first in line to promote the "two strikes you're out" (locking up Black males en masse) and the expansion of the death penalty.

The social sympathizers of the 60's and 70's are part of the lynch mob in the 90's and into the 21st century. In essence, they gave us the rope to hang ourselves.

Criminal Justice and Welfare Reform

More insidious means of implementing these policies have been through criminal justice and welfare reform. This will eventually give way to a more violent means of eradicating these "human pests" for the survival of the "master race". Utilizing the death penalty, abortion, infanticide (becoming a reality with late term and post-birth abortion) euthanasia, fetal tissue research, melanin extraction, human experimentation, and organ removal from healthy individuals particularly prisoners and aborted babies; human lives are being exploited and eliminated.

How can Blacks expect to survive this onslaught by those who wish to annihilate all nonwhites via contraception, abortion, sterilization, imprisonment and poor medical care? Black ministers have been virtually silent to this holocaust as more unborn Black children are painfully executed. While these innocents (victims of unplanned and or undesired pregnancies) are blamed for a multitude of social problems, the greed of the rich continues to absorb a greater and more unequal share of God's kingdom which was created for all of his children, regardless of man's standard for poverty or wealth.

Sanger's Negro Project and Planned Parenthood mandates have been so successful in indoctrinating Black leaders that today, Blacks politicians are the most consistent promoters of exterminating future generations of our children through abortion. They also are often the major supporters of harsh mandatory sentencing for young Black men and supporters of the death penalty (Anti-Terrorism and Effective Death Penalty Act 1995) which are all part two of the plan for peaceful genocide of Black Americans proposed by Margaret Sanger and other racist eugenicists.

While our leadership attacks our youth in response to Black-on-Black crime, they are willing to tolerate abortion's human sacrifice, a more violent form of Black on Black crime, to appease white political allies. Like the unwillingness to speak for the innocent unborn, there is a similar unwillingness to speak for the thousands of innocent Black men and women and children who are unjustly incarcerated.

The 21st Century

Now, in the 21st century, America is on the brink of overly unleashing Margaret Sanger's genocide plan against Blacks, the poor, minorities, the handicapped, the elderly and all who are perceived as burdens on the elite. It's no wonder that the perceived differences in the political parties have become fewer and fewer.

Though pseudo-liberals have a plan to get you in the wash (abortion and choice) and the conservatives have a plan to get you in the rinse (criminal just-us and welfare reform), the agenda is the same—the extermination of nonwhites. Most recently, Democrats have become increasingly pro-incarceration and pro-death penalty and Republicans are becoming more and more pro-abortion, and both promoting the Sangerian philosophy of "the cruelty of charity."

By promoting and advancing the payment of over $365 million federal tax dollars a year to Planned Parenthood, our nation's political leaders are sending us a message. In essence, they are telling us that they will pay abortion supporters over a million dollars a day to control the population.

We should rise up and demand that Planned Parenthood be defunded and that the tax dollars go to education and prison reform that will regenerate and affirm the lives of those who are currently deemed "useless eaters" and burdens on society.

We must urge Caucasian prolife advocates to stand firm under attacks that would label them "racist" for telling the truth about Black Genocide. These Caucasian allies against Black Genocide are not racists, they are 21st Century Abolitionists, and the Pregnancy Care Centers are the Underground Railroads, rescuing womb babies from the womb lynchers.

As Jesus Christ stated, even Beelzebub (Satan) knows that a kingdom divided against itself cannot stand. Therefore in coming days we can expect to see greater unity amongst these men of evil. In urgency, God's people must unite, mindful of the fact that the destruction of all mankind is the ambition of Satan!

Faithfulness to the laws of God, the Master Creator of all life, and willingness to protect the innocent could avert this impending doom. "All that it takes for evil to conquer is for the good to do nothing." My people shall perish for the lack of knowledge. Those who can't remember history are bound to repeat it.

Dr. Loretto Grier Cudjoe Smith is past President of the Coalition for Equal Justice Project Truth Representative, L.E.A.R.N.

CHAPTER 32

Sexual Risk Avoidance

Dr. Freda McKissic Bush

If you could change your community to make it better, what would you do? If you knew your community was endangered near extinction, what changes would you be willing to make to save it?

People often get caught up valuing "rights" and "freedom" more than the life of a human being, valuing the right to choose over the right to life. As a practicing OB/GYN for the past twenty-nine years and a health professional specializing in women's health for over forty years, I have become increasingly aware of an imminent threat to the survival of the Black race.

Initially presented as a way to help save women's lives and empower them to take charge of their own health, abortion was viewed as a "right." Now after thirty nine years, the truth is known. Abortion is a "wrong." Abortion not only hurts women, it also kills babies, families and communities.

Understanding this information empowers you to decide whether to continue down this path of death and destruction or turn and choose the path of life and liberty. With our history of slavery and disempowerment for generations, it was easy for us to latch on to the catchy phrases of "right to choose," "reproductive rights," and "freedom of choice." We quickly forgot that what is done to the least of us is eventually done to all.

Three consequences of our shortsightedness and ignorance that disproportionably affect Blacks will be addressed below. This does not include the physical consequences associated with abortion as hemorrhaging, infection, injury to the bowel and bladder, possible infertility, hysterectomy and death of the mother.

Consequences of Induced Abortion

First, according to the Institute of Medicine 2006 report on preterm birth causes, consequences and prevention, induced abortion is noted as an immutable risk factor for premature labor (Swingle, Colaizy, Zimmerman & Morriss, 2009). Stated simply, if there's a history of a previously induced abortion, premature labor in future pregnancies is an unalterable risk factor. Black women deliver their babies prematurely three times as often as white women. We also obtain 35% of all abortions in the United States, although we are only 13% of the population.

The second consequence is the psychological affect evidenced most in the post-abortion syndrome. After the initial feelings of relief, there are long term studies that reveal a linkage between abortion and a woman's mental health resulting in depression, substance abuse, and suicide in young women (Coleman, 2011).

The third unintended consequence of abortion is the breast cancer risk. When this natural pregnancy process is interrupted abruptly by abortion, the breast cells are left in an immature state and vulnerable to develop cancer. The association between abortion & breast cancer has been documented by many studies (Laing et al, 1993).

Every organ system is affected and changed in some way by pregnancy. It is natural for the woman to nurture the child—the product of her womb. It is unnatural for a woman to sacrifice her child for herself. Without pregnancy and birth, the race becomes extinct. There is no one left to fight for rights.

A Scientific Reality

The scientific reality is that the instant a human egg and sperm unite (fertilization), the newly formed being contains the full complement of DNA in which hair and eye color, gender, and all other physical characteristics are determined. During its journey down the fallopian tube, the fertilized egg is actively growing and dividing. It will then implant in the uterine lining where it will continue to grow.

Body changes also begin immediately in the woman. The hormone progesterone prepares the endometrial lining in the womb to receive the embryo. Once implanted in the endometria, a special process occurs for the nourishments to be transported to the baby through a thin membrane without exchanging blood.

Estrogen grows the breast tissue and the milk glands. Progesterone matures the breasts for milk production to nourish the child after birth. Later, a brain hormone, oxytocin, stimulates the uterus for labor to evacuate the womb. After birth, when the baby cries or when it is time to feed, the oxytocin stimulates the milk to "let down" and the natural bonding of the mother and baby.

No Replacement Value

For every 100 Black babies born, there are seventy-seven other Black babies killed by abortion. That is a ratio of four to three. A fertility rate of 2.1 is needed to continue a race and replace the ones present who will naturally die. The 0.1 is needed for the expected miscarriages. Current fertility rate in Blacks is 1.9. We are not even at replacement value. As a race we cannot survive at that rate.

"Play It Forward" is a popular saying to evaluate future consequences of what we are doing now. Put aside labels like liberal, conservative, right, left, politically correct, Christian, Republican or Democrat. I read recently that the reason for a higher rate of abortion in the Black community was a function of healthcare disparity. The author proposed if Black women had access to birth control information and services including condoms, and if they had better healthcare and affordable healthcare for their children, then they would not have such a high rate of unintended pregnancies, and thus would not need abortions.

The fact is millions of dollars are being spent annually on Title X for free family planning services at health departments and Community Health Centers where they already dispense all birth control measures including condoms. The problem is that we have disconnected sex from procreation (reproduction) and we view sex mainly as a recreation seeking pleasure and stress relief.

Mistake . . . Intrusion . . . Burden?

When pregnancy occurs, even with the use of condoms and contraceptive measures, we are not prepared. We see the pregnancy as a mistake, intrusion and burden; thus, we treat it as such and seek to eliminate it. We are blindsided when we deny that the purpose of sex is not only for pleasure but also procreation and relationship or the 3 R's—recreation, reproduction and relationship.

The right of the woman to choose what to do with her body should be exercised *before* pregnancy is conceived. The right of the baby to life—to be born and exercise its rights to choose—is the first right after conception. If pregnancy is not desired, the woman has freedom and can exercise her right to avoid the risk of pregnancy by abstinence or birth control measures.

Pregnancy Resource Centers

Pregnancy Resource Centers (PRC) are nationwide to provide women with alternatives to abortion. They provide counseling, material services, referrals to financial assistance and medical services. PRCs also provide post-abortion counseling. I am the medical director for the two centers in Jackson, Mississippi. One is dedicated to the Black community since we obtain the largest number of abortions.

The thought process is to identify with the women and men of color and penetrate the communities with the information that would wake us up to the devastation abortion is causing. Being able to identify the root causes will help avoid the perceived necessity for abortion.

You have heard it said that to get a different result, one must do a different thing. I do not want to leave you hopeless or in despair after reading this article. Here are my proposals for action:

We must come together and genuinely love each other—unselfishly, expecting nothing in return.

We must practice the universal principles of self-control, self-discipline, respect and responsibility.

We have to take personal responsibility for our own actions first. Changing our worldview will save the children for they are our future.

Freda McKissic Bush, MD, FACOG, is a board-certified OB/GYN in private practice in Jackson, Mississippi and a member of the American Association of Prolife OB/GYN.

REFERENCES

Coleman, P. (September 1, 2011). Abortion and mental health. *The British journal of psychiatry* (BJP).

Lazovich, D., Thompson, J.A., Mink, P. J., Sellers, T.A., Anderson, K.E. (2000). Induced abortion and breast cancer risk. *Epidemiology.* 11(1):76-80.

Laing, A.E., Demenais, F.M., Williams, R., Kissling, G., Chen, V.W., Bonney, G. E. (1993). Breast cancer risk factors in African-American women: the Howard University tumor registry experience. *Journal National Medical Association.* 85:931-9. *http://www.ncbi.nlm.nih.gov/pubmed/8126744*

Preterm Birth Report. (2006). Institute of Medicine.

Swingle, H. M., Colaizy, T. T., Zimmerman, M. B., & Morris, Jr., F. H. (2009). Abortion and the risk of subsequent preterm birth: A systematic review with meta-analyses, 54 J. *Reproductive Medicine.* 95-108.

CHAPTER 33

Abstinence vs. Condoms and Comprehensive Sex Education

Dr. La Verne Tolbert

Imagine.

A person is lost in the heat of a sexual encounter about to have sexual intercourse. Just before the act itself, the illicit sex partner flippantly mentions that he or she has HIV and reaches for a condom. Would the sex partner continue to revel in kissing and snuggling, or would he or she *flee* the scene before the condom were slipped out of its candy-colored plastic shield?

Abstinence stresses avoiding such scenes altogether. Teaching kids to abstain from sexual intercourse until they are married, or "celibacy-based sex ed," should be applauded because it saves lives and avoids heartache. Instead, abstinence has been accused of having little impact on adolescent sexual behavior and failing to protect kids from HIV (Barr, 2008). Along with Barr's article is a map of the United States of America covered in Crayola-colored condoms. The caption says, "One nation under confusion: Our teens need better sexual education."

Here is what's confusing. Condoms are everywhere! One need only to walk into almost any high school—especially those with school-based clinics or health centers—to find condoms in buckets in the hallway, in school bathrooms and in health education classrooms. Every teen in America knows how to get a condom.

Kids and Condoms

Why aren't kids *using* condoms? Because the immature and inexperienced teenage mind feels invincible . . ."Nothing 'bad' will happen to me". While condoms in the environment have little impact on students' use, studies demonstrate that where condoms are present, boys have the attitude that sexual intercourse is *expected* and *accepted* by parents, principals and teachers. In other words, adults give condoms to kids because they approve of kids having sex. Makes sense?

Girls disagree that handing out condoms implies permission to have sex. So why are boys getting this message? Because condoms are a male contraceptive. And since they feel encouraged to have sex, more virgin girls respond to the pressure and become sexually active. This is especially true in schools with school-based clinics where the peer-pressure to have sexual intercourse is high (Tolbert, 1996).

To suggest that adults teach teenagers (whose mood swings and romantic interests flip flop in dizzying acrobatic speed) to protect themselves against a deadly disease like HIV/AIDS by using a condom is nothing short of irresponsible. In fact, faced with the truth of how diseases are transmitted and the irreversible consequences of warts and infertility, not to mention eventual death, one teen in stunned awareness shouted, "Then why aren't they telling us *not* to have sex?"

Why indeed, because the words "celibacy" or "purity" or "abstinence" are counter culture to the humanistic values that rule in our schools. Comprehensive sex education—which teaches kids *everything about everything*, or all there is to know about sexual activity, including "outercourse," oral sex, self-sex, same-sex, and anal sex—is preferred.

In comprehensive sex education classes, for example, kids are taught how to use oral condoms to prevent herpes of the throat. Wouldn't it be more intelligent to recommend a *better* solution to catching oral herpes than wearing a condom? Of course, comprehensive sex education offers the disclaimer that condoms don't guarantee *safe sex* but *safer sex*, meaning condoms are safer than nothing.

Condoms are not safer than abstinence, but abstinence education is viewed as fear-based religious instruction. Additionally, studies to discredit abstinence education are conducted with more rigorous criteria than are studies that affirm comprehensive sex education. And the researchers who evaluate abstinence programs and deem them ineffective are researchers hired by, working for, or associated with the Department of Health and Human Services' Planned Parenthood.

Incapable of Self-Control?

The primary reason abstinence isn't taught to Black children is this: social science research depicts African American children as if they are animals, incapable of self-control. Our children are portrayed in the most demeaning terms along with Black parents and the Black community as a whole.

Reading these papers led me to select a team and develop a six-week abstinence curriculum for middle/high school students for the AC Green Foundation—"I've Got the Power!"—because our children *do* have the power of self-control. They are *not* animals! Black kids deserve to learn the same information that other children are privy to in white schools and in upscale communities.

> "I've Got The Power" is a tool for today's youth. Powerlessness is a universal feeling among today's youth. If our youth are taught, through abstinence-based curriculum, that they have the power to control themselves and to change their lives in the process, the result may be less promiscuity and increased personal effort to step out of the cycle.

> Research demonstrates that abstinence-based curriculum works (Olsen & Weed, 1987). Even school-based clinic proponent Kirby (1991) suggests that abstinence may be an effective message in the efforts to reduce teenage pregnancy. For inner city teenagers, a curriculum empowering students in a society that infers through sex education and condom distribution that they are powerless might well be the answer. (Tolbert)

Teacher Expectation

Unlike comprehensive sex education, abstinence does not assume that all teens are going to have sex anyway, so why not show them how. This has to do with teacher expectation. If the teacher *expects* students to achieve at a high standard, student performance increases. Similarly, if parents *expect* their children to live sexually pure lives and *model* fidelity and purity, their children will also do the same.

Abstinence education teaches that self-control, self-respect, delayed gratification, planning for the future, building healthy friendships and other values essential in successful adult life can be nurtured now. Just as drinking and driving poses potential risks, so, too sexual intercourse has risks . . . heartache and heartbreak, disappointment, betrayal and rejection, in addition to STDs including HIV/AIDS, unwanted pregnancy, and abortion.

Skyrocketing STD/HIV Rates

Proponents of comprehensive sex education argue that those who teach abstinence may be responsible for increased rates in STDs. The CDC reports that "approximately 19 million new infections occur each year, almost half of them among young people ages 15 to 24" (Centers for Disease Control, 2006). However, readers of the actual document will note that the rise in STDs may be attributed not to increased rates but to improved reporting methods.

> The increases in reported cases and rates likely reflect the continued expansion of screening efforts and increased use of more sensitive diagnostic tests; however, the continued increases may also reflect an actual increase in infections . . . The availability of urine tests for Chlamydia is likely contributing to increased detection of the disease in men, and consequently the rising rates of reported Chlamydia among males in recent years (from 126.8 in 2002 to 173.0 in 2006). (CDC, p. 1, 2)

Although syphilis rates have increased among women, it is important to note that the "rising rates [are] driven largely by cases among men who have sex with men" (p. 4). This increase is a whopping 54 percent over the past five years.

Why not teach teens about Chlamydia's potential to cause pelvic inflammatory disease (PID), ectopic pregnancy, and infertility, and about the cancer-causing human papillomavirus (HPV). Or, why not teach them that HPV also causes genital warts that are impossible to cure and ask how many would voluntarily have sex if they knew their boyfriend would infect and re-infect them with this disease?

Or, explain to children that the CDC reports a significant challenge with curing gonorrhea. "While gonorrhea is easily cured . . . drug resistance is an increasingly important concern in the treatment and prevention of gonorrhea" (CDC, 2006, p.3). Or tell them that the CDC reports that syphilis, "like many other STDs, facilitates the spread of HIV by increasing the likelihood of transmission of the virus," (CDC, 2006, p. 4).

Rates Double in Black Communities

In Black communities where school-based clinics are concentrated because of the DHHS governmental mandate that hires Planned Parenthood to provide reproductive health services to children under the guise of health care, STD rates are *double* that of other communities. Yes, school-based clinics are in inner-city schools to distribute condoms, remove children for abortions, and offer sterilization if the child desires, all without parental notification or consent.

If there isn't a clinic in the school, it's probably down the street or around the corner from the school. These are called school-linked clinics (Tolbert, 1996).

Parents, principals, pastors, and community leaders are soothed into compliance when they are told that the clinic will provide essential health care for this poor, underserved population. Except the care that's essential for to these health-care providers is making sure that reproduction among Blacks is monitored through population control.

How is it that with comprehensive sex education in schools, widespread condom distribution—Planned Parenthood mails condoms to children at home!—and clinics that cost over $90,000 per school that the rates of STDs where Black children live are twice that of white communities? If children are using condoms, which means that the clinics are working, why are STD rates consistently so high?

Pro-abortion researchers use the statistics to prove that clinics and comprehensive sex education are needed because STD rates are high in Black communities. But something is wrong if condoms have been the norm for 30-plus years but STD rates have not decreased.

Birth Rates Decrease

The only rates that have decreased are birth rates (Roan, 2011).

The birth rate for teenagers aged 15-19 has declined for the last three years and 17 out of the past 19 years, falling to 34.3 births per 1,000 teenagers in 2010-a 9 percent decline from 2009 and the lowest rate ever recorded in nearly seven decades of collecting data. Birth rates for younger and older teenagers and for all race/ethnic groups reached historic lows in 2010. (CDC Press Release, 2011)

This data was summarized for the Centers for Disease Control press release. The report itself especially highlights the *ethnic groups* in which the birth rates declined.

Births were down for all race and Hispanic origin groups, declining 5 percent for Hispanic women, 4 percent for American Indian or Alaska Native (AIAN) women, 3 percent for non-Hispanic Black women, and 2 percent for Asian or pacific Islander (API) and non-Hispanic white women. (Hamilton, Martin, & Ventura, 2011, p. 2)

Planned Parenthood clinics are in schools and throughout the Hispanic community, too. (The report also notes that at this national decline, the total fertility rate is below replacement.) While birth rates decline, STDs are high. This is so, even with clinics in our children's schools.

Los Angeles

The Sexually Transmitted Disease Morbidity Report (2010) for Los Angeles reveals trends that are nothing less than startling for the Black community in this, the second largest city in the nation. In the chart, compare South Los Angeles (formerly South Central) where Blacks are concentrated to the rest of the city. Teens 15-19, and young adults 20-24 have the highest rates (Surveillance Summary, 2010). Note the population percentages.

Chlamydia		Gonorrhea	PID	% Pop.
Antelope Valley	1,837	321	9	3.8
East	5,597	722	16	14.0
Metro	6,121	2,279	24 12.8	
San Fernando	6,536	1,155	46	22.6
San Gabriel	5,361	582	13	17.7
South	**10,367**	**2,413**	**52**	**10.9**
South Bay	5,093	1,047	32	11.4
West	1,616	515	10 6.7	

HIV Infections

Nationwide, according to the Centers for Disease Control, African Americans lead in the rate of HIV infections (Diagnoses, 2008):

> 51% Black/African American
> 27% White
> 19% Hispanic/Latino

Here is one STD that is . . . fatal. Yes, people with HIV are living longer, but they are not living as long as they would have had they not contracted the virus. Illicit sex—sex outside of the safe boundaries of marriage between a man and a woman—is killing us.

Just Say No

Abstinence is *not* taught in California schools. When grants were available, California just said "No" and refused to accept abstinence education funds. Since 1997, California rejected approximately $64.8 million dollars of the Title V, A-H Abstinence Education State Block Grant (Tolbert, 1998). When refused, this money was not recycled to fund abstinence education projects in other states. Instead, it was returned to a general fund. The children who might benefit most—inner-city African American children—were deprived from learning resistance skills that help them say "No" to non-marital sexual intercourse.

If parents knew that monies dedicated to protecting the lives of their children were being refused and that abstinence education isn't even an option in public schools, they might be outraged. What if every mother asked her legislator this simple question: *Why?*

Good News

With abstinence education, attitudes are changing and initiation to engage in sexual intercourse is delayed. One of the largest and most comprehensive studies of teen sex education conducted by Stan Weed, Ph.D., of the Institute for Research and Evaluation in Salt Lake City, demonstrates that abstinence is the most successful method of preventing the physical and emotional complications resulting from pre-marital sexual activity. The study tracked the education and behavior of over 400,000 adolescents in 30 different states for 15 years.

According to Dr. Weed, sexual activity rates among teenagers have decreased in the last 12 or 13 years coinciding with the national launch of abstinence education. Abortion, pregnancies and out of wedlock births rates have also decreased among teens during this same time period. However, pregnancy, abortion and out of wedlock births have been rising for the older ages, between 19 to 25, a group that has not been targeted by abstinence programs (Weed, 2007).

Don't Drink and Drive

Abstinence education is rejected because it is seen as "fear-based" instruction. Does abstinence teach fear . . . or truth? We teach our teenage children to say *No* to drugs by showing the film of junkies and addicts hooked on heroin and cocaine. We teach our teenage children to say *No* to drinking and driving by showing them mangled cars and highlighting the death rates associated with driving under the influence.

Perhaps it's time to speak with one voice and to encourage our teenage children and young adults to say *No* to sex by emphasizing the warts, herpes, infertility, and HIV/AIDS, crushed dreams, and broken hearts that result from teenage experimentation. Teaching abstinence cannot be credited with the rise of STDs. A closer look at this argument may prove that nationally, abstinence has helped millions of teens to say *Yes* to their futures.

La Verne Tolbert, Ph.D., is a former board member of Planned Parenthood, New York City, from 1975 to 1980 where she learned the truth about abortion detailed in her book, Keeping You & Your Kids Sexually Pure. She is founder/ CEO of Teaching Like Jesus Ministries, a parachurch ministry that equips leaders in the local church www.teachinglikejesus.org.

REFERENCES

Barr, N. (April, 2008) Sex and teens: Why abstinence isn't working. *O the Oprah Magazine.* p. 152. *http://www.oprah.com/relationships/Teens-Abstinence-and-Putting-Sex-Back-In-Sex-Ed*

Centers for Disease Control (CDC). *STD Surveillance 2006: Trends in Reportable Sexually Transmitted Diseases in the United States, 2006 National Surveillance Data for Chlamydia, Gonorrhea, and Syphilis, p.1. www.cdc.gov/std/stats/trends2006.htm*

Centers for Disease Control. (2006). Interpreting STD surveillance data. *2006 STD Surveillance Report*

Centers for Disease Control (CDC). 2011. Press Release. Retrieved on March 1, 2012 from *http://www.cdc.gov/media/releases/2011/p1117_teen_birthrate.html*

Diagnoses of HIV infection among adults and adolescents, by population of area of residence and race/ethnicity, 2008-37 states. *Centers for*

Disease Control. Retrieved from *http://www.cdc.gov/hiv/surveillance/ resources/reports/2009supp_vol17no2/*

Surveillance Summary of Sexually Transmitted Diseases Reported to the Los Angeles County Sexually Transmitted Disease Program. (2010). Sexually transmitted disease morbidity report. *County of Los Angeles Public Health Sexually Transmitted Disease Program.* Retrieved March 2, 2012 from *http://publichealth.lacounty.gov/std/docs/annualreport_2010_v1.pdf*

Hamilton, B. E., Martin, J. A., & Ventura, S. J. (November, 2011). Births: Preliminary data for 2010. National vital statistics reports. *U.S. Department of Health and Human Services Centers for Disease Control and Prevention.* Retrieved on March 1, 2011 from *http://www.cdc.gov/ nchs/data/nvsr/nvsr60/nvsr60_02.pdf*

Roan, S. (March 31, 2011). Drop in U.S. birth rate is the biggest in 30 years. Los Angeles Times. *http://articles.latimes.com/2011/mar/31/news/ la-heb-us-birth-rate-falls-20110331*

Tolbert, L. *I've got the power abstinence curriculum for middle and high school students.* A. C. Green Youth Foundation. *http://www.acgreen.com/ abstinence/curriculum.html*

Tolbert, L. (1996). Condom availability through school-based clinics and teenagers' attitudes regarding premarital sexual activity. (Doctoral Dissertation, Talbot School of Theology, La Mirada, CA, 1996). *Dissertation Abstracts International,* 57/08A, 3409. [Ed.D. Awarded Ph.D. May 29, 1999]

Tolbert, L. (1998). Teaching Abstinence: Legislators Just Said No. *Los Angeles Times* [Essay].

Weed, S. Institute for Research and Evaluation. Retrieved from *http://www. lifesite.net/ldn/2007_docs/CompSexEd.pdf*

CHAPTER 34

Not a Hint: A Message for Young Christians

La Nej Garrison, M. A.

Over ten years in ministry and from Africa to Asia, the answer to the following question has not changed. Why do young people have sex? Whatever your answer is, sorry to say, it has been said before. But doesn't that give you hope, at least a little?

This struggle is not new. The reasons why young people have sex don't vary by region, neighborhood, social status, ethnic background or even age. The reasons are the same and the excuses are the same. And the answers will not surprise God. "No temptation has overtaken you except such as is common to man . . ." (1 Cor 10:13). God did make it a point that Mary was a virgin, so I think he knows a little about sex.

This scripture needs to be imbedded in every Christian's mind and heart. It ends the debate about what God says about sex before marriage, "Flee sexual immorality" (1 Cor 6:18). The funny thing about the word flee is that it is an active verb. Every time you read the word flee, it is still saying, "Run!", "Get out!", "Stay away from . . . !", and basically, "Don`t do it!"

A Good-Looking Guy

When I was younger I wore glasses the size of dinner plates. They were huge and no one told me that my glasses were enormous. There was a guy in our church, slightly older and very beautiful. I mean this guy was gorgeous,

214

fine, or whatever word you want to use for extremely good looking, this describes him.

I prayed that he would notice me, but to no avail. Maybe it was the glasses. I figured that God made him that fine and obviously He wanted me to date him. But he did not notice me until I was older. We were both working at the church office when our paths crossed. Obviously God was working in my favor. He came in my office and acted nervous to ask *me* out. "Do you want to go to dinner?"

After I picked myself off of the floor, I asked if he were hungry *now*. I was that anxious to go out with him. We started dating and I was in love before our first date, or rather in lust. One of the big clues that he was bad news was my mother's reaction. She HATED him! Regardless of what she says now, she hated him and wanted him to fall off the face of the planet.

By the time we were dating I was beginning my ministry and speaking at different churches. This guy knew about my ministry and even went with me sometimes. But he was not moved. He never said that he wanted to have sex, but he kept pushing the boundaries that I had set.

When I asked my friends about him, they never told me to break up with him. These were friends who had grown up in church with me. "Do not be deceived, evil company corrupts good habits," (1 Cor 15:33).

The Book of Life

I had this fear—I would die and go to heaven and run up to the God excited about having made it into the pearly gates. God would flip through the Book of Life searching for my name. He would look at me and then look at the book, again.

Because I am so funny, I would joke with Him and say the line was getting long, so He should stop playing. God responded, "Your name is not in here."

I am outraged. "How can this be? I went to church, sang in the choir, and I even cried during services. How could my name *not* be in the book?"

In response, the Lord catalogued the names of my friends. "These were your gods. I am not your God. You chose to listen to what *they* had to say about how you should live your life. Their words were the ones that you lived by, not mine."

I was on the path of doing well, but I chose to associate with other Christian friends who were not as committed. For me, loyalty is a big thing. These were my best friends! How could I walk away from them? So when the struggle of my life came with this "fine" guy, I had the wrong words in my head.

I was around friends who were disobedient for so long that it seemed easily justifiable. I watched them justify sexual sin for themselves, and I began to hear the same excuses in my own head. It's not that they were deliberately trying to persuade me, but they would have approved if I had given into temptation. Just as the Bible says, their habits began to rub off on me. I wasn't changing them. They were changing me. Now, I understood why Romans 1:32 says that we should not even associate with those who approve of sexual immorality.

How Far is Too Far?

One of the main questions teens often ask me is this, "How far can we go?" We cannot have sex, but how far is too far?

The problem begins with the question itself. It's not how far is too far, but rather, how close to God can we stay? We've created this imaginary line and then tell ourselves not to cross the line. Instead of staying as far as possible *away* from the line, we try to get as *close* to the line as possible.

This is wrong! "But among you there must not be even a hint of sexual immorality," (Ephesians 5:3 NIV). There should not even be a hint . . . ?

My first question was, "To whom is the 'you' referring?" because I am not trying to do extra stuff as a Christian. The answer is in the text. The 'you' refers to those of you who claim to be Christians.

My next question was, "What's a hint?" A hint is anything that might look like anything *but* sexual purity! My goal was not simply to remain a virgin. My goal was to remain sexually pure. That was how I was raised. I needed to change my vocabulary, and I needed to change my strategy. I repented. To repent, means to literally go the other way, change direction. True repentance is not tears, but termination of previous actions . . . no tears, but termination equals repentance.

Room to Sin

Romans 13:14 cautions that we should not make any provisions for the flesh to fulfill its lusts. In other words, don't make room to sin.

Get off the phone and Internet late at night when your hormones are raging. Don't go over to his (or her) place alone to "watch movies." Seriously, God is not dumb! Don't put yourself in situations where you will be tempted. Plan ahead and decide if you are going to obey God or not.

And please make the decision today, because there are too many Christians who say they love God but they are living foul lives. If you love God, then John 14:15 says that you will *keep* his commandments. If you are not keeping His commandments, then you don't love God.

Too many Christians are living the Christian life with excuses. You've had a rough life? I've had a rough life, too. I was born to a paranoid, schizophrenic, manic depressive birth-mother who abandoned me in a cab with my twin siblings (we were all adopted a few years later).

So let's not try to compare stories and personal tragedies. God's word is still His word regardless of our excuses. Live for God. Or don't.

Period.

A Forever Gift

That's what I told a new friend I met overseas. Let me explain . . .

I married my best friend from college. He's a basketball pro, so we travel a lot to different countries, which I love because I'm always excited to meet new people. In nearly every country, there are other professional basketball teams who are considered to be the NBA for that country.

In one country that will remain nameless (details omitted for privacy's sake), we met other Americans who played on different teams. There was a female basketball team, and since Americans were few, we all tended to socialize together.

Soon, one player started dating one of the female basketball players. She was attracted to him because he was rich, and he had a great contract. He owned a few homes and had a few children but no wife. So this female basketball player—let's call her, Cleo—was in love! Even though she claimed to be a believer, she was sexually active and having intercourse with this super nice super rich guy.

I asked how she could have sex and be a Christian, but felt that God understood. Cleo said she believed in God and specifically Jesus and felt this man was going to be her husband. No matter what I said, having sex was alright with her.

One morning Cleo came to the door. She told me she had been crying for hours. Cleo slowly walked in our unit and proceeded to explain what was wrong.

That morning, she was taking a shower and felt something "down there" . . . a sore in her vagina that was very painful. She told me that when she got dressed, she had not put on underwear because the friction caused her extreme pain.

She went to the doctor and was told that she had Herpes. She was freaked out and went to tell her `lover`. You cannot imagine what he said! "Oh, I did not know it could show up that fast."

What? I was shocked and she was devastated. He gave her $200 for medication, and he went out to a club that night. He showed no remorse.

For the rest of her life, she will have this disease. For the rest of her life, she will have this horrible reminder—a consequence to her disobedience. And when she finally does meet the man of her dreams, she will have to tell him that she has Herpes and pray that he wants it too.

We think that God is trying to keep us from having fun, but He is not. The consequences of disobedience are serious and they may last the rest of your life. We all know this scripture:

> *The thief comes only to steal and kill and destroy; I have come that they may have life, and have it to the full.* (John 10:10 NIV)

And that's the truth. What seems like fun may end up stealing your future, killing your dreams, and destroying your life. Jesus died so that we can experience life in all of its fullness, in all of its beauty.

Do We Believe in God?

Today in public schools, we are taught that God does not exist. Although there isn't room here for a cumulative defense for the existence of God, I do want to share a few tools that I pray will strengthen your faith.

Evolution teaches that the earth existed for an infinite amount of time in the past. Reread that sentence. Okay. So let's say you're driving on the freeway and the directions tell you to exit at Hill Street. But before you get to Hill Street, there are an infinite amount of exits. When will you get to Hill Street? Never!

If there was infinite time in the past, when will we arrive here today, to the present? The answer is . . . we'd never arrive. So time had to start at some point. And if it started, what was the catalyst that made time begin? And if something made time begin, that something had to be outside of time. This is called the Infinite Regress Argument.

There had to be a first Cause and the cause had to be greater than whatever it was causing. In addition, consider the earth and our fragile our existence. Life is no accident. There are fine tuning points of our universe that are undeniable. From the gravitational force to the expansion rate of the universe, to the velocity of light and even to the very salinity of ocean, if any of these were to change .01 positive or negative, the nature of universe—even life itself—would be in jeopardy. These ideas, coupled with the emergence of consciousness, argument from morality, and more provide a cumulative argument for the existence of God.

> *For since the creation of the world, His invisible attributes are clearly seen, being understood by the things that are made, even His eternal power and Godhead, so that they are without excuse.* Romans 1:20 (NKJV)

Therefore, we should be able to look in the world and see evidences of the existence of God and allow those evidences to lead us to Jesus Christ. Sadly, it is not the lack of good philosophical arguments that keeps many from accepting Jesus, but God's existence is questioned because those who claim to know Him don't live as if He really exists.

Regardless of where you come from or what your personal story may be, let today be the day that you allow Jude 24 to govern the rest of your life.

> *Now unto Him who is able to keep you from stumbling, and to present you faultless before the presence of His glory with exceeding joy, to God our Savior, Who alone is wise, be glory and majesty, dominion and power, both now and forever.* (Jude 24)

God is able to keep you. This is His desire for your life. God wants you to live a life of purity.

As for me, I was able to walk away from that fine guy in the nick of time. With tears in my eyes and clothes melting away, I told him to leave, and I was able to save myself for my husband.

What we believe about God will be demonstrated in our lives. I think that we have a lot of Christians that are Satanists and don`t know it. Why, would I say that? Well, the slogan for the Church of Satan is, "Do what thou wilt." There is no moral standard; just do what you want.

Secretly, a lot of Christians live like this. We need a generation of people who believe God and their lives reflect their belief. Do you believe in Jesus?

Prove it!

La Nej Garriso, M. A., is the first African American female to graduate with a Master's degree in Philosophy of Religion and Ethics from Talbot School of Theology/Biola University. She speaks to youth groups all over the world and is currently writing a book on sexual purity. www.teachinglikejesus.org

CLOSING WORDS

Our year of Jubilee

Dr. Alveda King

In helping Dr. Tolbert prepare this volume, I was touched by the opportunity to work with such wonderful warriors. Because many of our contributors are authors in our own rights, we are all seeking to bless our readers with a broad representation of our "prolife ministries."

As we began to compile the submissions for the book, we quickly realized a need for a second volume, and perhaps more. The goal is to touch hearts of our readers, and to illuminate the shadows of death that have plagued the world for far too long.

In our "history" chapter, we introduced the ancient origins of genocide and brought you along through the ages, the decades, and the years of "man's inhumanity to man." We wanted to show that slavery isn't just about skin color, and that oppression can include babies in the womb, the young, the old, the sick and the well, the rich and the poor.

We say this because in order for there to be a slave, there must be a slave master. In order for there to be an aborted baby, there must be an abortionist. In either case, the oppressor is involved in the act of oppression, even as the victim is oppressed. Consider this: you can lock someone in chains, but you must watch over your prisoner lest he or she escape. So both the oppressor and oppressed are bound until a force more powerful than either sets the captives free.

Jubilee

American slave traders and slave masters often misquoted the Bible as justification for slavery. I often ask those who point to the Bible as justification for slavery why then, if the Bible is to held up as a standard for slavery, why the slave masters didn't honor the command the set the slaves free and give them wealth and property after seven years of service? The Bible describes this process as *Jubilee*.

Obviously the ancient bondages of slavery and racism still exist in the 21st Century. Now, along with oppression due to skin color, babies in the womb are counted in the masses of the oppressed. The sick, infirm and elderly are not far behind in the onslaught.

It will take yet another brief history excursion to discover why the African American or Black communities of America are being targeted by racism, segregation, genocide and the onslaught of social ills. Please take a deep breath and hold on to your hat. What you are about to read may shock you.

Possibly, many African Americans are the biological and spiritual seed of Abraham. This is what makes the mandate of Jubilee as cited in Leviticus 25 relevant to Black people in America. Consider this excerpt from the book, *Who We Are in Christ Jesus*:

> God wants us to have a greater knowledge of who we are, and how we fit into His eternal arrangement. By coming to understand God's heavenly plan, we will be able to conceptualize how we as a nation of people came to be known as "The Black Man," also known as "The Slave," "Nigger," "Colored," "Negro," "Black," "Afro-American," and "African American."
>
> Here in America for over 400 years, we Black Americans have longed for a name and home, and yet our destiny lies in two covenants. The term remnant in the Old and New Testaments, reveals that we, like our oppressed Hebrew brothers of old, have been living in bondage, but have been a major source of energy in the building of our country (like Joseph in Egypt.). Also like Joseph in Egypt, we came in as slaves, but have risen to the top of the political and social platforms of our great nation, as we ourselves are critically entrenched in the mechanisms of its influences.

If we consider how the Hebrews ran into all parts of Africa just after the massive slaying by the Roman Empire, we can also discover how the Hebrew nation came into captivity at the hands of African nations (Deut. 26:5-8; Ps. 105:32-27; 106: 19-22; Isaiah 11:11; Amos 9:7; Zeph. 3:10Mi. 5:7-8; Acts 2:5). The Hebrew nation was no stranger to bondage on the continent of Africa. Moses, in the dramatic Exodus of the Bible, answered God and led the people out of Egypt. But once again, in the first century A.D., Israel returned to Africa seeking refuge, only to find themselves in certain situations causing them to be re-enslaved!

The children of Ham largely accepted the children of Shem, as they intermingled into one people (Judges. 3:5-6; Ezra 2:1-2; Ezek. 16:1-3). Remember, the God of Israel also embraced the children of Ham. At that time in history, the Afro-eastern religions had a toehold in every aspect of the African society. For fourteen centuries, the blood of Abraham mingled with the blood of Ham. Now if we could keep in mind that God knew before day one, just what would occur, would definitely help us to understand that He knew that Abraham's seed would mingle with the African people of Ham.

Religious differences made the now Black skinned, broad nosed Israelites easy prey for their Hamitic relatives, who sold them into the profitable slave trade of the 16th century. It would be some time before people of conscience such as Wilberforce and the abolitionists leaders in America would rise up against the forces of darkness, and once again echo the cry of Moses: "Let my people go!" The wheel was set in motion, and slavery had a course to run.

At the height of the more recent oppression, when the slave traders reached the "dark continent," they attained help from the native Black people in order to "capture" the Black Jews, then placed them on the treacherous slave ships to a "new land."

Here, we can observe how the "Black Jews" went into bondage for another 400 years, which lasted from the 1500's to the 1900's. These Black Jews carried with them their heritage in their music. The old "Negro Spirituals," "Go Down Moses," "Joshua Fit De Battle of Jericho," "Jordan River Crossing," and many others give credence to a history that the Black Israelite slaves in America did not learn such rituals in Africa, nor from their slave masters in America. These children in a strange land had carried those songs from their Mother Land Israel, to their Mother Land Africa, then to the remote regions of the earth.

Later, during this same period, the blood of Abraham crossed with the blood of Japheth, when the "White" slave masters, took the Black slave girls into their beds. These acts irrefutably initiated a breeding system that would alienate the slaves from each other by forming a system of color differentiations; a system that taught the darker skinned slaves to resent the lighter complexions; a practice that did not avoid consequential preferences.

Then, another spiritual Exodus, similar to the times and experiences of Moses, which occurred hundreds of years before Martin Luther King, Jr., certainly brought Blacks up from the dregs of oppression. Like Moses, Dr. King did not "reach the promised land." God has raised up another "Joshua generation" to lead the people into another spiritual warfare, toward possessing a promise land.

Unlike our Hebrew brothers of old, we are not seeking milk and honey, even though the stakes are the same, since we want the richest of God's promises. We, as Blacks who have accepted the heritage offered by the Salvation of the Messiah, are heirs to an unlimited source of power and wealth. Naturally, God's promise is for everyone, regardless of color or gender. Yet, while God's promise is not limited, it is certainly for us as well as others, since we are a special people. It is plainly understood that the Word acknowledges that God has vested interest in us, and that all people, including African-Americans are definitely members of the family tree of Adam (Acts 17). People around the globe acknowledge this truth. Yet, it appears that the American Blacks still stumble in unenlightened confusion, leading many to cry out that we must discover who we are in Christ Jesus!

In light of the context of the ancestry of the African American "nation" or "village" living in America in the 21st century, many are connected to ancestors of the ancient Hebrew bloodline. Following this trail of evidence, we can conclude that descendants of slaves in America are entitled to the Jubilee Mandate of Leviticus 25:39-55:

If any of your Israelite relatives go bankrupt and sell themselves to you, do not treat them as slaves. Treat them instead as hired servants or as resident foreigners who live with you, and they will serve you only until the Year of Jubilee. At that time they and their children will no longer be obligated to you, and they will return to their clan and ancestral property. The people of Israel are my servants, whom I brought out of the land of Egypt, so they must never be sold as slaves. Show your fear of God by treating them well; never exercise your power over them in a ruthless way . . .

So, according to the Bible, our "foreign" slave masters were required to release us after seven years, and give us land and gifts as we departed from the years of slavery. They were not supposed to hang us, lynch us, bomb us and otherwise abuse us. They were not supposed to enslave us for generations, even into the 21st century, and keep us on "the plantation."

So, can we then conclude that greed and manipulation caused American slave masters to disregard the Bible mandate of Jubilee? Is this same spirit of greed and rebellion at the basis of racism, genocide and other atrocities of man's inhumanity to man at the root of America's social ills today?

This is a question that must surely be considered in the next edition of our Anthology. We want to hear from you as we prepare to launch our next volume. Please send your questions and feedback to *Blackprolifeanthology@ gmail.com.*

Friends, there is a cry for revival in the land. There is a longing for a Jubilee. Set the captives free we cry. At the time of this publication, we are months away from the 50th anniversary of Dr. Martin Luther King, Jr.'s 1963, "I Have a Dream" speech. The number 50 marks the time of Jubilee. As we approach or, as some say, as we are in the era of the end of a dispensation, we look towards the new where liberty and freedom will take on heaven's appearance.

We long for liberty and redemption, not just for some, but for all, regardless of skin color, gestational condition, age or physical restraints. This is a season to cry out for revival. Oh Lord, send revival. LET FREEDOM RING! Amen.

A Prayer for Revival

Dear Heavenly Father, because you are my Creator and my Judge, I want you to be my Father.

Please forgive me for my sins, and show me the way to you as my Father through Christ Jesus. Teach me Your ways, and fill me with Your Holy Spirit. Help me to forgive my oppressors, and all who have sinned against me and hurt me and my ancestors, so that you can forgive and heal me. You are LOVE Father and YOU never fail! Lord, send revival to my heart and life, and to our families, our communities, to America and to the world. In Jesus' Name I pray. Amen.

—Dr. Alveda King

REFERENCE

Preserving families of African Ancestry. (January 2003) Retrieved March 5, 2010, from *http://nabsw.org/mserver/PreservingFamilies.aspx*

Selected Poetry by Dr. Alveda King
For Generations to Come

Our family tree
means more to me, Than silver
or gold, or a
Rolls Royce.

I can rejoice and be glad,
that Mother and Dad, loved each other
—and GOD
Who blessed their union.

.

From one to another, we are linked
to each other . . .
Through the blessings and mercy of our awesome
CREATOR

Our Creator, the Artist, Who reminds us of
ETERNITY

In the smiles of our children, who have the
Spirit of our ancestors—
Twinkling out from their eyes . . .

Reminding us
Of GENERATIONS to COME.

Ripples
(In Time and Space)

Libations, fluids rippling on the sands bringing time and space together;
Bringing souls and spirits together . . . pebbles on the water, water
making ripples,
Ripples in time.
"Behold I show you a mystery; We shall not all sleep, but we shall all be
changed
In a moment, in the twinkling of an eye, at the last trump;
For the trumpet shall sound, and the dead shall be raised
Incorruptible
And we shall be changed."

II

Libations, shadows rippling on the sand
The earth beneath my feet changes from my dark and musky
Mother, becoming red and alien, harsh,
As the waters ripple and the great ship rolls.

III

I am carried away from my familiar jungle of fruits and passion flowers,
wild animal friends and even wilder beasts;
Four legged animals, predators and yet, magnificent creations of God,
with skins and furs . . . and fangs.

IV

Yet, change carries us over waters that no longer
Ripple.
The water becomes an awesome, rolling jungle of waves
That carries us on in the Middle Passage
Washing us away from our home ground to a new land of tears and
sorrow,
Our newfound home in a new world.

V

And yet, wherever we were bought,
Beaten and scattered, over continents and islands,
New blood was added to our veins; and yet the Blood of our Motherland
remained,
True and deep.
In our new world, we learned to harvest new crops;
Some not quite so different from our jungle fruits and vegetation.
We tamed fields of cotton and tobacco
Even as our wild, free spirits were tamed by the new predator; Two-legged
beasts, still creatures of God, yet not quite so magnificent in their
borrowed skins and furs. But still their fangs, though changed Remain
deadly.

VI

The libations continue
The spirits that were summoned bring new birth to memories
Reflections of time itself.
We see ourselves in a new jungle—still a part of God's creation,
And yet, the earth has changed.
The soil is not dark and musty between our bare and braceleted feet,
Nor is it red and cracked beneath our chained and callous feet.
It has become rock, concrete,
A machine-made improvement on nature,
And yet still part of nature.

VII

The tribal dancers before the sun, the wind, the rain and the Moon have
become whirling disco bodies beneath a myriad of simulated starlight,
Lightning and thundering electro phonic sounds.

VIII

The hunter's spears and darts have become a mania for Money;
And guns bring down men and the bloodthirsty prey upon the weak who
become Homeless, Jobless, and
Dreamless.

IX

The savagery continues, though times and methods change. The lie of
racism causes us to forget that we are all of one blood. Slaughter begins in
the womb, and the terror rains down across the ages. Humanity seems to
have forgotten why we are here.

Humankind has changed, and yet has not changed, only
Shimmered and rippled in the reflections of time.

X

For though one generation passeth away, another generation cometh.
As the sun rises, it sets only to rise again.
The wind goes to the south only to return to the north,
Whirling continually, returning again according to its circuits.
And the rivers run to the sea, yet the sea is not full,
For the rivers return again to that place from which they came.
For that which has been, shall be again, and that which has been done,
Shall be done again.
For as all things change, they remain because: "There is no new thing
under the sun." There are only rippling images of change, all belonging to
the universe, The Old, the New created by the Omnipotent
The Lord GOD! Who changes not.

APPENDIX I

The Beloved Community and the Unborn

As our nation pauses to recommit itself to fulfilling the dream of Dr. Martin Luther King, Jr., we invite our fellow citizens to reflect on how that dream touches every human life. Dr. King taught that justice and equality need to be as wide-reaching as humanity itself. Nobody can be excluded from the Beloved Community. He taught that "injustice anywhere is a threat to justice everywhere."

In his 1967 Christmas sermon, he pointed out the foundation of this vision: "The next thing we must be concerned about if we are to have peace on earth and good will toward men is the nonviolent affirmation of the sacredness of all human life . . . . Man is a child of God, made in His image, and therefore must be respected as such . . . . And when we truly believe in the sacredness of human personality, we won't exploit people, we won't trample over people with the iron feet of oppression, we won't kill anybody."

Scripture teaches, "Seek first God's Kingdom and His righteousness and all else shall be yours as well" (Matthew 6:33). Dr. King humbled himself before God and became increasingly dependent on Him. Dr. King's search for the "Beloved Community" was really part of his search for the Kingdom of God. Because "God is Love" (1 John 4:16), His Kingdom is founded on love (agape). That is why, in his search for the Beloved Community, Dr. King discovered God's love.

The work of building the Beloved Community is far from finished. In each age, it calls us to fight against poverty, discrimination, and violence in every form. And as human history unfolds, the forms that discrimination and violence take will evolve and change. Yet our commitment to overcome them must not change, and we must not shrink from the work of justice, no matter how unpopular it may become.

In our day, therefore, we cannot ignore the discrimination, injustice, and violence that are being inflicted on the youngest and smallest members of the human family, the children in the womb. Thousands of these children are killed every day in America by abortion, throughout all nine months of pregnancy.

We declare today that these children too are members of the Beloved Community, that our destiny is linked with theirs, and that therefore they deserve justice, equality, and protection.

And we can pursue that goal, no matter what ethnic, religious, or political affiliation we have. None of that has to change in order for us to embrace Dr. King's affirmation of the sacredness of *all* human life. It simply means that in our efforts to set free the oppressed, we include the children in the womb.

We invite all people of good will to join us in the affirmation that children in the womb have equal rights and human dignity.

Dr. Alveda King
Director, African-American
Outreach, Priests for Life
Niece of Martin Luther King, Jr.

Mrs. Naomi Barber King
Wife of the late Rev. A.D. King
(brother of Martin Luther King, Jr.)

Fr. Frank Pavone
National Director, Priests for Life

Gloria Y. Jackson, Esq.
Great-granddaughter of Dr. Booker T.
Washington
President of the Booker T.
Washington Inspirational Network

APPENDIX II

Reducing the Number of Young Black Americans Lost through Abortion and Imprisonment Restoring Respect for Life and Liberty

Sponsored by: Georgia State Conference of Branches NAACP
Unit Number: Date Adopted: April 28, 2007

Whereas, the National Association for the Advancement of Colored People was organized in 1909 during the height of lynching and brutality against Americans, and was formed for the establishment of civil rights for nonwhite people, and for the protection of their human rights.

Whereas, for more than 95 years the National Association for the Advancement of Colored People has fought to establish and protect basic human rights, civil rights, and the constitutional rights of all people especially those with little or no legal protection, mainly people of color.

Whereas, unborn children, no matter how viable, have no legal rights or political protection in the United States, abortion being legal all nine months of pregnancy.

Whereas, the abortion rights movement has long been linked to the politics of eugenicist Margaret Sanger, founder of Planned Parenthood, who assisted in organizing the Negro Project, which was devised as a systematic plan for "peaceful genocide" to reduce the Black population in the United States via "placement in work camps and on farms" (prisons), and/or "birth control", including abortion and sterilization.

Whereas, according to the Center for Disease Control and Prevention more that 13 million African-American children have been lost through legalized abortion since 1973.

Whereas, the loss of these children has had a detrimental effect on the voting strength of the Black community and has relegated Black Americans to now be only the second largest minority group in the United States; recently surpassed by the Hispanic population.

Whereas, the high rate of incarceration of young Black males, with legislation in place to insure that the length of their sentence exceed their reproductive capabilities, also serves to curtail growth in Black population, serving as another form of genocide against Black people.

Whereas, the fact that the ratio of Blacks continue to grow in grossly disproportionate numbers in America's prisons, jails, and youth detention, not only diminishes Black population, but also stifles the political and economic viability of the entire Black community and creates dysfunction in many Black families.

Whereas, statements made by William Bennett in 2005, linking the crime rate to the Black birth rate and putting forward the insidious notion that killing Black children, America can reduce its crime rate, should awaken Black Americans to the existence of racial population control, and the fact that active genocide is taking place against Blacks via the abortion industry and the prison industrial complex and should cause Blacks to become more proactive in reducing the Black abortion rate and the Black imprisonment rate.

Whereas, the year 2007 is a Jubilee Year

Therefore, Be It Resolved that the NAACP will undertake efforts to reduce America's disproportionately high Black prison inmate population:

— By undertaking all efforts to reduce crime in the Black community and to assist in the release of thousands of wrongly incarcerated, or unfairly sentenced, or presently rehabilitated Black prison inmates needlessly languishing in federal and state prisons throughout America,

— By reaffirming its support for the repeal of Georgia's SB 440 and SB 441 which mandates long prison sentences (no parole) even for children; and similar legislation in other states throughout America,

— By requesting that a commission be formed by the federal and state governments, which the specific purpose of reducing prison population, with the engagement of civil rights organizations and faith communities in partnership with prison systems, parole boards, and aftercare providers for the specific purpose of selecting prisoners for release and for providing aftercare to them once released,

— By requesting that federal and state governments immediately engage in an effort to begin a "Jubilee Year" release of prisoners, this year 2007.

Be it also resolved that the NAACP will undertake efforts to reduce the high abortion and infant mortality rate in the Black community and the great number of Black children lost for these reasons by:

— Encouraging the development of pregnancy care and crisis centers and safe havens for mothers with young children to be located in the Black community and near Black college campuses,

— undertaking efforts in the Black community to educate our youth on fetal development and the miracle of life,

— Educating Black females of childbearing age on proper diet and nutrition that will assure healthier babies,

— Educating young Black males on parental rights and responsibilities,

— Encouraging public and private support for prenatal, infant and early childhood care and public policies which are supportive of the mental and physical health of pregnant women and mothers with young children which are fostered by the attitude that motherhood is one of the greatest contributions to society,

— Highlighting Black mothers, who have historically chosen life, in spite of the overwhelming adversities of slavery, discrimination, oppression, and poverty, and who held on to help and continued to give birth to new generations,

— Studying why Black women are having abortions at such unprecedented rates,

— Educating the Black community on the political, economic, physical, and mental impact of abortion, infant mortality, and a stifled birth rate on the Black family and the entire Black community; and the racist origins of the abortion movement and industry,

— Supporting efforts of the faith community that promotes the sacredness of human life; and by working to dispel the notions and stereotypes that view Black life as less valuable and dispensable and Blacks as violent lacking respect for human life.

APPENDIX III

Dear President Obama: Americans Prayerfully United to Advance the Culture of Life

"For Life, Liberty and Family"

To sign on to this letter, please visit *www.africanamericanoutreach.com* where you can print a PDF of the letter and encourage your elected officials to sign the letter. Once you and/or your elected official have signed the letter, email to aao@priestsforlife.org or mail to Priests for Life, c/o African American Outreach, PO Box 141172, Staten Island, NY 10314

Adapted from original letter posted January 7, 2009

Dear President Obama, Members of the U. S. Congress, Governors of State and Legislative Bodies, All Political Candidates and all elected and appointed leaders of the people of the United States of America:

Objective: To restore respect for human life, liberty and family, as a means of reducing crime; America's grossly disproportionate prison inmate population; and the number of pregnancies ending in abortion.

Violent crime reflects a basic disrespect for the lives and liberty of other individuals. Crime often destroys human life or the liberty to enjoy freedom or pursue happiness. As crime has skyrocketed in the United States, so has the cost of defending one's freedom be it as a criminal defendant or as a community burdened by the cost of law enforcement and imprisonment of those convicted of crimes so that others may enjoy the freedoms promised by the Constitution. Abortion is an act of violence against God and humanity. Life and Liberty are joint partners, anchored by the family. The challenge of this country has been to balance the freedom of one individual against the freedom of others. The essential duty of protecting the lives of its citizens must not be subjugated to the protection of the liberties of a few.

We the undersigned respectfully submit for your consideration the following strategic plan with the desire to accomplish the betterment of all Americans. We would appreciate the opportunity for open dialogue at town hall meetings, or at any venue you so choose.

1.) Remove all federal and state funding including Title 10 funding that is used to promote or commit acts against the family.

2.) Remove all federal and state funding that is used to support, promote or commit acts of genocide, abortion and prenatal murder, including Title 10 funding.

3.) Support legislation and allow funding for development of a Human Life Curriculum for schools; youth detention; centers and prisons. Said curriculum would include pertinent information regarding nutrition; natural family planning; the link between fertility, breast feeding and continuation of the species and other non-invasive prevention strategies. The race issue would be addressed with information regarding the knowledge that all human beings are one race rather than the currently accepted concept that there are separate races of human beings on the earth. Essential parenting concepts, fatherhood and motherhood principles and other information regarding human life and development would be included.

4.) Support legislation and provide funding for enabling mothers and fathers to be actively involved in the educational choices of their children.

5.) Provide legislation, funding for and support of Public Service Announcements heralding the benefits of embracing family life as opposed to practicing the use of harmful chemical and surgical procedures such as artificial birth control and abortion. Such announcements would be similar to those of those Surgeon General's warning that smoking is hazardous to your health.

6.) Support legislation and provide funding that enables provision of Birthing and Crisis Pregnancy Centers throughout America.

7.) Support legislation and provide funding for Re-establishment of the Federal Parole System:

8.) Support legislation and provide funding for Municipal Transition Centers: (The Clinton Administration directed funding to local government for the funding of new prisons and jails. Similar funding should be directed to local governments for the funding of locally operated transition centers for newly released prisoners)

9.) Provide funding for and support the development of Local Parole Advisory Boards: made up of local citizens who assist state parole boards in making parole decisions.

10.) Support legislation and provide funding for Re-established Prisoner/ Parolee Exchange Programs to maintain balance in state and federal prison population with parole population and to limit the growth in prison population.

11.) Provide funding, legislation and plan for utilizing Parolee Labor to rebuild America's infrastructure as opposed to privatizing prisons.

12.) Provide legislation and funding for federal and state establishment of a commission made up of civil rights advocates, spiritual and community leaders, lawyers, law enforcement etc. for a "jubilee release project" to review individuals for release first considering those who may have been wrongly convicted, unjustly sentenced and then those who have demonstrated rehabilitation, targeting a reduction in federal and state prison populations.

As leaders and lay members of the populations you serve, we welcome the opportunity to assist and support efforts such as those outlined above in this letter. We commit ourselves to communicating this information to you through the channels you provide, and expect to find other creative, loving and non-violent ways of communicating with you, respectfully acknowledging your authority to govern, with the expectation of fostering a better life for all human beings.

Your signature here represents your commitment to this pledge and to a better America.

Signed: _____ (Political Leader)

We are looking forward to your response.
Prayerfully and sincerely,
Americans for Advancing the Culture of Life, Liberty, Justice and Family in America

Signed: _____ (US Citizen)

APPENDIX IV

Contributors' Bios

BIOS

The Editors and Cover Designer

Dr. Alveda King

Dr. Alveda King is a Minister of the Gospel of Jesus Christ, a grateful mother and grandmother. She is a former college professor, author, mentor, stage and screen actress and presidential appointee. She has been "honored" and "blessed" to sit on several boards, and has received numerous awards and honors. Through her ministry of King for America and her vocation as Director of African American Outreach with Priests for Life, she devotes her God-given gifts and talents of writing, singing, song writing, producing and directing media projects and other gifts "to glorify God in the earth".

Dr. King is the daughter of slain civil rights activist Reverend A. D. King and his wife Naomi Ruth Barber King. Her life in the "King Family Legacy" enables her to advance the message of Agape Love that her uncle, Dr. Martin Luther King, Jr. shared with the world. She attributes her accomplishments in life to the grace and love of God. Among those counted as her human mentors are her parents, her grandparents Daddy and Mama King, and her pastor, Allen McNair, and his wife Anna.

Reverend Dr. La Verne Tolbert
Author, educator La Verne Tolbert, Ph.D., has over 35 years' experience in the field of teen pregnancy prevention. Her interests began in 1975 when was invited to become a board member of Planned Parenthood in New York City where she volunteered until 1980. The education she received about abortion and population control during her five-year tenure turned her into a pro-life advocate before the term was coined and laid the groundwork for continued research in this field.

Her book, *Keeping You & Your Kids Sexually Pure* (Xlibris) was originally published by Zondervan and is based on her dissertation research about condom availability and school-based clinics. It has been endorsed by American Family Radio, Focus on the Family and Youth Builders.

Dr. Tolbert earned her undergraduate degree from Hunter College, New York, and her masters and doctoral degrees from Talbot School of Theology, La Mirada, CA. An ordained minister, she is an adjunct professor at Biola University and Golden Gate Baptist Theological Seminary (Southern California Campus).

Teaching Like Jesus Ministries, Inc., a parachurch ministry that equips leaders and parents in the local church in seminars and workshops, was founded by Dr. Tolbert in 2001 and is titled after her best-selling book, *Teaching Like Jesus: A Practical Guide to Christian Education in Your Church* (Zondervan). Her latest book, *How to Study and Understand the Bible in 5 Simple Steps Without Learning Hebrew or Greek* (Xlibris) is an easy-to-read ebook designed to help God's people fall in love with reading and studying God's Word.

Passionate about rescuing children from lifelong foster-care placements, Dr. Tolbert promotes adoption in conjunction with the Los Angeles County Department of Children and Family Services through her project, Covenants for Kids, "churches helping children in foster care." She is President of the Society for Children's Spirituality: Christian Perspectives, a scholarly organization that examines factors contributing to the spiritual development of children. Her husband, Elder Irving Tolbert, is a vice-president at a Los Angeles bank.

Ryan Scott Bomberger, M. A.

Ryan Scott Bomberger, M. A., has a rather unique perspective of the innate nature of Purpose as an adoptee and adoptive father along with his wife, Bethany. Ryan's biological mother was raped yet courageously chose to go through 9 months of pregnancy, giving him Life.

Ryan was adopted as a baby and grew up in a loving, multi-racial Christian family of 15, of whom 10 were adopted. His life defies the myth of the "unwanted" child. He was loved, and he has flourished.

Today, he is an Emmy® Award-winning Creative Professional who has made an unexpected impact in the pro-life movement with the bold *TooManyAborted.com* billboard/web campaigns. As the first pro-adoption themed ad campaign created to address the disproportionate impact of abortion in the black community, the effort received massive media coverage from The New York Times, USA Today, LA Times, CNN, MSNBC, the Associated Press, Washington Times, Fox News, ABC World News with Diane Sawyer, and, seemingly, the entire blogosphere.

The extensive media attention enabled The Radiance Foundation, and Ryan's personal story of adoption, to reach millions. He is a featured blogger on LifeNews.com and addresses the cultural dynamics of abortion, eugenics, and the beautiful act of adoption.

As Chief Creative Officer of The Radiance Foundation (TheRadianceFoundation.org), his work resulted in Planned Parenthood's launch of two national conferences to combat the campaign and the massive media frenzy it caused. Bomberger addresses a myriad of social issues in the context of individual and irreplaceable intrinsic value. Through creative ad campaigns, powerful live multi-media presentations, and compassionate community outreach the Radiance Foundation illuminates the truth about God-given Purpose. Ryan and Bethany are passionate about supporting adoption and foster care by connecting with churches, colleges, and civic organizations nationwide to help build a culture that values Life in all of its stages.

Contributors In Alphabetical Order
(By Last Name)

Minister Emmanuel Boose

Minister Emmanuel Boose is a community activist, pro-life activist, author and a minister ordained by Dr. Bill Winston. He was raised up out of the deadness of a worldly life and brought into the destiny that God had prepared.

The Lord has blessed Minister Boose with multiple ministries including hosting a radio show called "Changing Your Community," a broadcast that is empowering the lives of our community. Pastor Boose is also a police chaplain and founder of Counter Crime Unit Security.

Pastor Stephen Broden

Stephen Broden has served as Pastor of Fair Park Bible Fellowship in Dallas, TX for 20 years. A conservative on fiscal, social and national security issues, Pastor Broden has recently been proclaiming his pro-life conservative beliefs on the Glenn Beck and Mike Huckabee shows, Fox and Friends, James Robison program and many other venues across America.

As a board member of Life Always, he has been instrumental in helping to expose the abortion-related genocide that is rampant throughout the black community via thought-provoking billboards. Broden has a Master's Degree in

Communications from the University of Michigan, and a Master's Degree from Dallas Theological Seminary.

In 2010, he was endorsed by Republican National Coalition for Life in his unsuccessful Congressional campaign against an entrenched pro-abortion Democrat in Dallas. Prior to becoming a pastor, Broden worked in broadcasting and was a business owner.

Dr. Freda McKissic Bush

Freda McKissic Bush, M.D., FACOG, has been involved in women's health for more than forty years. Since 1987, she has been practicing OB-GYN in Jackson, Mississippi and is a Clinical Instructor in the Department of OB-GYN and Department of Family Medicine at the University of Mississippi Medical Center. Dr. Bush is a Board Member of the American Association of ProLife OB-GYN's and Chair of the Board of The Medical Institute for Sexual Health.

With Joe S. McIlhaney, MD she co-authored two books—*HOOKED, New Science on How Casual Sex is Affecting Our Children,* and, *Girls Uncovered, New Research on What America's Sexual Culture Does to Young Women.* She was also a contributing writer to *Faith Matters: How African American Faith Communities Can Help Prevent Teen Pregnancy* published by the National Campaign to Prevent Teen Pregnancy.

Dr. Bush has been married for 42 years to her husband, Lee Bush, an engineer. They have four children and seven grandchildren.

Reverend Clenard Childress

Reverend Clenard Childress serves on the boards of several pro-life organizations. He has been featured in World Magazine and has contributed commentary and editorials for Christianity Today, The Christian Post, Black Christian News, The Washington Times, and New Jersey Star Ledger and is a regular columnist on Alan Keys Renew America.

Reverend Arnold M. Culbreath

Reverend Arnold Culbreath is the Urban Outreach Director of Life Issues Institute, Inc., an organization established to serve the educational needs of the pro-life movement, internationally headquartered in Cincinnati, Ohio. He oversees its Urban Outreach Initiative, Protecting Black Life, with a primary objective of reaching the Black community with the pro-life message. He frequently travels nationally and internationally, educating audiences about abortion's devastating effects and equipping them with practical solutions to end this problem.

He is an ordained minister with 27 years' experience, holds degrees in Theology and Architectural Engineering, and has worked in Pastoral and Architectural roles for many years. Throughout his life, Arnold has been intentional in promoting racial reconciliation and developing cross-racial relationships, positively impacting lives on many different levels. He and Barbara, his wife of 26 years, have 2 children and reside in the greater Cincinnati area.

Catherine Davis

Catherine Davis is a seasoned community activist and human resources professional who has worked in a variety of environment, including a Fortune 40 corporation, non-profit and for-profit organizations, and state government. A former candidate for Congress in Georgia's 4th district, Catherine has worked on a number of campaigns at the local, state and federal level and is working to make the sanctity of life a politically urgent issue for the African-American community.

She has also served as Director of Minority Outreach for Georgia Right to Life and Legislative Director for the Network of Politically Active Christians, and is an active member in a number of political organizations. Catherine has been instrumental in organizing grassroots efforts on behalf of vital issues and is a sought after public speaker who routinely brings new insight from a Biblical worldview to political issues of the day.

Drs. Richard and Renée Durfield

Richard Durfield, Ph.D., CFLE, is an acclaimed psychologist, award winning author, educator, and international speaker. As creator of the Purity Key Talk—a youth abstinence program that impacted families throughout the United States—he ushered in a movement that helped countless teens enjoy personal success in confronting sexual pressures.

He and his wife, Renée, founded All About Marriage, which provides resources and seminars on cutting-edge strategies for marital stability, divorce tropism, and effective communication. Their innovative approaches weave decades of research with practical and sound solutions for successful marriages.

Dr. Durfield holds a Ph.D. in Marriage and Family Studies from the Fuller Graduate School of Psychology. He completed advanced studies in Marital Therapy at the Gottman Institute in Seattle, Washington. Dr. Durfield is a Certified Family Life Educator (CFLE) through the National Council on Family Relations and has received additional certifications as a JPEA Consultant, D.I.S.C. Consultant, Prepare/Enrich Consultant, and PREP Consultant.

He recently retired as an Associate Professor at Azusa Pacific University and has continued teaching at the university as an Adjunct Professor in the areas of Theology and Psychology.

Renée Durfield, D.D.

Renée Durfield holds an honorary doctorate and has earned wide respect as an international speaker and best-selling author. She and her husband, Richard, are dynamic and entertaining speakers with a wonderful ability to inform and inspire audiences toward peak performance and high levels of achievements. They have addressed thousands of couples, including pastoral staffs, executives and members of many of America's largest churches, on the subject of marriage and family and have spoken in public/private schools, Pregnancy Crisis Centers, as well as other national organizations. Their exciting seminars and conferences on gender roles, self-esteem, marriage, parenting and teen sexuality have inspired immediate changes and long term results.

As a young girl, Renée King, participated in the Civil Rights movement with Dr. Martin Luther King, Jr., and was honored to sit with him as an invited guest to her home. As a fair-skinned African American, she served a vital role in the attempt to break racial prejudice in restaurants and other public establishments.

Ric and Renee recently celebrated their 46th anniversary. They enjoy spending time with their grandchildren and reside in southern California.

Dr. Day Gardner

Dr. Day Gardner made history when, as Miss Delaware, she became the first black woman to be named a semifinalist in the renowned Miss America Pageant, breaking through numerous racial and stereotypical roadblocks. Presently, Dr. Gardner is the founder and president of the National Black Pro-Life Union headquartered on Capitol Hill. She is a wife, mother and author of the novel *If Not for Grace*.

La Nej Garrison, M.A.

La Nej Garrison, M. A., has been in the forefront sponsoring no-nonsense educational seminars on the risks of non-marital sex for over ten years. In addition to teaching teens and young adults about sexual purity, she is passionate about equipping Christians with tools to successfully defend the faith. La Nej believes understanding what you believe is essential to live a life of righteousness.

La Nej has ministered to teens and their parents in public schools, in churches and in several mega-ministries including Youth for Christ, American Baptist Churches, the Christian Educators Association, Biola University and more. A licensed minister, she has also taught in Japan and on missions trips to South Africa.

La Nej completed her Master's Degree in Philosophy of Religion and Ethics from Talbot School of Theology, La Mirada, CA. She earned her Bachelors in Communication with an emphasis in Theatre Arts and a minor in Bible from Biola University. She is married to Matthew Garrison and they are proud parents of three boys—Josiah, Judah, and Jeremiah. La Nej is currently writing a book on sexual purity.

Rev. Walter Hoye, II

Walter Hoye, II, is both Founder and President of the Issues4life Foundation. He is author of the book, *Leadership from the INSIDE Out* and is in demand as a speaker and consultant.

"Walter embodies the Martin Luther King, Jr. legacy, standing up for the least of these, the vulnerable mothers and their babies."—Dr. Alveda King, niece of Dr. Martin Luther King Jr. (Tuesday, March 31st, 2009)

Dr. Johnny Hunter

Dr. Johnny Hunter is an inspirational speaker, educator and consultant. For 30 years, he has given the invitational sermons at national Christian conferences, church celebrations and youth meetings. His fervent style of speaking is sought after for national banquets and conferences. Dr. Hunter has also spoken on college campuses across America and in South Africa.

A wise leader, Dr. Hunter is regularly sought after to advise and to counsel new pro-life and pro-family organizations. He has also been called upon to serve as a facilitator for racial healing and reconciliation.

Because of his experience and knowledge about creating charitable organizations, he is a consultant for businesses and nonprofit organizations that wish to work with minority communities. In this capacity, he advises leaders on the allocation of funds for outreach programs.

Dr. Tim Johnson

Timothy Johnson, Ph.D., is the Founder and Chairman of the Frederick Douglass Foundation. Dr. Johnson made history on June 13, 2009 when he was elected Vice Chairman of the North Carolina Republican Party, becoming the first African-American to hold the position since the party's inception March 27, 1867.

Born and raised in Cleveland, Ohio, Dr. Johnson graduated from Benedictine High School and was a member of two state championship football teams. It was there he got the bug to get involved with politics. In preparation, Timothy earned the Boy Scouts of America's highest rank, the Eagle Scout Award, at the age of 14. He has continued to be a servant leader throughout his adult life.

Dr. Johnson completed 21 years of military service with the United States Army, serving as enlisted soldier and commissioned officer. His military honors include the Joint Service Commendation Medal, Army Commendation Medal (3rd Award), Army Achievement Medal, Army Good Conduct Medal (2nd Award), National Defense Service Medal (2nd Award), Armed Forces Expeditionary Medal, Armed Forces Reserve Medal with Device, Army Service Ribbon, Overseas Service Ribbon, NATO Medal, and Soldier of the Month. Twice elected Chairman of the Buncombe County, NC, Republican Party, Dr. Johnson was a delegate to the 2008 Republican National Convention and a panelist at the 2008 Black Republican Forum in New York. He is an adjunct professor at Shaw University.

Dr. Johnson founded and leads The Frederick Douglass Foundation, a public policy and educational organization that brings the sanctity of free market and limited government ideas to bear on the hardest problems facing our nation. It is a collection of pro-active individuals committed to developing innovative and new approaches to today's problems with the assistance of elected officials, scholars from universities and colleges, and community activists.

Chaplain Ayesha Kreutz

Ayesha is a Bible-believing Christian striving to be a servant to those around her by acting as the willing hands and feet of God. She is the wife of Matt Kreutz and the mother of five children, three of whom are living.

Chaplin Kreutz serves her community as a corporate chaplain with Chaplain Fellowship Ministries, serves as a 21st century Abolitionist as President of the Frederick Douglass Foundation of New York, and works with many area pro-life groups and organizations.

Within the framework of these organizations, she focuses her time and skills on educating those around her through a comprehensive biblical worldview. This includes encouraging positive changes through preaching the Gospel of Jesus Christ in order to strengthen the family-unit and integrating peaceful initiatives involving education and civic participation. Standing up for life, for traditional family values, for Real History and for the economic solvency of the United States of America are some of the issues that she believes are vital to our survival.

Homeless by the time she was 14, Mrs. Kreutz is mostly self-taught with some formal education in psychology and marketing from Monroe Community College and the International Academy of Design and Technology. Ayesha shares her testimony of her own abuse and abortions, and emphasizes how God brought her through the pain of childhood. Her journey in life has taken her from broken and abused to a place of godly character through the forgiveness and healing of Jesus Christ.

Reverend Ceasar I. LeFlore III
Reverend Ceasar I. LeFlore III is the Associate Pastor of Lorimer Baptist Church of Dolton, IL and the Executive Director of The Beloved Community Development Coalition.

Reverend LeFlore is the past executive director of The African American Family Association, and presently sits of the boards of The Pro-Life / Pro-Family Coalition, The Southland Prevention Coalition, and LEARN.

Tegra Little
Born, raised and educated in Los Angeles (Sociology degree from USC), Tegra Little left a successful twelve year career as a respected music business executive to devote her energies to motherhood. Never in her wildest dreams did she imagine the journey to having children would be filled with ups and downs.

After struggling with eight years of infertility—multiple miscarriages, fertility cancer, and gestational surrogacy—God has opened the heart of Tegra and her husband to adoption. They're looking forward to pouring their spiritual DNA into the lives of the children God has ordained for them.

Her cancer challenge led her to an even higher calling. She formed her own company to promote the healing benefits of wholesome living foods that come straight from nature. She loves discipling women and founded No Longer Bound, an abortion recovery ministry for women who have been suffering in silence with the pain, guilt and shame of a past abortion(s). Her own personal story of abortion led her to be used as a vessel to heal broken women in this area.

Tegra attends Faithful Central Bible Church in Inglewood, CA. She is married to Marc Little, an attorney.

Reverend Dean Nelson

Reverend Dean Nelson is the Vice President for underserved outreach at Care Net, the Chairman of the Frederick Douglass Foundation and is an executive leader with over 20 years of experience in ministry and over 10 years in political activism on local, state and national levels. He has extensive experience working with leaders in the African-American community and is passionately committed to promoting a culture of life.

Dean has previously served as the executive director for the Network of Politically Active Christians (NPAC) and as vice-chairman for the Frederick Douglass Foundation (FDF). Under his leadership, both organizations informed thousands of faith leaders of relevant political developments and trained hundreds in biblical worldview and public policy. In addition, he recruited and equipped pro-life Christian minorities to run for office on the local, state and national level.

Rev. Nelson is a licensed minister from Salem Baptist Church and an ordained pastor with Wellington Boone Ministries. He is married to the love of his life, Julia Nelson, who works as a freelance writer and home schools their three children.

Dr. Loretto Grier Cudjoe Smith

Dr. Loretto Grier Cudjoe Smith is noted for her life of community service and active participation in the humanitarian cause of seeking justice for the unborn, the sick, elderly and incarcerated. She is a member of her state chapter of the NAACP. She is also a dentist with a practice in Georgia.

Reverend Dr. Eric Wallace

A man of vision and focus, Reverend Dr. Eric Wallace couples his rich educational background with a unique ability to challenge the status quo. His post-graduate degrees in Biblical studies (MA, Alliance Theological Seminary; ThM and PhD, Union Theological Seminary in Richmond, VA), together with his passion and strong message of conservative reform, are inspiring exciting change.

Dr. Wallace's publishing tenure spans well over 10 years. As former president and CEO of Wallace Publishing and Computer Graphics, he published the *Lamb's Book*, a Christian business directory, and the *New Life Journal*, a bimonthly magazine. He also served as editorial director for Urban Ministries, Inc. (UMI).

In 2004, Dr. Wallace dreamed of a multimedia company and began to implement that vision. However, he was encouraged to run for political office, and he chose to delay launching the company for two years. Dr. Wallace's campaign drew the attention of news sources and politicians. Over the last several years, he has served on the African American Advisory Board for the Republican National Committee, as Chairman of the African American Republican Council of Illinois, a member of the Outreach Advisory Board for the Illinois GOP and as a commissioner on the Illinois Transatlantic Slave Trade Commission among others.

Currently Dr. Wallace and his company are based out of Chicago, Illinois. He along with his wife, Jennifer, publish *Freedom's Journal Magazine*, in hopes of encouraging African-Americans to cling to their natural conservative principles. He has also authored two books. *Integrity of Faith: An Autobiography* is published by Integrity Books, a subsidiary of Wallace Multimedia Group and is currently available at *www.integritybooks. net*. *Jesus on Trial: A New Approach to Interpreting the Gospel of John* will also be published by Integrity Books.

Integrity of Faith is published by Dr. Wallace's strong commitment to revitalizing conservative principles within the African-American constituency—coupled with his desire to fight to uphold our nation's founding principles—are based on his philosophical premise that "our cause requires that we stand for what we say we believe, and that we actively engage in the political process that represents us."

Elder Levon Yuille

Elder Levon Yuille is Pastor of The Bible Church in Ypsilanti, Michigan and National Director of the Black Pro-Life Congress. Pastor Yuille participated in the only all Black Operation Rescue sit-in during the history of the movement which took place in Lansing, Michigan in the early 1990's.

Pastor Yuille has worked with Barbara Listing and Right to Life of Michigan for over fifteen years, and has been keynote speaker for Right to Life of Michigan auxiliaries throughout Michigan. Along with wife Sally, Pastor Yuille has received the Right to Life of Michigan Life Time Achievement award.

Pastor Yuille's ministries have taken him to Africa four times, where he took the gospel of Jesus Christ as well as the message of life to the countries of Uganda, Kenya and Tanzania. He is a recipient of an honorary Doctor of Divinity Degree, conferred upon him by Mid-Atlantic Conference of Methodist Episcopal Church-USA by recommendation of the National Clergy Council Board of Scholars.

Due to over 30 ears of community involvement, Dr. Yuille has received over 40 awards, plaques and letters of recognition which include being named "Person of the Year" by the Ypsilanti Press. On two occasions the City of Ypsilanti, has declared "Pastor Yuille Day." Dr. Yuille and wife Sally have been blessed to raise eight children, and have 20 grandchildren.

CPSIA information can be obtained at www.ICGtesting.com
Printed in the USA
LVOW061908150512

281776LV00001B/2/P